The Digest Enthusiast

Book Fifteen C

I0647277

Tom Brinkmann

Steve Carper

Peter Enfantino

Stephen Jones

Gary Lovisi

Anthony Perconti

Jack Seabrook

David A. Sutton

Bob Vojtko

Edited by Richard Krauss

The Digest Enthusiast (TDE) Book Fifteen
Published by Larque Press LLC

Editor/Designer: Richard Krauss
Cover: Rachel Krauss
Cartoons: Bob Vojtko (pages 99, 138, 139, 157 and 160)
Photography: Pixabay.com (unless otherwise noted)

Printed on demand from January 2022 in the United States of America and other countries.

Larque Press LLC
4130 SE 162nd Court
Vancouver, WA 98683

Visit <larquepress.com> for news about current digest magazines and vintage digest covers. Join our mailing list for exclusive updates on *The Digest Enthusiast* and other Larque Press projects. Sign up at <larquepress.com>

Back Cover Images
Fantasy Tales Vol. 1 No. 1 Summer 1977
Murder Mystery Monthly No. 31 1945
Asimov's Science Fiction September 2012
Manhunt Detective Story Monthly Vol. 3 No. 11 November 1955
Fantastic Vol. 1 No. 1 Summer 1952
The Vanishing Redhead 1948

Our thanks to our contributors for some of the cover images that appear in this edition. Cover images are retouched to remove defects from the original source material. When reference material is not available, retouched areas are "best guess." In some cases text may be reset in a font similar to the original work.

Contents Page Images:
People Today February 11, 1953 back cover with Alice B. Toklas.
Fantasy Tales Vol. 10 No. 1 Autumn 1988 back cover by Chris Achilleos.

The Digest Enthusiast
ISSN 2637-448X (print)
ISSN 2637-4498 (digital)
ISBN 978-1-7344548-9-5 (No. 15C color interior)
ISBN 978-1-7372299-0-2 (No. 15BW black-and-white interior)

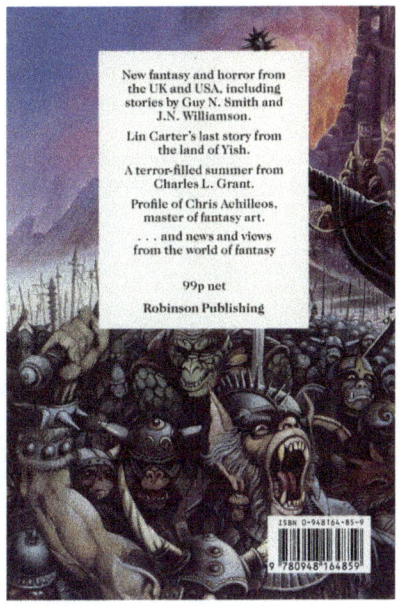

Interview

**22 Stephen Jones &
David A. Sutton**
Fantasy Tales

Articles/Synopses

46 A Look at Marijuana Girl
Gary Lovisi

**52 Howard Browne's
Fantastic 1952**
Richard Krauss

**74 People Today
February 11, 1953**
Tom Brinkmann

**78 Paragon: Thoughts on
William Preston's
Old Man Sequence**
Anthony Perconti

86 Manhunt 1955 part three
Peter Enfantino

**100 Murder Mystery Monthly
No. 31 June 1945**
Jack Seabrook

106 11 True Crimes
Richard Krauss

**124 Carl D. Hodges:
Crime On My Hands**
Richard Krauss

138 Carl G. Hodges Biblio

**140 The Strange, Short Life of
the Boys' and Girls' Fiction
Series**
Steve Carper

Reviews

**150 Startling Mystery
Stories No. 2**

Departments

4 News Digest

122 Vince Nowell, Sr.
Dedication

139 Supermarket Blues
Bob Vojkto

159 Opening Lines

My heartfelt thanks to **Stephen Jones** and **David Sutton** for their interview about the *Fantasy Tales* digest. It could well be this issue's highlight! I love the opportunity to document a slice of digest magazine history with those who helped make it. I think I first saw *FT* when **Peter Enfantino** sent a couple of extras he had—two of the earlier issues with covers by **Jim Pitt**. It was love at first sight. Over the years I've managed to put together a whole set, and fortunately they are still fairly easy to find at larger online used booksellers and ebay.

Peter wraps up *Manhunt*'s third year this issue, topped with his favorite stories from 1955. That *Verdict* cover shown in his article is from the title's second run, which I'll be reviewing for a future issue of *Bare Bones* in 2022.

I'm delighted to welcome **Steve Carper** back to our pages with his piece

No. 2 in 1977.

Our cover this time is by **Rachel Krauss**, my daughter, who gifted me her painting on Father's Day 2021. Follow her artistic journey on Instagram at Curly Ewe Studio.

Jack Seabrook returns with a review of *Murder Mystery Monthly* No. 31 along with background about its author **William Irish**, aka **Cornell Woolrich**. Jack's piece inspired me to dive into Woolrich's *Rear Window* collection. **Ellery Queen** was correct, "Woolrich can distill more terror, more excitement, more downright nailbiting suspense out of even the most commonplace happenings than nearly all his competitors."

Several of our contributors have suffered poor health on top of the pandemic. **Tom Brinkmann** managed to finish a review of an issue of *People Today* that dovetails with his previous

News Digest

on Boys' and Girls' Fiction, a short-lived children's series out of Kenosha, Wisconsin. Also returning is **Gary Lovisi** who explores the controversial *Marijuana Girl* digest-sized novel, and its author **N.R. de Mexico**.

New to our pages is **Anthony Perconti**, writing about the work of science fiction author **William Preston** and his "old man" series for *Asimov's*. Anthony's a regular contributor to *Pulp Modern*, where he examines the *Uncanny X-Men* in issue No. 8.

My favorite indie cartoonist, **Bob Vojtko**, retired just in time to avoid the pandemic out there in the world of retail. Still an avid gag cartoonist, he found time to provide four new cartoons this issue and granted permission for us to reprint a page that originally appeared in *The New Funny Book*

piece on *The Creature from the Black Lagoon* from *TDE10*. He's been working on another piece about **Jeanne Carmen** and her many appearances in pocket-size mags, but its status is uncertain. See Tom's bio on page 77 for more background information.

Vince Nowell, Sr. lost his battle with his bad heart in October. This issue is dedicated in his memory on page 122. Vince was thinking about a number of articles when he passed. He wanted to explore an Avon series and *Venture Science Fiction*, but left his thoughts incomplete, so here we are, feeling his absence in more ways than one.

My fascination with true crime digests leads us to a one-shot title, *11 True Crimes* by famed crime reporter **Joseph Gollomb**, this issue. The sensationalism here comes from the selected cases, rather than editorial hype. Every time I think I've discovered every true crime digest published, another one pops up somewhere. My latest edification was *International Detective Cases*, a saddle-stitched true crime digest that went 19 issues in the late 1930s. Incidentally, if you're looking for a great resource for true crime mags check out <pofoz.com/magazines/true-crime/index.html>.

As you'll read in the *Fantasy Tales* interview, putting out a indie magazine is a lot of work. After seven years of *The Digest Enthusiast*, I'm ready for a break. There are other projects on my bucket list, so I'm taking the first half of 2022 off to explore some other creative endeavors. There are some stories I'd like to write, and some thoughts I'd like to record while I'm still on this side of the crust. At the moment, I think I'll return to *TDE* in 2023, but that's a year out, so let's see what happens. In the meantime, many thanks to all our contributors and readers for your generous support.

The main feedback on *TDE* comes in terms of sales. Last issue, I tried something new, a comprehensive synopsis of an entire story, rather than the usual partials that avoid spoilers. There were no complaints about *20 Million Miles to Earth*, so this time we've got *Crime On My Hands* by **Carl G. Hodges**, along with what I hope is a full bibliography of his stories.

Over the years, limited reader feedback is split on our fiction. Some like it, some would rather see the space devoted to other features. This time, the latter get their wish. This issue is devoted entirely to features, without a word of original fiction. As the Brits put it: "Have your say." Send your comments to arkay@larquepress.com

---

Updates from the Editors, Writers, and Artists of today's newsstand and indie digest magazines.

Phyllis Glade: Fate

Coming in *Fate* No. 738: "The cover mockup is from **Timothy Wyllie**, who wrote the eight Rebel Angel books, plus others. It's about the war in heaven through the ages (dang, politics even in heaven!).

"Part two about the most famous contactees [by **Timothy Green Beckley**] and a listing of the types of extraterrestrials that have been identified so far. Pretty creepy, some of them.

"Well also have an article on iron coffins in the past, bodies completely preserved until the coffin is opened. "Rust in Peace" is the witty title of that one. Water Jar Diplomacy from 50 years ago, fascinating psychic

abilities in Sumatra, and **Uri Geller** still manifesting his amazing abilities."

Emily Hockaday: Analog

"On Thursday, December 9, 2021, as part of the City Tech Science Fiction Symposium, editor **Trevor Quachri** announced the winner and finalists for the first annual Analog Award for Emerging Black Voices. The winner is **Kedrick Brown**, and the finalists (in alphabetical order by last name) are: **Yazeed Dezele**, **Erika Hardison**, and **Jermaine Martin**. Kedrick will receive publication in *Analog* and a year of mentoring, including sessions with authors **Nisi Shawl** and **Steven Barnes**, literary agent **Kim-Mei Kirtland**, and the *Analog* editors. Each finalist will receive a mentoring session with the *Analog* editors. The 2022 award will open to submissions in March. Follow at @Analog_SF or check the website for details.

"Moving into 2022, we have a trove of fantastic fiction from the likes of **Stanley Schmidt**, **Naomi Kanakia**, **Marianne Dyson**, **Tom Jolly**, **Sean McMullen**, **Shane Tourtellotte**, **Steven Barnes** & **Larry Niven**, **Marie Vibbert**, **Marissa Lingen** & more!"

Tony Gleeson: Artist/Author

"At present I am hard at work preparing my fifth book for Wildside, *Find the Money*, a novel-length expansion from my original UK novella, packed with even more capers and craziness then the original. It's a procedural, like the others in my Personal Crimes series, but with a difference. Someone called it a 'gangster procedural.' I'm hoping it'll see publication before March, when the annual Paperback Collectors' Show returns to the Los Angeles area after a year's 'sabbatica' due to the pandemic. And that's where my other present project fits in, since I create the posters, program announcements, and all the other graphics for the show, as well as appear at it, and we are now gearing up for it as the proverbial excitement builds. My other current project—besides doing my best to retain my sanity in an uncertain and insane world—is my ongoing sketchbooks, which at some point I hope to begin gathering for publication."

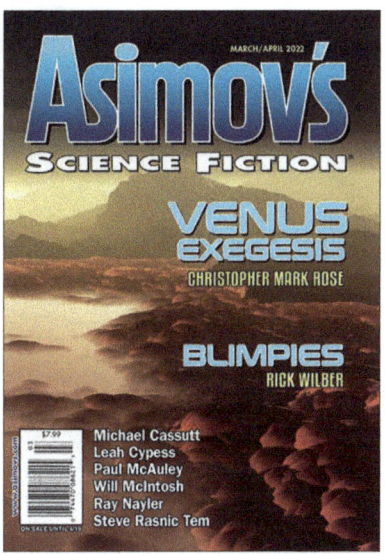

Emily Hockaday: Asimov's

"2022 brings a wide array of fiction to the magazine. From **Evan Marcroft's** far-future North American "Coyote-land" where borders are ever shifting, to the ambitious young "Rocket Girls" of **Kristine Kathryn Rusch**, to the future of punk rock in **Zack Be's** "Meryl's Cocoon," there will be something for everyone. Look out for names like **Greg Egan**, **Sheila Finch**, **Alice Towey**, **Oghenechovwe Donald Epeki**, **Robert Reed** & **Leah Cypess**!"

Steve Darnall: Nostalgia Digest

"With the new Winter 2022 issue, Funny Valentine Press is pleased to announce that *Nostalgia Digest* is now available in both print and digital formats, which means readers can take the nostalgia with them wherever they go! The new Winter issue includes a cover story about **Humphrey Bogart's** movie career and a conversation with the legendary **Carol Burnett** about her early days in television—in addition to articles about the great **Mel Blanc**, 'The Man of a Thousand Voices;' songwriter **Johnny Mercer**; Hollywood movies about Golden Age movie stars; how a controversial radio show changed the complexion of the toy industry and much more. Subscriptions and single issues are available from: <nostalgiadigest.com>.

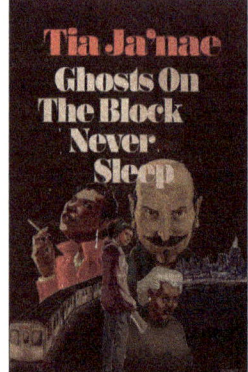

Alec Cizak: Uncle B Publications

Indie Publisher Uncle B is on a tear. Their latest books include *Crowmouth* by **Ronin Heck** and *Ghosts On the Block Never Sleep* by **Tia Ja'nae**. *L.A. Stories* with three grindhouse novellas about L.A. in 1979/1980 by **Alec Cizak**, **Andrew Miller**, and **Scotch Rutherford**, with an introduction by **Rex Weiner**. Other volumes by **Jim Towns**, **Rev. Joe Haward**, and **Mehmet Akgönül** are coming, as well as the second volume of the Drifter Detective series. Alec's latest novel, *Cool It Down*, is already available.

The new year will also bring big changes to *Pulp Modern*, along with the first in a series of Pulp Modern motion pictures! The next *Pulp Modern* (Vol. 2 No. 8) will be out in January 2022.

Jennifer Landels: Pulp Literature

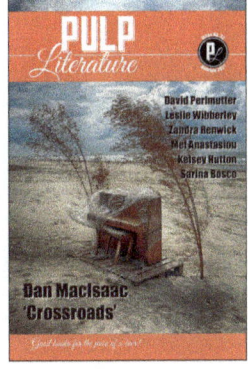

PL32 Autumn 2021: "**Tais Teng** offers this issue's opening notes with 'The Pianist Who Serenaded the Mermaids with Chopin's Nocturne in E Minor.' The wonders continue with short fiction from **Dan MacIsaac, Zandra Renwick, Kelsey Hutton, Sarina Bosco, David Perlmutter, Melissa Nelson, Leslie Wibberley**, and **Robin Malcolm**. There's poetry from the Magpie winners and a graphic short finale from **Matthew Nielsen**. **JM Landels** brings us Toinette's latest adventures, and **Mel Anastasiou** introduces us to an all-new mystery, 'Pretty Lies.'

PL33 Winter 2022: "Cover artist **Bronwyn Schuster**'s 'Space Cat' ricochets us into a pinball-inspired future with our feature author **Kate Heartfield**. Chickens, candles, fairies, and ponies dance through inspired short fiction from **Krista Jane May, Anne Baldo, Monica Wang**, and **Lulu Keating**, while **Douglas Smith** and **Kimberley Aslett** tug at our hearts. The Hummingbird winners flit across the page, and **JM Landels** and **Mel Anastasiou** give us a taste of their new novels.

"Novels coming in early 2022: *The Extra* by **Mel Anastasiou**, and the third book of the *Allaigna's Song* trilogy by **Jennifer Landels**. In *The Extra: A Monument Studios Mystery*, Vancouver schoolmarm Frankie Ray runs away to Silver Screen Hollywood to test her conviction that an actress who lacks glamour but has talent and an enterprising attitude can make it in the movies. But when a dissolute, womanizing matinee idol turns up dead on her sofa, Frankie's career hopes shatter. She'll need all her acting chops to sleuth out the murderer and clear her name.

Justin Marriott:
The Paperback Fanatic

Following a busy year, Justin expects the trend to continue in 2022. "*The Paperback Fanatic* No. 45 is due January 2022. It is a "visual guide" dedicated to Belmont and Tower Books, with over 300 full-colour reproductions of rare and unusual 60s and 70s covers, as well as plenty of factoids and trivia about the authors and artists."

If the approach clicks he'll continue the visual guide approach for other publishers, including DAW books.

In addition to paperbacks, Justin and the team have expanded their media coverage to include comics with the launch of a new title, *Battling Britons*. Launched in Sept. 2021, and intended as a one-off special, positive feedback from readers that included **Garth Ennis** writer of *The Preacher* and *The Boys* fame, convinced Justin to proceed with the title. He says, "Look for the second issue in Jan. 2022, with a mix of articles, reviews, and interviews. It's a fascinating insight to the unfashionable yet enduring genre of British war and adventure comics." All of Justin's publications are available through <amazon.com>.

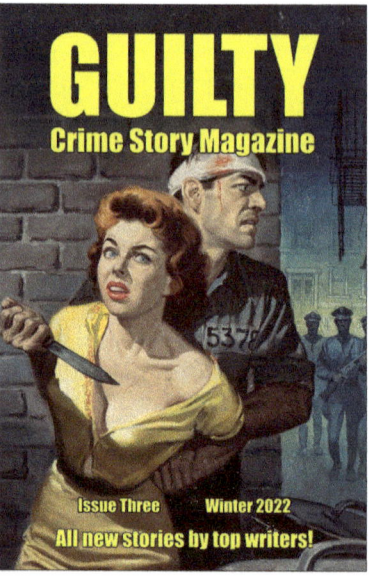

Brandon Barrows: Guilty Crime Story

"*Guilty Crime Story Magazine* issue three will be out in January and includes brand-new stories by **Robb T. White**, **Dustin Walker**, **Ethan Robles**, **Brandon Barrows**, **Mike McHone**, **Bruce Harris** and an article by **Anthony Perconti**. Issue four is tentatively planned to be a themed issue with a submissions window in late January/early February for an April/May release, so watch our website for details." <guiltycrimemag.com>

Susan Emshwiller: Author

"I have finished a new novel, *All My Ancestors Had Sex*, and am looking for representation for it.

"On her eighteenth birthday, it's clear that Izzy's ugly-duckling-phase isn't passing. She's a mess of mismatched limbs and features, insisting, 'My DNA wasn't stirred!' In contrast, her ten-year old brother is *GQ* perfect but, growing up in their cocoon of wealth and privilege, seems destined to become an entitled jerk. Izzy vows to save the little prick—by kidnapping him. On the road and on the run, Izzy's oddness grows more apparent. Not only is she a physically weird conglomeration but now these different parts are asserting themselves as distinct personalities. A young Black slave, a WWII German soldier and his girlfriend, a gay South-ern gentleman, a Gold-Rush prostitute, a Suffragette, and a Dragon Lady—the non-binary motorcyclist. They say they are Izzy's ancestors who have traumas seared into her genes and now they want revenge. Or maybe Izzy's nuts.

"A manuscript of 98,000 words, *All My Ancestors Had Sex* delves into a young women's growth: dealing with sexual harassment, finding strength from the past, and standing up to exploiters. Her ancestors hurl her into a world of terrifying and horrific situations, (at times absurdly funny with all these disparate personalities in one body) and finally bring a healing and transformation that allows her to leave that past behind and become a whole individual."

Leah R. Cutter: Mystery, Crime, and Mayhem

MCM No. 8 includes stories by by **Jason A. Adams, Joslyn Chase, Leah R Cutter, Diana Deverell, David H. Hendrickson, Kari Kilgore, Nicole Givens Kurtz, Steve Liskow, Cate Martin,** and **Annie Reed**. Sign up for the *MCM* newsletter at: <mysterycrimeandmayhem.com>.

Gordon Van Gelder: Fantasy & Science Fiction

"It looks like we have stories for the Mar/Apr issue by **Fawaz Al-Matrouk, Shreya Ila Anasuya, Megan Beadle, Ai Jiang, Aliya Whiteley, John Wiswell,** and others.

"And for the May/June issue, we have a new story by **Norman Spinrad** penciled in."

Douglas Draa: Weirdbook, Startling Stories

"*Weirdbook* No. 45 should be coming out in February 2022. The themed Annual for 2022 will be Vampires. *Weirdbook*'s existence is guaranteed for at least six more issues. We've filled, contracted, and paid for the contents of the next six issues. We'll decide what to do afterwards once No. 50 comes out. That should be sometime during the 2nd half of 2023.

"Another issue of *Startling Stories* will also be coming out next year. We hope to open a Kickstart campaign next year to finance much higher rates for *Startling*."

Weirdbook 2021 Annual: Zombies

Michael Bracken: Author and Editor

"Coming out in April: *Groovy Gumshoes: Private Eyes in the Psychedelic Sixties* (Down & Out Books) with stories by **Jack Bates, C.W. Blackwell, Michael Bracken, N.M. Cedeño, Hugh Lessig, Steve Liskow, Adam Meyer, Tom Milani, Neil Plakcy. Stephen D. Rogers, Mark Thielman, Grant Tracey, Mark Troy, Andrew Welsh-Huggins,** and **Robb White.**

"Coming out first quarter: *Black Cat Mystery Magazine* No. 11 with stories by **Mike Adamson, Lis Angus, Mar-** **lin Bressi, Mark Bruce, Leone Ciporin, O'Neil De Noux, Veronica Leigh, Robert Lopresti, Anita Murphy, David Rudd, Max Devoe Talley,** and **Elizabeth Zelvin.**

"I hope to get *BCMM* 12 out second quarter, but I'm not ready to announce contributors. And, there will be another season of *Guns+Tacos*. **Trey Barker** and I are currently editing the six novellas for season four and hope to deliver them to Down & Out before the end of December. We don't know yet if there will be a season five."

Art Taylor: Author

Productivity picked up for Art in 2021, he has several stories coming up: "Love Me or Leave Me: A Fugue in G Minor" will appear in *Music of the Night*, the new anthology from the Crime Writers Association and editor **Martin Edwards,** to be published in February in the United Kingdom by Flame Tree Press; "We Are All Strangers Here" in an upcoming *Ellery Queen's Mystery Magazine*; "After Their Convictions, Six Murderers Reflect on How Killing Mr. Boddy Changed Their Lives," co-written with Art's wife **Tara Laskowski,** in an upcoming *Black Cat Mystery Magazine*, and "Two for One" in an anthology produced by the group blog SleuthSayers.

Chris Rhatigan: All Due Respect

No details yet, but Chris has confirmed work on an *All Due Respect* anthology is in progress and will release in 2022.

Chuck Carter: Mystery Magazine

"*Mystery Weekly Magazine* shortened its title to *Mystery Magazine* in October 2021. I asked publisher **Chuck Carter** what factored into the change: "Our original intention back in 2015 was to start a weekly e-zine, hence the name *Mystery Weekly Magazine*. After only a few weeks we decided to become a monthly print magazine instead. Unfortunately, we kept the original name, and it's been a source of confusion ever since. In actual fact, we've never been a weekly magazine and our stories have never appeared online: we're a monthly magazine, available primarily through Amazon POD and by subscription on Kindle Newsstand.

"In 2022 we're planning to explore some new markets and distribution channels, so it seemed now was the perfect time for a name change. Using 'Mystery Monthly' was out of the question, because it locks us into a publication schedule again, and choosing an entirely new name would mean losing all of our hard-earned brand recognition—so we decided to simply remove the word 'Weekly.' Some will probably say "Mystery Magazine" sounds too generic, but that actually suits us, because we tend to choose stories that appeal to the widest possible mystery audience. And as you know, there's already been

a *Mystery Magazine* a century ago, so we're not exactly treading on uncharted territory.

"Within days of making the change we moved to the number one rank on Google for the search term 'Mystery Magazine.' We were also able to retain the familiar look of our covers by making only minimal changes to our masthead, and updating our sponsorships and distribution partners was relatively painless since it's obvious we're still the same publication. We also took the opportunity to update our mobile app and website while changing the name. So all in all it's been a positive change that sets us up for the next few decades."

Michael Neno: Cartoonist

Neno World's next public domain-sourced tiny mashup microcomics title is *Farmers vs. Astronauts* (see image) and it may be out by the time you read this. Check <facebook.com/michael.neno> for updates and order info.

Bob Vojtko: Cartoonist

Bob has several mini comics available, contact him through his page on Facebook for titles and costs. He's also planning a new one called *Last Week's Saurkraut* which will contain comics from the Vojtko Vault. Hopefully, there will be many more to come in 2022., so be sure to order.

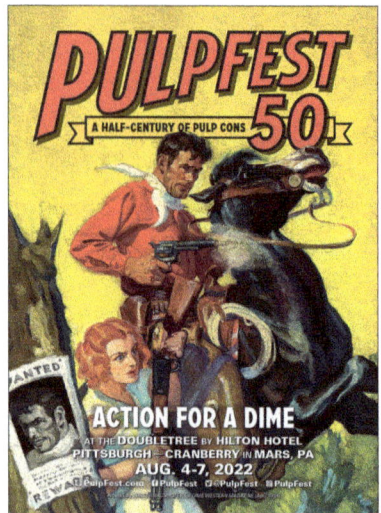 

Mike Chomko: PulpFest

"If you haven't visited our website <pulpfest.com> of late, you're in for a treat. Since the beginning of November, we've looked at the start of Popular Publications' line of 'Dime' pulps; featured biographies of pulp and comic strip artist **Stan Drake** and authors **Raoul Whitfield** and **Joel Townsley Rogers**; and saluted the beginning of **Ned Pines** and **Leo Margulies'** 'Thrilling' line of pulp magazines.

"In between, we profiled award-winning science fiction author **Allen Steele**, the writer who brought Captain Future into the 21st century. We've also looked at occasional pulp writer **William Lindsay Gresham**, author of *Nightmare Alley*, recently adapted to the screen by celebrated filmmaker **Guillermo del Toro**; profiled actor, writer, artist, and filmmaker **Mark Redfield**; and delved into the Fiction House line of 'North-West' and football pulps.

"In early January, we'll release our programming plans for PulpFest 50, taking place from Thursday, August 4, through Sunday, August 7, at the DoubleTree by Hilton Hotel Pittsburgh—Cranberry in Mars, Pennsylvania. The convention will be celebrating a half-century of pulp cons, the centennial of Fiction House, and the 90th anniversary of Popular's 'Dime' line of pulps. The convention's guest of honor will be **Robert Randisi**, called 'one of the last true pulp writers.'

"We hope you'll join us for 'A Half-Century of Pulp Cons' and 'Action for a Dime.' It's all planned for PulpFest 50. So be sure to bookmark <pulpfest.com> and visit often! It's where you'll find all the pulp that's fit to print!

"For those who enjoy the PulpFest programming book, *The Pulpster*, we have copies of our 2020 and 2021 issues available for sale.

"Visit <pulpfest.com> to order."

Rusty Barnes, Tough Crime

"I am planning to restart our digest series with a release date of June, but I don't have a cover or designer yet. I'm going to work on that between now and February."

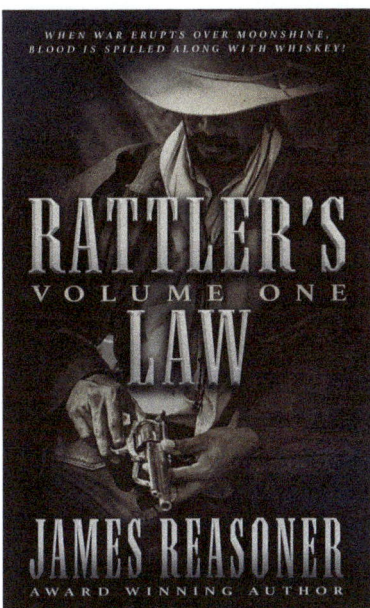

James Reasoner

Earlier this year, "I sold my little imprint, Rough Edges Press, to Wolfpack, which has relaunched it as a mystery/men's adventure line with me editing, and that's taking more of my time than anything else. Although I'm still writing Westerns under another name I can't claim. So I'm pretty anonymous at the moment.

"Next year I hope to carve out enough time to write at least one hard-boiled crime novel under my name. I have three good outlines sitting in my files, just waiting . . . they're all set in the Forties and Fifties and are Gold Medal-style plots."

Two of James' recent releases from Wolfpack are *Rattler's Law* Vol. 1 & 2.

Gary Lovisi: Gryphon Books

"*Paperback Parade* No. 114 will have an extensive article on the British Sexton Blake crime digests, a long run series; also SF writer **Allen Steele**, interview, booklist, and an article by him about SF. Also **Edmond Hamilton** and

more. Out in late December 2021 or early January 2022.

"I have been busy doing some books over the year that I hope will appear soon, more about these when I get publication dates."

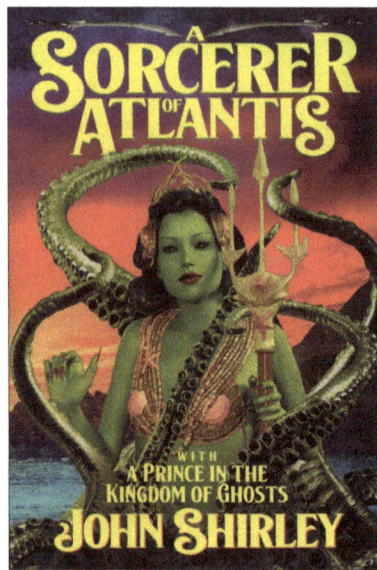

John Shirley

Hippocampus Press published *A Sorcerer of Atlantis* in May 2021. The title is taken from the lead novel, part of which originally appeared in *Weirdbook* No. 42. The book also includes a separate sword and sorcery story, "A Prince in the Kingdom of Ghosts" which runs nearly 70 pages. *Weirdbook*'s editor, **Doug Draa** interviewed author John Shirley for Black Gate in August 2021. <blackgate.com>. In March 2022, John's first book of a western trilogy, *Axle Bust Creek* is scheduled to debut from Kensington Books.

J.D. Graves: EconoClash Review

"*EconoClash Review* is riding dirty these days in the lowest of profiles. *ECR8* will be coming in late winter 2022, and may be the last of the classic formats you thrill seekers have come to love, and to say more would be to say too much."

In other news, Editor-in-Chief J.D. Graves in deep into work on a novel to be published by Death's Head Press sometime in 2022. He reports, "*Mayhem Sam* promises to be the wildest wild west tale in the Splatter Western line-up."

Steve Davidson:
Experimenter Publishing

In August, **Steve Davidson**, publisher of *Amazing Stories*, announced he would be unable to continue the print edition of the magazine. In a message to subscribers he wrote: "First, *Amazing Stories* will change to an annual format, producing one (over-sized) issue per year rather than quarterly (four) issues per year.

"Second, we are eliminating the print edition as a regularly available option. Print copies of each issue will remain available as a separately purchased Print On Demand (POD) product. All current print subscriptions will be converted to Electronic Editions moving forward. In addition, former print subscribers may select one of the *Amazing Select* titles, electronic edition, for each year of subscription that is being converted.

"These are necessary steps that will allow us to continue publishing the magazine.

"Please know that we are not happy with having to make these changes, but following long discussion, we believe that these changes offer us our best chance of moving forward."

In Sept. 2021, Experimenter Publishing released the final novel in the Captain Future tetralogy by **Allen Steele**: *The Horror at Jupiter*. The volume include the first *TDE* blurb: "Great read with clever plotting. Can't wait to get my eyeballs on the conclusion."

Josh Pachter

"*The Man Who Solved Mysteries: More Short Fiction* by **William Brittain** is my second collection of Brittain's *EQMM* stories from Crippen & Landru Dec. 2021. (Volume 1—*The Man Who Read Mysteries: The Short Fiction of William Brittain*—came out in 2018, and the third and final volume—*The Man Who Wrote Mysteries: The Rest of Brittain*—is scheduled for 2024.)

"KLDI," the fourth of my stories featuring Texas PI Helmut Erhard, will be in **Michael Bracken's** *Mickey Finn: 21st Century Noir* (Vol. 2), coming from Down & Out Books in Dec. 2021. (The fifth and sixth Erhard stories are coming in 2022 from *AHMM* and *Black Cat Mystery Magazine*.)

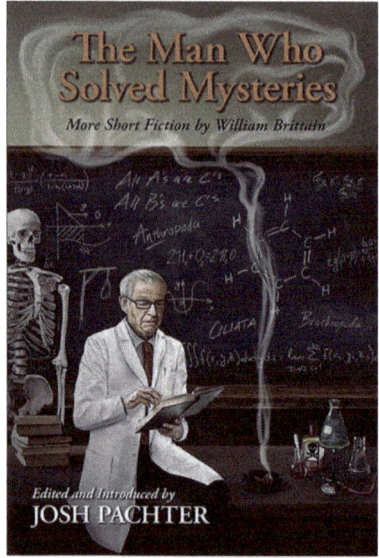

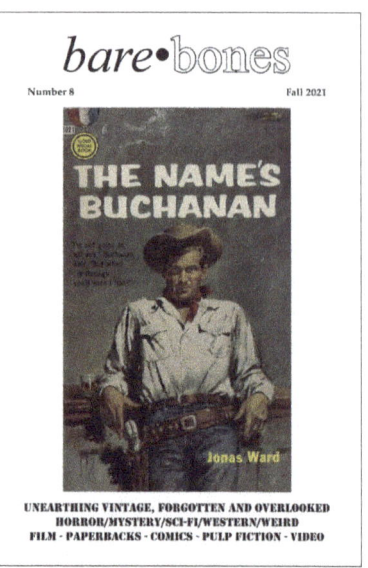

"Their Last Bow," the fifth and last of my Ellery Queen's Puzzle Club pastiches, will be in the Jan/Feb 2022 issue of *EQMM*, and Crippen & Landru will publish *The Adventures of the Puzzle Club*, which collects EQ's original five stories and my pastiches, in April 2022.

"Other stories in various pipelines include "The Brimley/Cocoon Line" (*Mystery Weekly*), "My Shit's Fucked Up" (*Lawyers, Guns, and Money: Crime Fiction Inspired by the Songs of Warren Zevon*, edited by **Art Taylor** from Down and Out), and "I Don't Like Mondays" (*I Just Died in Your Arms: Crime Fiction Inspired by One-Hit Wonders*, edited by **Jay Hartman** from Untreed Reads)."

Peter Enfantino:
Cimarron Street Books

"In 2022, Cimarron Street Books will release four new issues of *Bare Bones*, featuring the usual eclectic variety of articles spotlighting vintage, forgotten, and overlooked horror, mystery, sci-fi, western, and weird film, paperbacks, comics, pulp fiction, and video. We've got several surprises

awaiting our readers in '22, including some familiar faces and several surprising additions. Cimarron Street will continue publishing the works of **David J. Schow**, with at least three story collections (*Black Leather Required*, *Havoc Swims Jaded*, and *DJStories*) to be released in '22. And then there's the pet projects of publishers **John Scoleri** and I. John is working on a movie tie-in book and I'm finally finished my dissection of all the pre-code horror comics published by Atlas (Marvel) in the 1950s. Both books should see the light of day in the coming year. Check the <cimarronstreetbooks.com> website for up-to-the-moment details."

In the seventh issue of *Bare Bones* from Summer 2021, **Matthew R. Bradley** covers **H.P. Lovecraft** adaptations, **John Scoleri** leads a roundtable discussion of *Once Upon a Time in Hollywood*, **William Schoell's** cover story about comic book adaptations of fantasy and SF films, **J. Charels Burwell** and Peter review stories by **James McKimmey**, **S. Craig Zahler** talks pulps, Peter visits "Sleaze Alley," and **David J. Schow** examines novelizations.

Jackie Sherbow:
Ellery Queen and Alfred Hitchcock Mystery Magazines

"*EQMM* celebrated its 80th anniversary in 2021, concluding toward the end of the year with a trivia contest. The March/April 2022 issue, available in February, will contain a new novella by National Book Award winner **Joyce Carol Oates** and stories by other top authors, including Edgar winner **Wendy Hornsby**. The May/June issue, available in April, features stories by multiple Edgar winner **Doug Allyn**, O. Henry Prize winner **Sheila Kohler**, and Edward D. Hoch Memorial Golden Derringer winner **Michael Bracken**. It will announce the winners of the 2021 *EQMM* Readers Award. The award will be presented in the spring.

"*AHMM*'s March/April issue will feature stories by **Paul D. Marks**, **Michael A. Black**, and *EQMM* Readers Award winner **Gregory Fallis**. The Case Files column will address DNA testing and other law-enforcement related topics. The May/June issue, available in April, will contain stories by **Mary Angela**, **John M. Floyd**, and Edgar Award nominee **Stephen Ross**. The 2021 Black Orchid Novella Award winning story will be published in the July/August issue, available in June."

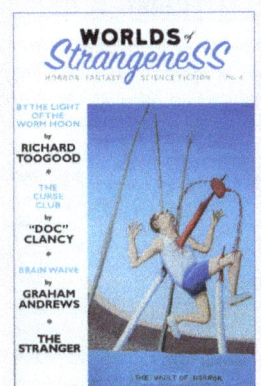

Nigel Taylor: Worlds of Strangeness

Shortly after *TDE14* launched, Nigel released the fourth edition of his genre fiction digest. *Worlds of Strangeness* No. 4, Spring/Summer 2021 features "By the Light of the Worm Moon," a sword and sorcery story by **Richard Toogood**; "The Curse Club," with Silver Sabremen, by **"Doc" Clancy**; "Brain Waive," a story by **Graham Andrews** riffing on a Fredric Brown theme; and Nigel himself writing as The Stranger with "A Farce in Metropolis," plus Micronicles (flash fiction) No. 10–12. Nigel reports issue 5 is in the works now but its launch date remains a secret. <worldsofstrangeness.com>

Stark House Press presents...

Staccato Crime is a new series that will offer affordable paperback editions of dificult-to-find noir action and true crime from the Jazz Age, 1899-1939.

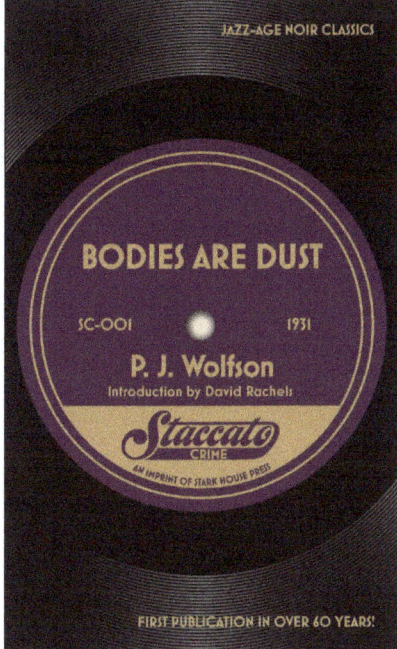

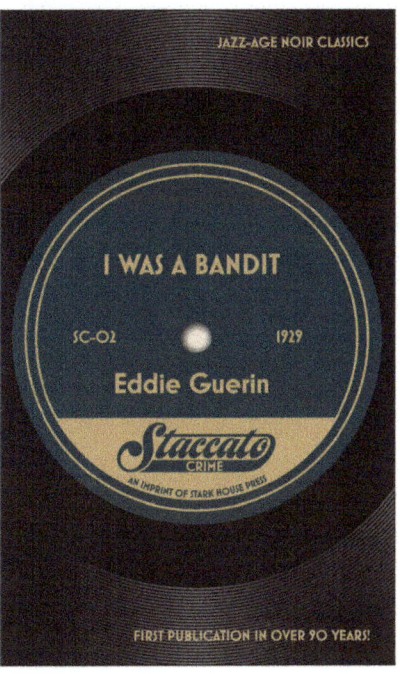

STACCATO CRIME #1
P. J. WOLFSON
BODIES ARE DUST

"...out-Hammetts Hammett. Same detached style, but the emotions are extraordinarily powerful. Astonishingly poignant dénouement."—Allan Guthrie.
New introduction by David Rachels.
August 2021.

STACCATO CRIME #2
EDDIE GUERIN
I WAS A BANDIT

The memoirs of Eddie Guerin, famous international criminal who escaped from the French penal colony of Maroni, near Devil's Island. New introduction by Jeff Vorzimmer.
November 2021.

1315 H Street, Eureka, CA 95501
707-498-3135
www.StarkHousePress.com
Available from your local bookstore, or direct from the publisher

Stephen Jones and David A. Sutton

Interviewed by Richard Krauss

"Fantasy Tales remained very true to its editors' aim, succeeding admirably in recreating the entertainment value of the pulps."

–Gordon Larkin, *Science Fiction, Fantasy, and Weird Fiction Magazines* Greenwood Press, 1985

The following interview with the creators of *Fantasy Tales* took place via email in Nov. 2021.

The Digest Enthusiast: What were the origins of *Fantasy Tales*, and how did it evolve?

Stephen Jones: In 1968, David had created the fanzine *Shadow: Fantasy Literature Review*, which ran for twenty-one issues until 1974, and he was one of the co-founders of the British Fantasy Society (BFS). He had also edited two volumes of the paperback anthology *New Writings in Horror & the Supernatural* for Sphere Books. When I entered the genre in the early 1970s, I was obviously in awe of him!

David A. Sutton: After I had wound-up *Shadow* in 1974, I'd already begun editing for Sphere and Corgi Books. Corgi published my stand-alone anthology *The Satyr's Head & Other Tales of Terror* in 1975. There were a number of great horror editors in the UK in the 1970s, such as Peter Haining, Richard Davis, Hugh Lamb, Herbert van Thal, Robert Aickman, Ronald Chetwynd-Hayes, and Richard Dalby, so I was in no illusion that I

The 1990s were cool. David A. Sutton and Stephen Jones, photographed by Seamus Ryan.

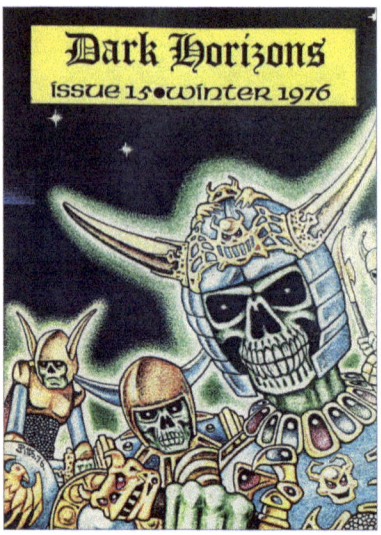

might be able to wedge my way further into a pretty busy field! So, I was looking for other areas to further hone my editing abilities.

Shadow had been my attempt at producing a 'zine that reviewed and evaluated the genre, and was almost totally dedicated to book reviews and feature articles on authors or themes in genre fiction. But based on my first forays into fiction editing, it was a short story magazine that was in my thoughts at this time.

Stephen: So David and I began corresponding, and I ended up editing the BFS' journal *Dark Horizons* in 1974. By this time, litho printing had pretty much replaced the old hand-duplicated method of printing fanzines in the UK, and I based my editions of the magazine on *Shadow* and Stuart David Schiff's American *Whispers*. I tried to make it more professional, and started getting writers such as Ramsey Campbell and Brian Lumley to contribute.

However, by 1976, I decided that I had taken *Dark Horizons* as far as I could. Britain had no semi-professional genre fiction magazines at that time—let alone any professional titles—so I

suggested to David that we collaborate on one.

David: Like Steve, I had been heavily involved in the British Fantasy Society and, alongside various committee jobs, I assisted with the production of a few issues of *Dark Horizons* and edited issue No. 7 in 1973 (I also edited several issues in the 1980s). As I recall, Steve and I were deep in conversation at one of the British fantasy conventions, Fantasycon. I can't recall how the discussion turned to magazines, but it was one of those serendipitous moments, because both of us wanted to edit and produce a fiction magazine of some kind, though we'd not discussed working together before. A collaboration was duly cemented, and the seed of *Fantasy Tales* was born . . .

Stephen: *Dark Horizons* No. 15 (Winter, 1976) was my final issue as editor, and it was basically a "pilot" for *Fantasy Tales*. Most importantly, although color printing was still prohibitively expensive in the UK, my printer had just got in a color Xerox machine, which was much more economical. We experimented with the cover of *DH* No. 15—by our artist friend Jim Pitts—and it seemed to work well enough that we felt confident to move ahead with our plans for Britain's first semi-professional fantasy and horror magazine.

TDE: What's the story behind the *Fantasy Tales* name?

David: Steve was creator of the magazine's title. But that name also suggested that it would be more than a purely horror or weird fiction title, of course!

Stephen: I had always been a fan of the classic pulp magazine *Weird Tales*, and I wanted something that reflected that. *Fantasy Tales* just seemed natural.

TDE: What inspired the early masthead's flowing typography?

Stephen: Again, it was *Weird Tales*. We wanted something that reflected that magazine's logo. At the time, I was

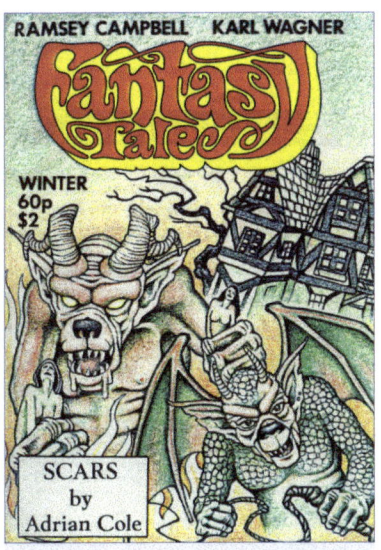

Fantasy Tales Vol. 1 No. 1 Summer 1977
Cover: Jim Pitts, BC: John Grandfield
"Naked as a Sword" by Kenneth Bulmer
"Fog Upon Ynth" by Gordon Larkin (verse)
"A Madness from the Vaults"
 by Ramsey Campbell revised from
 Doubt No. 1 1964
"Morvenna" by John Grandfield (verse)
"The Price to Pay" by Eddy C. Bertin
"Mylakhrion the Immortal"
 by Brian Lumley
"The Stone Thing" by Michael Moorcock
 from *Triode* October 1974
"The Dream Shop" by Brian Mooney
"Milk of Kindness" by Steve Sneyd

Fantasy Tales Vol. 1 No. 2 Winter 1977
Cover:Jim Pitts, BC: Jim Fitzpatrick
"Scars" by Adrian Cole
"The Hypnocosm"
 by William Thomas Webb
"Accident Zone" by Ramsey Campbell
"The Cauldron" letters column
"The Last Wolf" by Karl Edward Wagner
 from *Midnight Sun* No. 2
 Summer/Fall 1975
"City Out of Time" by Brian Lumley (verse)
"Borden Wood" by Sydney J. Bounds
"Undead" by Brian Mooney (verse)
"The Feast of Argatha" by F. C. Adams

working in the television and video industry in London's Soho, and we shot a lot at the ITN studios, which belonged to the UK's independent news network. I knew the head of design, Malcolm Beatson, very well. So I showed him an example of the *Weird Tales* masthead and asked him to come up with something similar in the distinctive red and yellow colors—on someone else's production budget!

The "flowing" logo was the result, and it was perfect. Remember, there was no such thing as personal computers back then—the logo was hand-painted onto a thin piece of clear ac-

etate, and we had to physically attach it to each new issue's cover art. I'm actually surprised it survived, and I still have it up in my attic somewhere.

David: I was bowled over when Steve showed me the logo design. It had something of the *Weird Tales* look to it, with the red and yellow lettering but even more, the flowing, curving letters contained within the F and Y of "Fantasy" fashioned a knock-out, bold and exceptional design. The studio designer had done a fantastic job.

TDE: *Fantasy Tales* always delivered a beautiful package, what factors drove its design and format?

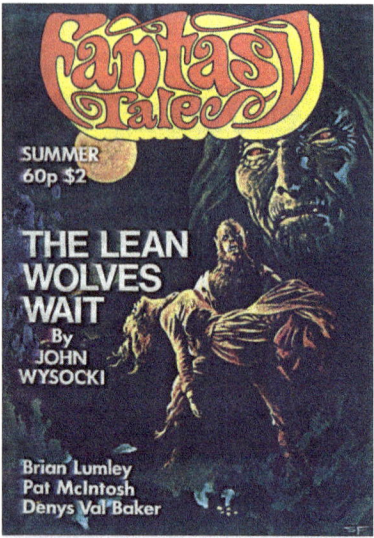

Fantasy Tales Vol. 2 No. 3 Summer 1978
Cover: Stephen Fabian,
    BC: Sylvia Starshine
"At the End of the Road"
    by Patrick Connolly
"A Sonnet for Insanity" by Marion Pitman
"Lean Wolves Wait" by John Wysocki
"Berúthiel" by Pat McIntosh (verse)
"The Last Sleeping God of Mars"
    by Andrew Darlington
"Fantasy Tales" by Brian Lumley (verse)
"The Inheritance" by Denys Val Baker
    from *The Face in the Mirror* by Denys
    Val Baker, Arkham House, 1971
"The Exhumation" by Peter Coleborn
"The Cauldron" letters column

Fantasy Tales Vol. 2 No. 4 Spring 1979
Cover: Jim Pitts, BC: Simon Horsfall
"First Make Them Mad" by Adrian Cole
"Love Philtre" by H. Warner Munn (verse)
    from *Weirdbook* No. 1 1968
"The Chinese Box" by Ken Dickson
"Mourning of the Following Day"
    by Karl Edward Wagner (verse)
    from *Dark Crusade* 1976
"Bloodgold" by Joe R. Schifino
"At Last the Arcana Revealed"
    by A. J. Silvonius
"Mausoleum" by Gordon Larkin (verse)
"Tomb-Time" by Steve Eng (verse)
"The Cauldron" letters column

Stephen: We always wanted *Fantasy Tales* to be as professional looking as we could make it, on the limited budget that we had to work with. Again, the interior design was very much based on the *Weird Tales* template—which involved using a whole raft of different elements.

As I said, no computers back then. I hand-typed all the text in columns on a IBM Selectric typewriter—changing the "golf ball" when I needed italics or another typeface.

The "display" faces for story titles and author bylines were created rubbing down individual letters from different sheets of Letraset typefaces.

I then had to hand-draw pencil grids for every page. Once that was done, I assembled all the different elements on my mother's kitchen table using a scalpel and several tubes of glue. Every element on a single page—including things like page numbers and running heads—had to be cut out, positioned, and then glued down. After that, I would erase the pencil lines and use whiteout correction fluid to hide the edges of as much as I could.

As you can imagine, it was a laborious process!

David: Laborious was exactly it. Although Steve did all the layout work for *Fantasy Tales*, with my *Shadow* magazine there was an even older, but just as laborious process. When I began production, lithographic printing for small fanzines was in its infancy, so my way of working was to type up text and columns using my (even then old) Remington office typewriter. This would be not on paper, but onto "stencils." These waxy sheets came with perforated backing paper, which had to be removed, before the stencil was attached to my hand-cranked Rex Rotary duplicator (mimeograph machine).

My machine was even more primitive than most, as it did not have an ink cartridge. I had to apply ink to the drum from a giant size toothpaste tube of ink, very messy and getting an even spread of ink was a nightmare. The drum duly inked, I would churn out the pages, changing the stencil for each side of the paper, 100 copies of each sheet (I think my print run was even more than that at one time). Then the whole set of pages had to be collated and side-stapled to make up the magazine.

For anyone who does not know what the hell I am talking about, there are some archive films about the process on YouTube, such as: <youtube.com/watch?v=XFIUm0DWA74>.

TDE: What was your network of writers and artists like when you started the magazine and how did it grow?

Stephen: Well by this time we knew a lot of writers and artists through the British Fantasy Society and our previous publishing ventures. We literally had no money to pay anyone on the first issue, so we contacted the professional authors we knew—like Eddy C. Bertin, Kenneth Bulmer, Ramsey Campbell, Brian Lumley, and Michael Moorcock—and, god bless them, they

Fantasy Tales Vol. 3 No. 5 Winter 1979
Cover: David Lloyd, BC: Randy Broecker
"Extension 201" by Cyril Simsa
"The Thing in the Moonlight" by H. P.
  Lovecraft & Brian Lumley from *The
  Arkham Collector* No. 4 Winter 1969
"An Agonising Choice"
  by Gordon Larkin (verse)
"For the Life Everlasting"
  by Brian Mooney
"Don't Open That Door" by Frances
  Garfield revised from "Forbidden
  Cupboard" *Weird Tales* Jan. 1940
"The Exiles" by H. Warner Munn (verse)
"Just Another Vampire Story"
  by Randall Garrett
"The Seafarers" by Simon Ounsley (verse)
"The Cauldron" letters column
"Morsel" by Steve Eng (verse)

supported our little venture by giving us new stories. That allowed us to make a bit of a "splash" with our debut issue, and things just grew from there.

David: Yes, that's right, we had a slew of writers and illustrators that came along with the growth of the BFS. I had also accumulated a number of writer contacts from editing for Sphere and Corgi. Soliciting for new short stories for the anthologies increased the resource of both established and be-

Fantasy Tales Vol. 3 No. 6 Summer 1980
Cover: Jim FitzPatrick, BC: Jim Pitts
"Ever the Faith Endures" by Manly Wade
    Wellman from *The Year's Best Horror
    Stories: Series VI* DAW, 1978
"The Wind-Walker"
    by Brian Lumley (verse)
"Lair of the White Wolf"
    by Joe R. Schifino
"The Blades of Hell"
    by Don Herron (verse)
"Dreams May Come" by H. Warner Munn
    from *Unknown* October 1939
"The Elementals" by Frances Garfield
"The Last Trick" by Dave Reeder
"The Cauldron" letters column
"The Story of the Brown Man"
    by Darrell Schweitzer from
    Fantasy Crosswinds No. 1 Jan. 1977
"Bone-Yowl" by Steve Eng (poem)

ginning writers who were looking for
outlets.

Some of my higher profile authors in
those early anthologies were Ramsey
Campbell, James Wade, Rosemary
Timperley, Robert Holdstock, and Joseph Payne Brennan. But for the most
part I was looking for new writers,
which meant an open market offering
opportunities for emerging talent. *Fantasy Tales* provided another outlet, but

for more than just horror tales.

TDE: *Fantasy Tales* was obviously a
labor of love, what did the financials
look like?

Stephen: Our plan was to use the
money we made on previous issues
to pay for subsequent issues. We had
enough "seed money" to pay for the
first two issues, and after that it was on
its own.

It almost worked. We were able to
start paying a minimal sum for fiction
from the second issue onwards, but
there was never enough to pay the artists or ourselves.

David: Our average author fee was
£10.00 (about $14.00) in the 1970s,
but most authors donated their work
for free, just contributor copies, in the
early days. We almost never paid for
verse or artwork, but stories attracted
a little more money in later issues, and
then more reasonable rates for the paperback series. The most we paid for a
story in the days of the magazine format was £60.00 ($84.00).

TDE: Before it launched, how did
you attract advertisers for your first
issue? Was it easier to sell ads as time
went on?

Stephen: Advertising was always
an important part of the magazine, and
it was one of the things that helped us
keep afloat, especially as a lot of the
bookstores and dealers who stocked
the magazine were often slow to pay us
(and, in one memorable instance that
nearly killed the title after the first issue, *never* paid us!).

Again, our links with the British
Fantasy Society helped a lot. I lived in
London and knew most of the publishing houses at that time. And we both
knew many specialist dealers on both
sides of the Atlantic, so we just contacted everybody we could think of.

It was always hard work getting advertising, but some of the dealers like
G. Ken Chapman and Fantasy Centre

were extremely supportive and booked advertising in every issue, which really helped us keep going.

David: I recall that both Fantasy Centre and G. Ken Chapman were our most frequent advertisers. The former was one of the best-loved second-hand genre bookstores in London, with its own inimitable atmosphere, always looking slightly down-at-heel, but what a treasure chest! The much-loved Ted Ball was the original owner. Chapman was an antiquarian bookseller, and the UK representative of Arkham House. It was my go-to mail order company to buy AH titles. Both were welcome supporters of *Fantasy Tales*.

TDE: As Editor and Associate Editor what was the division of labor?

Stephen: David mostly looked after the fiction and poetry submissions, while I handled the artwork, design, advertising, and commissioning some of the bigger names. However, it was never as clear-cut as that. From the very beginning, we worked together on every aspect of the magazine.

Looking back now, we should have just shared the "editing" credit but, again, I think the "Associate Editor" thing came from the pulp magazines. It basically means "co-editor" and just looked better on the page.

David: Steve is being a little modest, as he did *all* the layout work, with me offering suggestions as to design etc. I never had the hassle of gluing columns onto master sheets and getting the kerning right with Letraset transfers (although I had the experience and the fun of working with such material in the past). Steve had a natural ability with design and kept the look of the pulps in his mind at every stage of the process.

I got all the fiction and verse submitted to the magazine, so I read all the material first and dealt with acceptances and rejections, while Steve

Fantasy Tales Vol. 4 No. 7 Spring 1981
Cover: Jim Pitts, BC: Stephen E. Fabian
"The Other One" by Karl Edward Wagner
     from *Escape!* No. 1 Fall 1977
"The Wedding Guest"
     by Steven Edward McDonald (verse)
"Reflections on a Dark Eye"
     by Peter Tremayne
"Payment in Kind" by Caradoc A. Cador
     from *Gnostica* August 1975
"A Death-Song for Gondath"
     by Marion Pitman (verse)
"Wrapped Up" by Ramsey Campbell
"The Woodcarver's Son"
     by Robert A. Cook
"Limbo" by H. Warner Munn (verse)
     from *Omniumgathum* 1976
"The Last Horror Out of Arkham"
     by Darrell Schweitzer from
     Fantasy Crosswinds No. 3 Jan. 1977
"Bleak December" by Dave Ward (verse)
"The Cauldron" letters column

sought out new and reprint fiction from some of the high-profile authors and old-timers. Steve would then read all the fiction and poetry and, after discussing the various submissions, we'd come up with a final contents list for an individual issue.

Steve's approach, thinking especially of *Fantasy Tales* being a new slant on *Weird Tales*, meant that we could in-

DENNIS ETCHISON • BRIAN MOONEY

fantasy tales

SUMMER
75p $2.50

A PLACE OF NO RETURN
by Hugh B. Cave

Fantasy Tales Vol. 4 No. 8 Summer 1981
Cover: Dave Carson, BC: Alan Hunter
"The Dark Country" by Dennis Etchison
"A Place of No Return" by Hugh B. Cave
"The Elevation of Theosophus
     Goatgrime" by Brian Mooney
"The Legacy" by James Glenn
"Sic Transit..." by Mike Chinn
"Shadows from the Past" by Mary Clarke
"Swamp Call" by Brian Lumley (verse)
"Weirwood" by Michael D. Toman
"The Cauldron" letters column

clude some of the then living greats from the "Unique Magazine." So, we ended up with a new fiction magazine that tipped its hat to *Weird Tales* in a very tangible way. It was issue No. 4 that started this very real link to *WT*, with a poem by H. Warner Munn, who Steve had met while attending World Fantasy Conventions.

Stephen: After that, we published work by such original *Weird Tales* contributors as Robert Bloch, Fritz Leiber, Hugh B. Cave, Manly Wade Wellman, and Frances Garfield—we were happy to take reprints from them which most of our readership had never seen before. In fact, Cave, Garfield, and Wellman all ended up contributing original

work to the magazine as well.

TDE: In the introduction to the letters column, "The Cauldron," in issue No. 4, you mentioned most of your sales came from bookstores. How did that come about?

Stephen: Because, back then, bookstores were mostly where you bought your books and magazines. There was no Internet, no Amazon. Just bricks-and-mortar stores that sold these things. So those were our major markets to aim for.

Of course, there were some mail-order dealers who ordered copies but, as with the advertising, it was always an uphill struggle trying to get *Fantasy Tales* into stores. Again, we had some outlets that had standing orders (such as Fantasy Centre and Forbidden Planet in London), and that was very useful for the cash flow, although they were invariably slow to pay. We also sold copies directly by subscription.

David: Looking back now, before the days of Amazon and the Internet, it was much harder to get your stuff out there. I think the UK specialist book dealers and shops were our main places to sell and although most were based in London, where Steve could deliver copies by hand, there were also the odd out-of-town bookshops, such as the famed Andromeda Books in Birmingham. Everything was pay on invoice, so you had to wait at least a month, but probably longer, to get paid.

One thing we did to publicize the magazine was a "teaser" campaign prior to the launch of the first issue, which consisted of an advertisement with the *FT* logo and something like "Coming Soon!" with no other information. I think it generated a lot of interest.

TDE: What were the initial print runs of the magazine and how did they increase over the years?

Stephen: The simple answer is that they didn't. The print run for *Fantasy*

Tales remained at 1,000 copies for its entire seventeen-issue run.

When we started out in 1977, we pretty much sold out of the entire run, but by the time we ended the magazine a decade later, we probably had a sell-through rate of around 500–600 copies. I still have piles of back issues in my garage.

David: When you think how many people read genre material, it's always been odd that you can't sell to a wider audience—your fan base has always been the limit of sales for fan or small magazines. That *Fantasy Tales'* sales dropped over time mirrors the situation with paperback anthologies in the 1970s and '80s, although they were from mainstream publishers. Early *Pan Books of Horror* volumes, for instance, went through multiple reprints, but later volumes did not, and I daresay a lot of returned copies probably ended up being pulped.

There seems to be reader fatigue that sets in and sales decline . . . that seems to be the natural evolution in publishing. It doesn't diminish the work put in, or the esteem in which a book series or magazine is held, but it's just a natural

Fantasy Tales Vol. 5 No. 9 Spring 1982
Wraparound cover: Jim Pitts
"Dead Bird Singing in the Black of Night" by Adam Nichols
"The Changeling" by H. Warner Munn (verse) from *Weirdbook* No. 4 1971
"The Grey Horde" by David Malpass
"The Frolic" by Thomas Ligotti
"In Lieu of Applause" by Steve Eng (verse)
"The Laughter of Han" by Lin Carter
"Initiation" by George A. McIntyre (verse)
"The Strange Years" by Brian Lumley
"October Treat" by Phillip C. Heath
"Lee Brown Coye" by Karl Edward Wagner
"The Cauldron" letters column

progression.

TDE: A sister publication, *Fantasy Media*, was launched in 1979. What can you tell us about it?

Stephen: *Fantasy Media* wasn't really a "sister" publication to *Fantasy Tales*. It was basically a news and reviews magazine, along similar lines to *Locus* or *Science Fiction Chronicle*.

David and I have always ploughed some of the money we've made back into genre publishing. By this time we weren't happy with the direction the British Fantasy Society publications were going, so we set up our own

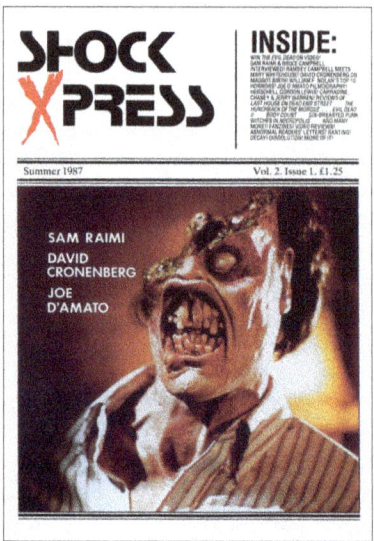

Fantasy Tales Vol. 5 No. 10 Summer 1982
Cover: David Lloyd, BC: Dave Carson
"The Voice of the Beach"
    by Ramsey Campbell
"A Witch for All Seasons" by Manly Wade
    Wellman as by Gans T. Field from
    Witchcraft & Sorcery No. 9 1973
"Death Wish" by Charlotte Dean (verse)
"But the Stones Will Stand…"
    by Mike Chinn
"Thatcher's Bluff" by James Anderson
"The Gardens" by Peter G. Shilston
"The Motel Room" by Scott E. Green
"The Cauldron" letters column

genre newszine with two other editors. It was quite successful for a while—we even had an exclusive interview with Stephen King in the first issue. *Fantasy Media* ran for eight issues.

We also published the one-off title *Airgedlámh* and the influential 1980s horror movie magazine *Shock Xpress*. In fact, we still support various genre publishing ventures to this day.

David: What Steve hasn't said is that there was a surprising amount of work involved in *Fantasy Media*. We had to trawl through tons of news clippings and media reports and extract information on films, books, comics, events, everything genre-related. Again, no

copy and paste from electronic documents or files, it was a lot of typing-up copy first! The magazine ran from 1979–80, and it was always a race to get the material ready for each issue. *Shock Xpress* ran from 1985–87 and was mostly edited by Stefan Jaworzyn.

Both this and *Fantasy Media* came out of Steve and myself putting money into projects that we were interested in. We have also helped to develop publications under our Airgedlámh imprint, such as various book titles with The Alchemy Press.

TDE: The stories you published in *Fantasy Tales* were a mix of reprints and originals. What considerations went into reprint selections?

Stephen: I think the reprints were marginally cheaper!

David: Reprints did attract smaller fees, but the magazine was small press, so there was never much of a difference between payment for new stories and reprints. It wasn't like we paid a pittance for reprints and tons of cash for new yarns—we paid quite low fees for all material, because that's all we could afford.

Stephen: The secret of any successful magazine is the names you put on the cover. We never really had the budget to attract the "Big Names" (although writers such as Ramsey Campbell, Brian Lumley, Dennis Etchison, even Clive Barker, gave us original material from time to time). Therefore we were happy to accept reprints, particularly if those reprints had never been published in the UK before, or had only appeared a long time ago or in some obscure publication.

David: Our strength came if writers wanted to contribute to this new magazine even if we couldn't pay much, and to our great joy they did. There was support that went beyond money, even though most writers in this field do not earn a proper income. It was only when the Robinson paperback editions came

Fantasy Tales Vol. 6 No. 11 Winter 1982
Cover: Jim Pitts, BC: Ian Hicks &
    Graham Crossland
"A Sprig of Rosemary" by H. Warner Munn
    from *Weird Tales* June 1933
"The Storm Devil of Lan-Kern"
    by Peter Tremayne
"To Welcome One of Their Own"
    by C. Bruce Hunter
"Seven Kings"
    by Robert E. Howard (verse)
"Dead to the World" by Allen A. Lucas
"At the Mouth of Time"
    by Joe R. Lansdale
"The Worm" by Joel Lane (verse)
"Legacy of Evil" by Peter Bayliss
"A Lady's Retribution"
    by Charlotte Dean (verse)
"The Story of Lallia the Slave Girl"
    by Dray Prescot
"The Cauldron" letter scolumn

Fantasy Tales Vol. 6 No. 12 Winter 1983
Cover: David Lloyd, BC: Stephen E. Fabian
"A Question of Identity" by Robert Bloch
    from *Strange Stories* April 1939
    as by Tarleton Fiske
"You Can Go Now" by Dennis Etchison
    from *Mike Shayne Mystery Magazine*
    Sept. 1980
"The Stones Would Weep"
    by Darrell Schweitzer
"The Zulu Lord"
    by Robert E. Howard (verse)
"The Summer House Party"
    by Peter A. Hough
"Ballad" by Marise Morland (verse)
"In the Labyrinth" by Simon R. Green
"The Green Man" by Kelvin Jones
"A Rock That Loved"
    by Jessica Amanda Salmonson
"Pharaoh's Revenge" by C. Bruce Hunter
    from *Sorcerer's Apprentice* No. 15
    Summer 1982
"The Cauldron" letters column

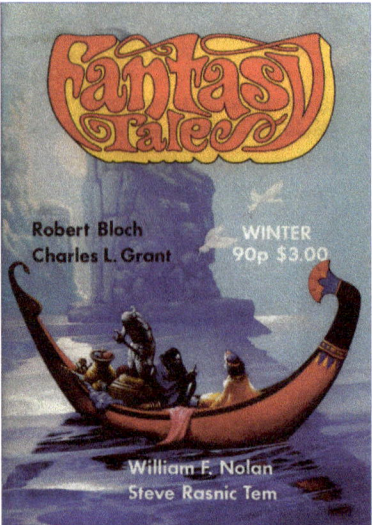 

Fantasy Tales Vol. 7 No. 13 Winter 1984
Covers: Stephen E. Fabian,
"The Sorcerer's Jewel" by Robert Bloch
    from *Strange Stories* Feb. 1939
    as by Tarleton Fiske
"The Last Guest" by Steve Eng (verse)
"Of Time and Kathy Benedict"
    by William F. Nolan
"The Generation Waltz"
    by Charles L. Grant
"The Bad People" by Steve Rasnic Tem
"Tongue in Cheek" by Mike Grace
"Vigilance" by Gary William Crawford
"The Cauldron" letters column

Fantasy Tales Vol. 7 No. 14 Summer 1985
Cover: Jim Pitts
"The Sneering" by Ramsey Campbell
"The Pushover" by Ardath Mayhar
"Yuggoth"
    by David Cowperthwaite (verse)
"The Castle at World's End"
    by Chris Naylor
"House of Ill Repute" by Jeffrey Goddin
"The Forbidden" by Clive Barker from
    Clive Barker's Books of Blood, Vol. V
    Sphere 1985
"The Other Side" by C. Bruce Hunter
    from *Mike Shayne Mystery Magazine*
    Nov. 1982
"The Cauldron" letters column

out that fees started to diverge and increase, with our ability to pay more for the well-known authors, based on our assumptions that sales would cover the expenses!

TDE: How were originals chosen? Did you solicit stories from authors you knew? What was the typical mix of requested work versus blind submissions?

Stephen: David can probably answer that question better than I can— he had the job of "first reader" of all the unsolicited submissions. Because I knew so many of the old-time or emerging writers personally, it was my job to try to hit them up for submissions at conventions or when we met up socially.

David: Over the time *Fantasy Tales* was published, we received many hundreds of unsolicited submissions. It was a completely open market, and as few outlets were available in the UK, we began to accumulate a large reserve of new material. There were plenty of good writers and good stories out there. The mix or percentage of unsolicited submissions against material sought directly from authors was, I imagine, more than 90%, though this is a rough estimate.

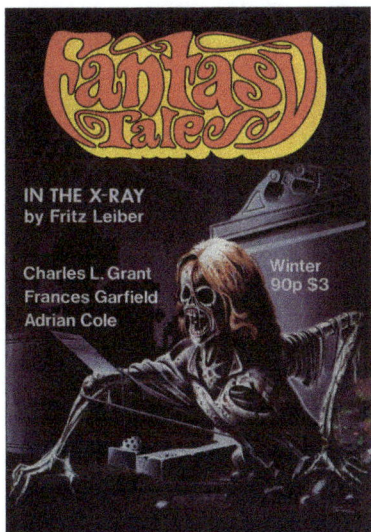

Fantasy Tales Vol. 8 No. 15 Winter 1985
Cover: Tom Campbell,
"In the X-Ray" by Fritz Leiber
    from *Weird Tales* July 1949
"Amorous of the Far" by Frances Garfield
"Book of the Dead" by Joel Lane (verse)
"The Terminus" by Kim Newman
    from *Sheep Worrying* 1981
"Shadrezzar" by Phil Emery (verse)
"Long Walk Home" by Charles L. Grant
"Down by the Sea" by Malcolm Furnass
"The Exile of Earthendale"
    by Adrian Cole
"After Nightfall" by David A. Riley
    from *The Year's Best Horror Stories*
    Sphere 1971
"The Farthing Lord" by Jon Bye (verse)
"Take Five" by Samantha Lee
"The Cauldron" letters column

Fantasy Tales Vol. 8 No. 16 Winter 1986
Cover: J. K. Potter, BC: Allen Koszowski
"The Olympic Runner"
    by Dennis Etchison
Tribute to Manly Wade Wellman
    by Karl Edward Wagner
"The White Road" by Manly Wade Wellman
    (verse) from *Weird Tales* June 1928
"Red" by Richard Christian Matheson
    from *Night Cry* Summer 1986
"The Singing Stone" by Peter Tremayne
"After the Funeral" by Hugh B. Cave
"Twins" by David Case
"Zerail" by Josepha Sherman
"Eradication's Rise" by Christina Kiplinger
    (verse)
"Our Christmas Spirit"
    by George A. McIntyre
"Bon Appetit" by Samantha Lee
"The Cauldron" letters column

Stephen: I was always on the look-out for stories that had been "bounced" or had been deemed "unpublishable"—that's how we picked up some of our most memorable contributions, such as Dennis Etchison's award-winning "The Dark Country" and "The Olympic Runner". We got those stories because nobody else saw them as genre. We weren't so fussy about labels.

TDE: The editorial comments often highlighted stories for the upcoming issue. How far out did you plan things? How many issues were in the works at the same time?

Stephen: That was something I got from *Weird Tales* as well—the "coming attractions." As David will tell you, we had quite a big slush pile to draw upon, but we only planned ahead one issue at a time. That's because we never knew if there would be another issue!

Our finances were always somewhat precarious . . .

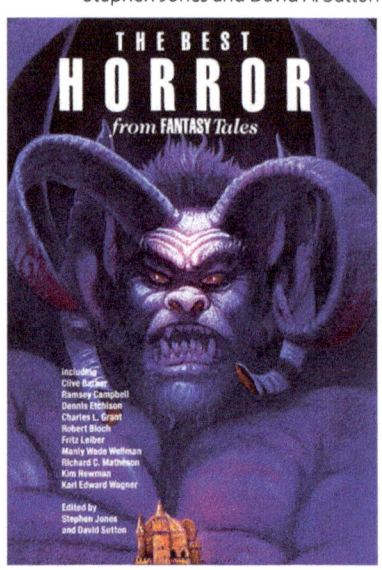

Fantasy Tales Vol. 9 No. 17 Summer 1987
Cover: Stephen E. Fabian,
"The Dandelion Chronicles"
    by William F. Nolan
"Writer's Curse" by Ramsey Campbell
    from *Night Flights* No. 1 1980/81
"The Last Call" by Michael Moorcock
"North Sea Lament" by Steve Eng (verse)
"The Traveling Salesman and the Farm-
    er's Daughter" by C. Bruce Hunter
"Ebony Rose" by Leilah Wendell (verse)
"Hell Is a Personal Place" by Brian Lumley
"Six Commonplaces" by Clive Barker
    (verse) from *Weaveworld* Simon &
    Schuster 1987
"The Hollywood Mandate" by Mike Chinn
"An Outworn Story"
    by Robert E. Howard (verse)
"The Ghoul of the Four Winds"
    by William Thomas Webb
"The Cauldron" letters column

David: That's right, only one issue
ahead was planned. The stories and
verse accumulated would sit there until
Steve and I got together to select material for the next issue.

Our publishing schedule was about
two issues per year. So, I always felt
guilty about hanging on to material
for so long, as we wouldn't always pick
earlier accepted material over later sub-

missions. We had to balance an issue
with a wide range of fantasy fiction. Of
course, in those days an author might
expect to wait a year or more before
seeing a story in print in an anthology,
so it wasn't so bad, except that a magazine format with greater frequency
would have served authors somewhat
better. Our aspirations were always
curtailed by ensuring the finances covered the next issue.

TDE: In 1988, the magazine grew
from saddle-stitch to perfect binding,
with more pages, a new design, and expanded distribution. What drove these
improvements?

Stephen: Well, firstly, I'm not sure
I would call them "improvements."
David and I made the decision to end
Fantasy Tales with an all-star No. 17,
dated Summer 1987. Other things were
happening, and we just didn't have the
time to devote to the magazine any
more. At least I didn't.

Then we had an advantageous meeting with the late and lamented Nick
Robinson in the bar late one night at
a Fantasycon. He had just started up
his own imprint, Robinson Publishing, and over a beer he asked us if we

Fantasy Tales Relaunch Flyer from 1988.

had ever considered putting together a "Best of" volume from *Fantasy Tales* as an anthology.

We looked at each other and then, with straight faces told him that we hadn't and it was a brilliant idea. In fact, we'd been trying to sell such a book for the past year or so and had been rejected by every publisher that we had approached!

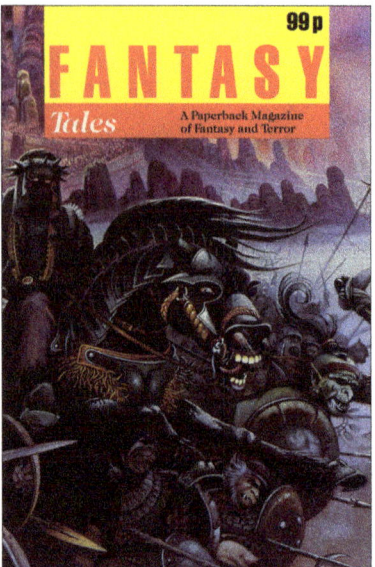

Fantasy Tales Vol. 10 No. 1 Autumn 1988
Wraparound Cover: Chris Achilleos
"Now and Again in Summer"
    by Charles L. Grant
"The Thievery of Yish" by Lin Carter
"Vampire Village" by Guy N. Smith
"The Farmer and the Travelling Sales-
    man's Daughter" by C. Bruce Hunter
"Fancy That" by J. N. Williamson
"Touching" by Chris Morgan
"A Vision of Rembathene"
    by Darrell Schweitzer from *Fantasy
    Crossroads* No. 10/11 March 1977
"Writer's Cramp" by David A. Riley
"The Cloven Cross"
    by Chris Naylor (verse)
"Memories" ("Shall We Remember")
    by Robert E. Howard (verse)
"The Cauldron" letters column
Cover Artist: Chris Achilleos
    by Stephen Jones

So we ended up doing a deal for *The Best Horror from Fantasy Tales* with Nick. It was my first anthology, and I think it turned out pretty well. It was published in both the UK and the USA, and there was even a Spanish translation.

Well, the thing about Nick Robinson was that he was always eager to try out any new publishing ideas. And so it was he who suggested that we revive *Fantasy Tales* as an inexpensive trade paperback—something that might be picked up by someone as an "impulse buy."

The problem was that he wanted to "modernize" the look of the magazine (including changing our distinctive logo), and it was also priced far too low to earn back enough to be profitable. As a result, the paperback edition not only lost its identity as a tribute to *Weird Tales*, but it also never made any money. It was an honorable experiment, and the trade paperback version lasted for seven volumes.

David: Nick Robinson was a great publisher to deal with, but the paperback *Fantasy Tales* didn't really work well. Like other magazines that turned into a paperback format, the look could never be as good. I'm forever grateful that Nick published those seven issues, in which we continued to work through the backlog of stories, as well as showcase some of our great genre writers, such as Charles L. Grant, Neil Gaiman, Brian Lumley, William F. Nolan, David J. Schow and many notable others. But, Steve has said it, the so-called "modern" look meant we lost the identity of the magazine as well as the nod of gratitude to *Weird Tales*.

But that first encounter with Nick—when he suggested publishing a "Best Of"—was a peculiar reversal of what normally happens when you try to get an anthology published: we didn't have to prepare a proposal, or submit the one we'd already been circulating . . . So Nick did us a lot of good. It was just that the paperback *FT* lost its way because of Nick's desire to change the look of the magazine and then underprice it.

TDE: How many *FT* anthologies were published?

Stephen: As previously mentioned,

THE 1988 WORLD FANTASY CONVENTION STARTS AT

FORBIDDEN PLANET

WITH A PRE-HALLOWEEN SIGNING BY

CLIVE BARKER
RAMSEY CAMPBELL
DENNIS ETCHISON
CHARLES L. GRANT
BRIAN LUMLEY
KARL EDWARD WAGNER

AND MANY, MANY MORE WHO WILL SIGN COPIES OF

The Best **HORROR** *from* **FANTASY** *Tales*

Robinson H/B £11.95

ON THURSDAY 27TH OCTOBER FROM 5.00-6 30PM

THE SCIENCE FICTION AND COMIC BOOK SHOP
71 NEW OXFORD STREET, LONDON WC1A 1DG, ENGLAND
OPENING TIMES 10AM-6PM; THURSDAY AND FRIDAY 10AM-7PM
TELEPHONE: 01-836 4179 AND 01-379 6042

The Best Horror from Fantasy Tales book signing flyer October 1988.

David A. Sutton and Stephen Jones, clad in *Fantasy Tales* T-shirts, accept the 1982 British Fantasy Award in David's backyard. Photograph by Jo Fletcher.

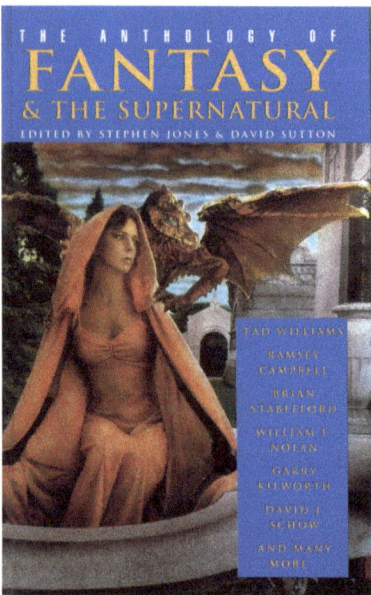

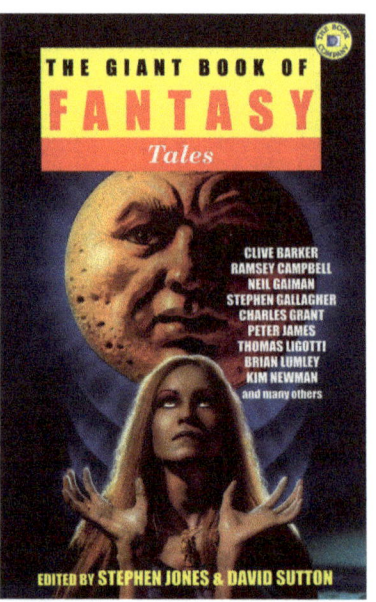

The Best Horror from Fantasy Tales was published in 1988 as a hardcover by Robinson in the UK and two years later in America by Carroll & Graf. It finally came out in paperback in the US from C&G in 2003.

David: Of course, *The Best Horror from Fantasy Tales* was also lavishly illustrated, and demonstrates how accommodating and open to suggestions Nick Robinson was.

Stephen: *The Anthology of Fantasy & the Supernatural* was a second *Fantasy Tales* anthology (it's indicated as such on the back cover), which we put together for Robinson in 1994. It was published as an "instant remainder" hardcover under the Tiger Books imprint in the UK, and reprinted in trade paperback two years later under the budget Magpie Books and Parragon imprints. For this, we mostly used stories that David still had left over in the *Fantasy Tales* inventory.

David: I was particularly pleased were we contracted to do *The Anthology of Fantasy & the Supernatural*, because we were able to use a pile of yarns that had been in the *Fantasy Tales* vaults for a long time. Although it was published as an "instant remainder," the Tiger Books edition was very attractive, with illustrations by several artists working for *Fantasy Tales* at the time.

Stephen: Finally, we followed that up in 1996 with *The Giant Book of Fantasy Tales*, which was basically another "Best of" volume, most of the contents of which was culled from the Robinson trade paperback run. It was done as another "instant remainder" for Magpie, but was only published in trade paperback under The Book Company imprint in Australia. It's never been reprinted.

David: All three *FT* anthologies we did for Robinson were very desirable books.

TDE: During the first decade, issue numbering was consecutive, with volumes assigned to years. When Robinson Publishing took over, the numbering system changed, and when a US edition with Carroll & Graf began it changed again. Can you sort out the numbers and editions for collectors?

Stephen: Oh, my god! That was a complete nightmare and, in my opinion, contributed to the failure of the Robinson/Carroll & Graf paperback revival. Robinson took its eye off the ball, and US readers were totally confused about the issue numbering—as were we!

To set the record straight: the UK trade paperback editions of *Fantasy Tales* No. 1, 2, and 3 were only published in Britain. No. 4 appeared in America as No. 1, but they left the numbering off the spine. The UK No. 5 was numbered No. 2 in the US but then, just to confuse everybody even more, No. 6 appeared under that number in *both* countries! Finally, No. 7 was issued as No. 4 in America, but by then it was too late. Nobody cared any more.

So, to summarize: there were seven volumes published in the UK, numbered sequentially, as you would expect. In the US there were four volumes, numbered No. 1, 2, 6, and 4. Don't let anyone tell you that dealing with publishers is easy!

David: What more can I add? I think I have my personal copies filed in the right order on my shelves, but who knows!

TDE: The covers of the Carroll & Graf editions repurpose cover artwork that appeared a few years earlier on a horror digest called *Night Cry*. What's the background on this?

David: I wasn't aware initially that the Carroll & Graf covers were all originally from *Night Cry*. Probably didn't do us any favors, although J.K. Potter is an artist whose work I admire, so I loved those covers.

Stephen: In fact, the covers on all the Robinson trade paperback editions were reprints. Because the books were priced so cheaply, they just didn't have the budget to buy in new cover artwork. In fact, the cover on No. 2 by Les Edwards had been previously used on

Fantasy Tales Vol. 10 No. 2 Spring 1989
Wraparound Cover: Les Edwards
"Ice and Fire" by Kenneth Bulmer
"The Cure" by William F. Nolan
    from *The Horror Show* Summer 1988
"The Dispossessed" by Joel Lane
"The Man Who Felt Pain"
    by Brian Lumley
"Vampire Sestina" by Neil Gaiman (verse)
"Stepping Out" by Will Johnson
"The Cauldron" letters column
"Future Fantasy" by Mike Ashley

a central heating advertisement! For those last four editions we were lucky to get "second rights" to his art from J.K. Potter. I guess it was just coincidence that they had all originally appeared on *Night Cry*. Probably the thinking at Robinson was that most readers would not have seen them before in the UK.

TDE: The final issue of *Fantasy Tales* appeared in Winter 1991. Why did it end? What happened to the stories and artwork (if any) in your backlog?

Stephen: As I've said, it was simply no longer sustainable. After discounts, there was just not enough profit there. Plus, I don't think that either David or I were entirely happy with the new in-

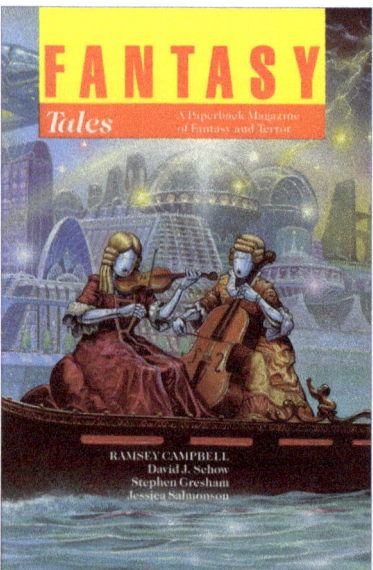

Fantasy Tales Vol. 11 No. 3 Autumn 1989
Wraparound Cover by Angus McKie
"The Sustenance of Hoak"
     by Ramsey Campbell from
     Swords Against Darkness Zebra 1977
"The One Left Behind"
     by Stephen Gresham from
     SPWAO Showcase No. 1 1980
"Wayland's Smithy" by Jon Bye (verse)
"John and the Magic Skillet"
     by Jessica Amanda Salmonson
"The Embracing" by David J. Schow from
     Ares No. 9 July 1981
"Worms" by Charles Whateley (verse)
"Fatal Bellman" by Alan W. Lear
"The Cauldron" letters column
"Future Fantasy" by Mike Ashley
Cover Artist: Angus McKie

Fantasy Tales Vol. 11 No. 4 Spring 1990
(Vol. 1 No. 1 Carroll & Graf, US edition)
Cover: J. K. Potter
"The Drain" by Stephen Gallagher
"Alice Smiling" by Charles L. Grant
"Into the Dark Land" by Darrell Schweit-
     zer from *Alien Worlds* Void 1979
"The Man Who Collected Barker"
     by Kim Newman
"Sea-Reverie" by Steve Eng (verse)
"Initiation" by Don Webb
"In the Trees" by Steve Rasnic Tem
"The Death and Afterlife of Sam McKay"
     by C. Bruce Hunter
"The Cauldron" letters column
"Future Fantasy" by Mike Ashley
"FT Forum" by Brian Lumley

carnation—it just wasn't "our" *Fantasy Tales*.

The artwork was commissioned on an issue-by-issue basis, and I think we pretty much used up any fiction backlog putting together *The Anthology of Fantasy & the Supernatural*. So far as I can recall, anything that was left over was returned to the authors.

David: In actual fact, there were still about sixty pieces of fiction and poetry still in the files when *Fantasy Tales* ceased publication, and that was after we had used up a good number of stories still in the vaults in *The Anthology of Fantasy & the Supernatural*.

I contacted everyone and apologized that in the end we weren't able to use their material. That's even worse than sending a rejection letter, because you have accepted the material for publication. There's an expectation on behalf of the writer, and for my part I felt like I had let them down. Hindsight's always a good thing to have and, had I been psychic, I would probably have set a time-limit on submissions, exactly as you do with anthologies; this would have kept me in check if nothing else!

TDE: Your beloved magazine seems a natural for a revival from one of today's small press publishers. Have you ever been approached in this regard?

Stephen: Funny you should say that. We are currently in the early stages of planning a one-off 45th anniversary tribute to *Fantasy Tales* with a small UK publisher, which is due to appear towards the end of 2022. I might even try to dig out that original acetate logo from up in the attic.

David: If the anniversary tribute goes ahead, I'd certainly like to see that old logo again… it's been a long time hidden away . . .

Stephen: It's probably also worth pointing out that *The Best Horror from Fantasy Tales* has never been published in paperback in the UK. *The Anthology of Fantasy & the Supernatural* has only appeared in the UK and nowhere else, while *The Giant Book of Fantasy Tales* was only ever published in Australia. I'm sure I speak for both of us when I say that we would be happy to see all those books back in print sometime . . .

David: Yes, I agree, the *FT* anthologies are long overdue a new airing!

TDE: Thanks so much for this behind-the-scenes look at *Fantasy Tales*. What's the best way for readers to keep up with your work?

Stephen: For me, it's probably through my Facebook page, but I'm very picky about who I let in.

David: I have an occasionally-used Facebook page and a modest web presence for my small press, Shadow Publishing <shadowpublishing.net>. These days when I get the occasional short story published in anthologies or magazines, I'll tend to mention them on Facebook.

Fantasy Tales Vol. 11 No. 5 Fall 1990 (Vol. 1 No. 2 Carroll & Graf, US edition)
Cover: J. K. Potter
"The Cauldron" by Stephen Jones & David A. Sutton
"Invisible Boy" by Roberta Lannes
"The Changer of Names" by Ramsey Campbell from *Swords Against Darkness* II Zebra 1977
"Night Bloomer" by David J. Schow from *Seeing Red* Tor 1990
"On the Wing" by Jean-Daniel Brèque (translated from the French by Nicholas Royle) from *Breves* No. 33/34
"Family Ties" by Elsa Beckett
"Black the Water" by Jessica Amanda Salmonson (verse)
"Dead on Time" by Nik Morton
"The Bridge People" by J. N. Williamson
"The Gnarl" by Randall D. Larson
"Scoop" by Samantha Lee
"The Cabinets" by Gary William Crawford
"Honour Bright" by Lee Barwood
"Networks" by Garry Kilworth

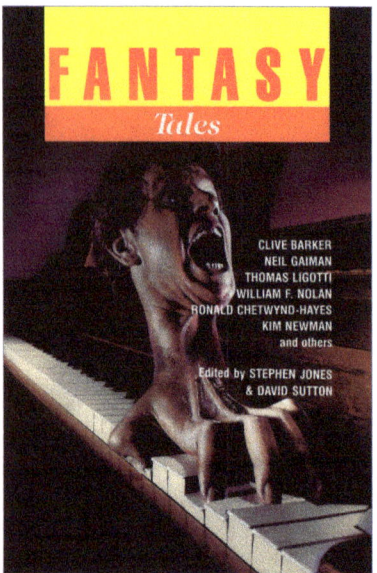

Issue contents primarily copied from Galactic Central website.

Fantasy Tales No. 6 1991
(Vol. 2 No. 3 Carroll & Graf, US edition)
Cover: J. K. Potter
"The Cauldron" by Stephen Jones &
    David Sutton
"FT Forum: Speaking from the Dark"
    by Clive Barker originally "Keeping
    Company with Cannibal Witches"
    from *The Daily Telegraph*
    January 6, 1990
"Foreign Parts" by Neil Gaiman from
    Words Without Pictures
    Eclipse Books 1990
"The Monster" by R. Chetwynd-Hayes
    from *The 5th Fontana Book of Great
    Horror Stories* Fontana 1970
"How Jaquerel Made War in Bel Azhurra"
    by Janet Fox
"The Revenant" by Shawn Ramsey (verse)
"Mother Hen" by Kim Newman
"The Spectacles in the Drawer"
    by Thomas Ligotti from
    Etchings & Odysseys No. 10 1987
"Happy Hour" by Marvin Kaye
"The Old Laughing Lady"
    by Michael D. Toman
"Day of the Dark Men" by Mike Chinn
"The Sorcerer to His Long-Lost Love"
    by Darrell Schweitzer (verse) from
    Eldritch Tales No. 21 Fall 1989
"Gobble, Gobble!" by William F. Nolan
    from *Weird Tales* Winter 1990/1991

Fantasy Tales No. 7, 1991
(Vol. 3 No. 4 Carroll & Graf, US edition)
Cover: J. K. Potter
"The Cauldron" by Stephen Jones &
    David Sutton
"The Supernatural—Fiction & Fact"
    by Peter James from 1990
"The Pit of Wings" by Ramsey Campbell
    from *Swords Against Darkness* III
    Zebra 1978
"Rehearsals" by Thomas F. Monteleone
    from *The Sun Magazine*
    October 1987
"The Medusa" by Thomas Ligotti
"Rejuvenation" by Edward Darton (verse)
"Living to the End" by Kathryn Ptacek
"Only Human" by Adrian Cole
"Unnamed" by Trevor Donohue &
    Paul Collins
"Bag of Bones" by Phillip C. Heath
"Nirvana" by Evelyn K. Martin (verse)
"Island with the Stink of Ghosts"
    by Garry Kilworth from
    *In the Hollow of the Deep-Sea
    Wave* The Bodley Head 1989
"Jelly Roll Blues"
    by Samantha Lee

Right: Stephen Jones and
David A. Sutton photographed
by Peter Coleborn in 2019.

Stephen Jones lives in London, England. A Hugo Award nominee, he is the winner of four World Fantasy Awards, three International Horror Guild Awards, five Bram Stoker Awards, twenty-one British Fantasy Awards and a Lifetime Achievement Award from the Horror Writers Association. A former television producer/director and genre movie publicist and consultant (the first three *Hellraiser* movies, *Nightbreed*, *Split Second*, etc.), he has written and edited more than 160 books, including the The *Art of Pulp Horror*, *Fearie Tales: Stories of the Grimm and Gruesome*, *A Book of Horrors*, *Curious Warnings: The Great Ghost Stories of M.R. James*, *The Mammoth Book of Folk Horror* and the *Best New Horror*, *Zombie Apocalypse!* and *Lovecraft Squad* series.

David A. Sutton lives in Birmingham, England. He is the recipient of the World Fantasy Award, the International Horror Guild Award and twelve British Fantasy Awards for editing magazines and anthologies (*Fantasy Tales*, Dark Terrors). More recently he has edited *Phantoms of Venice*, Houses on the Borderland and *Horror on the High Seas*. He has also been a genre fiction writer since the 1960s with stories appearing widely in magazines and anthologies, including *Phantasmagoria*, *Gruesome Grotesques*, *The Ghosts & Scholars Book of Shadows* and *The Ghosts & Scholars Book of Folk Horror*. Collections of his stories are *Clinically Dead & Other Tales of the Supernatural* and *Dead Water and Other Weird Tales*. In addition, he is the proprietor of Shadow Publishing, a small press specialising in collections and anthologies.

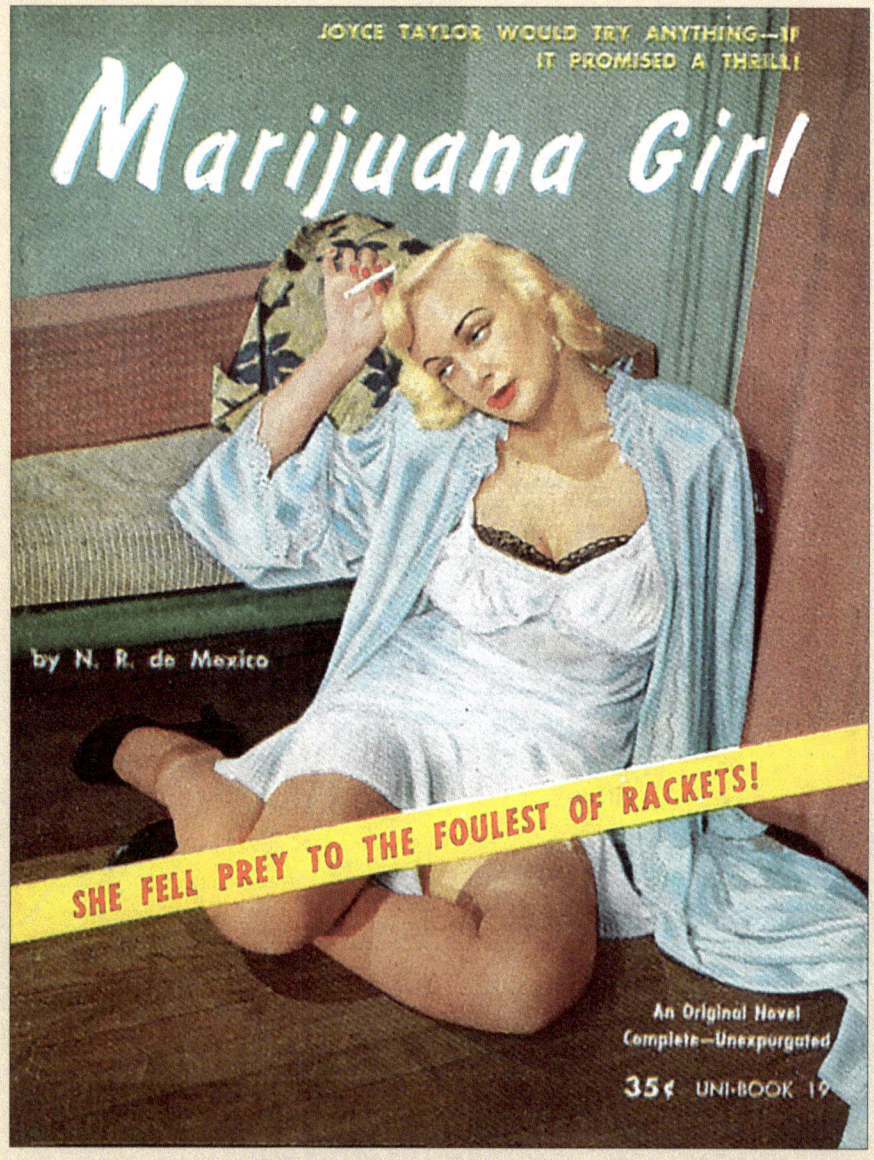

"This book epitomized the sort of paperback that conservatives regarded as licentious and immoral. Tame by today's standards, it nevertheless came under scrutiny and criticism by the U.S. House of Representatives' Select Committee on Current Pornographic Materials, otherwise known as the Gathings Committee."
–*Dope Fiends* Card Set (card No. 12) compiled and annotated by Doug Aanes (Kitchen Sink, 1995)

A Look at Marijuana Girl

Article by Gary Lovisi

There's nothing I like better than reading a vintage paperback in the original edition. Especially ones that are 40, 50, or more years old. It's like going back in time; when that book was first published, you get a glimpse of a real feel for the days and the people in such a book.

And such a book is *Marijuana Girl* by the enigmatic and mysterious N. R. de Mexico. It was originally published in a 127-page digest paperback by Uni-Books (No. 19) in 1951, and sports an excellent 'bad girl' photo cover. It's a real beauty and quite scarce! The book was reprinted a couple of years later in another digest-size paperback, this time from Stallion Books (No. 204) with identical cover and contents.

At the time I originally wrote this article, back in 1992, almost 30 years ago, I had no idea who N.R. de Mexico is (or was), perhaps only a pseudonym? However, he is credited with writing quite a few similar exploitation digests in the 1950s. Sex and drugs seemed to be a large part of this author's stock in trade and he seemed to know his stuff, especially around the drug and Jazz club scene of the early 1950s Greenwich Village in New York City. More about him later, in the meantime let's take a look at the book he wrote.

Marijuana Girl begins in the sleepy Long Island town of Paugwasset and is about a young high school girl, Joyce Taylor, a blonde bombshell ready to try new thrills and adventures in the big bad world of Paugwasset and beyond—and that eventually means New York City.

Joyce is a 17-year-old high school senior and begins her adventures when she is kicked out of her school for doing a striptease in study hall. Study hall was never like that when I was in high school! I must have went to the wrong school. Anyway, Joyce is obviously a wild girl, but she gets more than she bargains for with cheap thrills, bad

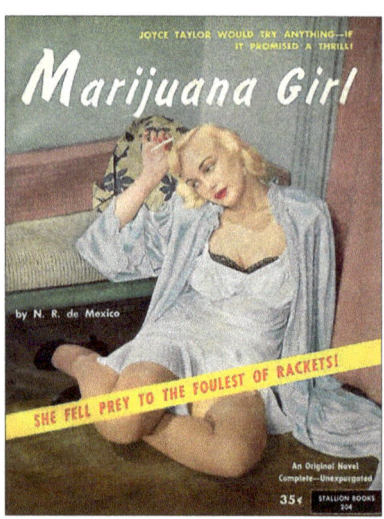

Back cover of Uni Book No. 19: *Marijuana Girl.*   Stallion Books reissue of *Marijuana Girl.*

company, and pot! The cover blurb tells us, "Joyce Taylor would try anything . . . once!"

On the first page of the book, one of the high school boys notices Joyce, and he immediately calls out, "Hubba, hub-ba," and from there on she is on every red-blooded male's radar.

Joyce is on the fast track down in this sleazy exploitation-titillation nov-el, and we all get to take a ride with her. And it's not a bad ride. The book is well-written, interesting, and seems fairly accurate in its limited delving into sex, drugs, and the Jazz scene of the early 1950s. A sleazy period piece, but enjoyable—and there is a story told here as well. What more could you ask for? This is, after all, a sleaze digest on the lowest-end of the publishing scene in the 1950s.

One of the charming aspects of the book is an actual "Jive" glossary includ-ed in the back of the book that defines such enigmatic and hip words from long ago as "horse," "smack," "reefer," and other mainstays of the Jazz and drug culture back then. There's a lot of stuff here, much of it has since found

its way into our language today and is nothing special—but back in 1951 it must have been way off the beaten track for almost everyone.

Not too soon after the story opens, there is an older guy who enters the picture. This is Frank Burdette, the 31-year-old city editor of *The Courier*, who loves Jazz, and as the blurbs tell us, has ". . . also brought the cult of the weed—marijuana." In this novel, as in a lot of similar books from this era, Jazz and drugs are inextricably linked—which is the way a lot of it was in those olden days.

Frank takes things as they come, "he was conscious of wrong doing in indulging himself in a smoke now and then, though in Paugwasset he kept its use secret from everyone but Janice, his understanding wife. She knew that it was an almost inescapable part of his background, a product of formative years spent in the company of musi-cians, entertainers, and others who took 'tea' smoking as much for granted as others take tobacco smoking."

But as things so often happen, when Frank's wife leaves with their son for a three-month visit to Maine, Joyce Tay-lor comes into the picture. Joyce fasci-nates Frank when she comes to work on the paper as a copy girl and they go out for lunch together—then they go out to a Greenwich Village Jazz club—and then one thing leads to another, as it so often does, and . . . you can guess the rest!

There are some decent descriptions of the early Village Jazz scene in this book that almost make it worth read-ing by itself. Almost, but not quite, and there is the sex/drug angle which I have to admit is very mild and incredibly campy by today's standards. Or lack of them!

The Jazz club Frank and Joyce go to is on 8th Street in the Village. It's called The Golden Horn. I don't know if any place with that name ever existed. It's described in an interesting manner:

"The air-conditioning was insuf-ficient, the seats were wire-backed and hard to the touch of spine or buttock. But the music was the best. Here, from time to time, came Sidney Bechet, Louis Armstrong, and other greats of native Ameri-can music. Here had played such supermen as the immortal Bix Beiderbecke. Here was the temple of a noble art."

And further:

"Here they came to attend the important business of drinking, smoking and listening to music. In taxis, and afoot, by bus and sub-way and private car, they came to have their pulses speeded by the hammering rhythms, their minds diverted by a spectacular run of guitar or piano—to have their at-tention caught, breathless, by glit-tering arpeggios. Here, too, came Frank and Joyce."

And, of course, there was the smell of marijuana throughout the club, "an odd smell that clung to everything

The same model used on Uni Book's *Mari-juana Girl*; was back again for *Gang Girl* by Leo Rifkin, Uni Book No. 74.

and damped down the atmosphere. It smelled a little like burning hay—old hay. But there was something else of the odor that made it different. It was a touch of sweetness that made the odor nearly pleasant . . ."

Well, now . . .

So Frank and Joyce enjoy the club and the music, and eventually go out-side near the NYU campus with two Black musician friends of Frank's.

"Wait a minute," Frank said [to Joyce] *as Jerry started to pass the case. "You know what this is?"*

"No. I—you mean . . ."

Newspaper stories of Jazz musi-cians floated through her mind.

"Is it marijuana?"

Jerry said, "That's right, honey. That's the grass. It's the greatest."

And that's how it happens in this novel. Joyce is on her way down the marijuana road to a life of misery and sin and we all take a ride with her.

It's hard with today's knowledge to take the content of this book seriously, since it may seem silly today. How-

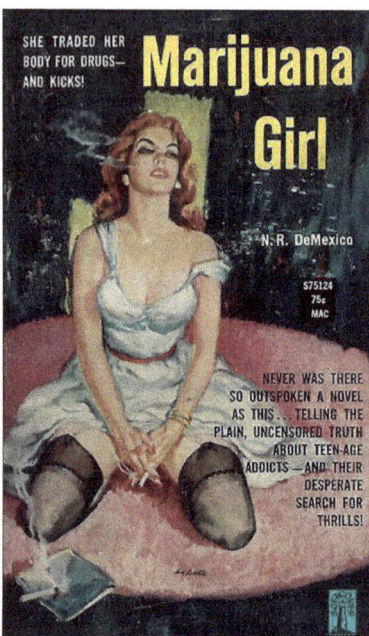

Beacon Books (No. 328, 1960) reprint.

ever, this book was looked at seriously enough at the time for it to be cited in Congressional committee hearings.

On a historical (or perhaps hysterical?) note, in May 1952, the United States House of Representatives authorized a probe of paperbacks, magazines, and comic books for so-called immoral, obscene or otherwise offensive matter. These were the notorious Gathings Hearings (named after their sponsor, E.C. Gathings, Democrat–Kansas) and one of the books they commented on was *Marijuana Girl*. They stated:

"Other paper-bound books dwell at length on narcotics and in such a way as to present inducements for susceptible readers to become addicts out of sheer curiosity. As an example of how this subject is handled by current books, one need only read Marijuana Girl *by N.R. De Mexico. A more appropriate title would be: 'A Manual of Instructions for Potential Narcotic*

Addicts!' ..even the evil effects of drug addiction are made to appear not so very unattractive by artful manipulation of the imagination. While the analysis of this book has been directed chiefly to its narcotic phase, that should not be construed as implying that it is not replete with lewdness and vulgarity."

Come on, guys! This book wasn't that bad, even for the narrow standards of the 1950s, when you look at what was going on in comic books and the horror pulps at that time. (Of course, these guys did just that, they looked at comic books and pulp magazines as well).

I wonder if the committee members ever saw a copy of *Junkie!* By William Lee (an Ace paperback original actually written by Beat poet William Burroughs, which came out after the hearings), which also had a glossary of dope terms daringly subtitled "Confessions of an Unredeemed Drug Addict!" Unredeemed? I think their heads would have exploded over that one. As it turned out, others would notice this book very soon and write about it.

So *Marijuana Girl* has this bit of history and consistency behind it, and that makes it all the more interesting as a curio and collectable. It was pretty popular in its day, and continues to be popular today among rabid paperback collectors. The book was reprinted as a digest paperback only once in a scarce Stallion Book No. 204 digest a few years later. It is an almost identical edition, but is even more scarce than the original Uni-book edition!

Marijuana Girl was also reprinted twice in rack-size paperbacks years later. First by Beacon Books (No. 328, 1960), which was affiliated with Uni-Books, and still later on from Softcover Library (a continuation of the Beacon series) in No. S75124 in 1969.

Many years later, sometime in the

2000s, I believe, because my copy has no publication date on it, it was reprinted in a facsimile edition in a small size paperback (4" x 5.5") by Fender Tucker's Ramble House Books.

Most importantly, there is also a Stark House reprint in trade paperback, under the title *A Trio Of Beacon Books* (2019) which contains a fascinating and important introduction by collector and scholar Jeff Vorzimmer.

In this book, Jeff unearthed the true author behind the N. R. de Mexico byline and he gives us some information on the enigmatic pseudonym—and the real man behind the N.R. de Mexico name. It seems that de Mexico was a mystery until about ten years ago when Kim Bragg, the son of the author, came forward to claim that the name was a pseudonym of his father, Robert Campbell Bragg.

Bragg, it turns out, was a writer who wrote many sleaze digests as de Mexico and under other names. He was also the editor of *Suspense* magazine.[See TDE4.] So he was a talented author and editor. Unfortunately he tragically died too young, at just 36 years of age in February, 1955. Bragg died in a Greenwich Village grocery store. Since the Gathings Committtee witch-hunt was well underway in 1952, soon after *Marijuana Girl* was published in 1951, it is assumed Bragg did not want to draw attention to himself as the author of such a controversial book, and since he died so soon afterwards, his credit for the pseudonym had become lost in time.

A Trio of Beacon Books contains *Marijuana Girl*, as well as *Call South 3300: Ask For Molly* by Orrie Hitt; and *The Sex Cure* by Elaine Dorian. Jeff's introduction to all three of these classic sleaze noirs, and the story behind them and their authors, is fascinating and important. If you can not afford the original Uni-Book, or the even more

Stark House's reprint of *A Trio of Beacon Books* edited by Jeff Vorzimmer.

rare, Stallion Book digest of *Marijuana Girl*, this is the book you must get. You will enjoy it—even if it goes against Congressional recommendations!

Author's Note: This article is expanded and updated from one that appeared in *Paperback Parade* No. 28, March 1992 issue. For more information on *Marijuana Girl*, see *Hardboiled America*, pages 116-117; *Two-Bit Culture*, page 235; and of course Jeff Vorzimmer's introduction to the Stark House Press edition of *A Trio Of Beacon Books*.

Gary Lovisi is the editor and publisher of *Paperback Parade* and Gryphon Books.

Howard Browne's

fantastic

1952 Article by Richard Krauss

"The *Fantastic* experiment had clearly been successful, highlighting what an editor can achieve when the publisher gives him a free hand and a reasonable budget."

–Mike Ashley from *Science Fiction, Fantasy, and Weird Fiction Magazines* edited by Marshall B. Tymn and Mike Ashley Greenwood Press, 1985.

By the time Ziff-Davis launched the pulp magazine *Mammoth Detective* in May 1942, Howard Browne (1908–1999) had already sold two stories to them featuring a skip-tracer named Wilbur Peddie. Davis liked the stories well enough that he called Browne in for a meeting and offered him the editor's position working under Ray Palmer, who was then Managing Editor of the Ziff-Davis lineup.

In 1950, the company announced they would move their editorial offices from Chicago to New York in the following year. Ray Palmer didn't want to go, so he resigned, staying in Chicago to start several new magazines of his own. Davis offered Browne the posi-

tion of Managing Editor if he'd move to New York and Browne accepted.

"I had never been happy with the pulps we had—almost immediately I tried to get them to change the make-up of the magazines and go to the digest size. *Amazing* was to be a slick, but the Korean War intervened, and we ran into paper problems, as we had before in WWII, when we had to keep cutting the page count down."

Browne reworked his ideas a year later and Ziff agreed he could prepare a sample issue of a new digest-sized magazine to be called *Fantastic*. The first three issues were published in 1952.

Although described as a home for

The debut issue of *Fantastic,* Vol. 1 No. 1, Summer 1952. Cover by Barye Phillips.

science fiction and fantasy, the first year's content leaned more toward fantasy stories, Browne's preference. He gathered work from many of the biggest names in the field and added Raymond Chandler and Truman Capote from the "slicks" to draw even more readers.

Premium production values, 162 pages, and a 35¢ cover price were fur-

Fantastic No.1 back cover by Pierre Roy "Danger on the Stairs."

Fantastic No. 1 Summer 1952
162 pages, cover by Barye Phillips

Six and Ten are Johnny

by Walter M. Miller, Jr., art by Virgil Finlay

Like *The Thing* and *Alien*, "Six and Ten are Johnny" creates a sense of dread that nearly flips its science fiction label to horror. A six-man launch from the starship Archangel drops rapidly toward the surface of a newly discovered planet that is blanketed by an unbroken sea of clouds. The dense cover nearly scuttles the mission, but as the launch nears the surface, visibility improves enough for the pilot, Hal Rogan, to spot the lone plateau selected for landing. A spot identified earlier on one of several scouting missions manned by Lieutenant Rod Esperson. But Rogan and his crew are the first to land.

On his fly-overs, Esperson had detected no signs of intelligent life on the planet. Only plant life—scattered stretches of jungle that seemed to billow and roll, but not in the way a wind would sway it. Rogan and his crew are tasked to land and collect samples, then return to the Archangel. The landing party will have a little over three days to complete their work; including the period of about forty hours when the orbiting mother ship will fall out of communication range.

At fifteen hundred feet, the launch is at last below the clouds. "Jeeziss! The color of that jungle!" Rogan reports to Esperson. "Putrid-looking—everything is. You can almost smell the stink, just looking at it." Esperson had the same impression from his fly-overs.

The launch lands safely. Up close, the crew realizes the plateau is covered in vines. One crewman reports a glimpse of something flying above the jungle, but no one else can confirm. Rogan suits up and prepares to exit the launch. With him are two dogs who don't seem

ther proof the digest-sized *Fantastic* was something new. The cover of issue one was a painting by Barye Phillips, reproduced in a six-color run on premium cover stock, backed up with one by Pierre Roy, courtesy of the Museum of Modern Art.

Response was tremendous. Browne reported the magazine was promoted from quarterly to bi-monthly status ten days after it hit the stands. Of course, publishing lead-time meant readers wouldn't see this effective change until its third issue, dated Nov/Dec 1952.

The interior paper stock was also an upgrade, much to the benefit of the magazine's detailed illustrations by Virgil Finlay, Ed Emshwiller, L. Sterne Stevens, and Leo R. Summers. The artwork of these "old school" stylists was nicely balanced by more contemporary commercial illustrators like David Stone and B. Frenkenberg. A second color was added to much of the artwork in the second and third issues, an embellishment seen in many of the best-selling digests of the day.

eager to leave the craft. When they do, even Esperson can hear the reaction over the communicator. "What's wrong with the pups? Sound[s] like they had their rumps painted with Tabasco sauce."

It's decided the atmosphere's high carbon dioxide content is responsible for the dog's unruly behavior. Although the planet's night is near, the rest of the crew exit the launch and begin collecting soil samples, taking photographs, and examining the plant life. "Everything looks like it's joined together. Vines grow right over the side of the cliff and down into the jungle. I can't make out any individual trees either. It looks like one solid tree with a million trunks, only the foliage looks more like the vines."

The Archangel's commander, Isaacs, returns to the control room after a nap, and takes the radio from Esperson. He and Rogan have history. Despite the impending darkness, Isaacs orders Rogan to descend into the jungle and report back. The dogs have settled down now, for no explicable reason, so Rogan takes them with him. Before long, the launch pilot reports, "There's a house."

"It's a log house with a thatched roof. Got a light in it, and there's a fat man standing in the doorway. I can see his silhouette. He waved at us."

The radio goes dead. Did Rogan cut it off or did something else interfere with the reception? The spotty communication with Rogan resumes, but his reports cast doubt on a clear picture of what's happening on the ground.

As the cabin's occupant approaches Rogan and his men, the dogs again lose control. They seem intent on attacking the stranger. So much so they have to be put down! The man identifies himself as Johnny. He is alone, yet insists two other men are plainly with him now.

As the story unfolds, the encroaching

Virgil Finlay's illustration for "Six and Ten are Johnny" by Walter M. Miller, Jr.

jungle wraps itself physically around the launch and mentally around the crewmen's minds; with Johnny somehow pivotal to the infiltration.

Eventually, a second launch is dispatched to investigate things first hand. As Esperson lands, he wonders if the rescue mission will succeed or become another victim of this strangely hostile planet's jungle.

Walter M. Miller, Jr. (1923–1996) wrote several dozen short stories throughout the 1950s. His work was known for its complex characterizations. In 1955, his story "The Darfsteller" (*Astounding* Jan. 1955) won the first Hugo Award for Best Novelette. His most famous novel, *A Canticle for Leibowitz* is a fix-up of three short stories that originally appeared in *Fantasy & Science Fiction* in 1955–1957. The award-winning novel was published in 1959 and has never been out of print since.

For Heaven's Sake by Sam Martinez, art by David Stone

Clarissa Crumm brings new mean-

A Canticle for Leibowitz by Walter M. Miller, Jr. Lippincott, 1959. Dust jacket artwork by Milton Glaser.

ing to the phrase "Holier than thou." She died of food poisoning at the annual picnic of the Women's Anti-Nicotine League. Fourteen others were hospitalized, but Crumm must've ingested a particularly bad portion of tainted meat, for she died in transit to the emergency room.

Her lifetime of activism and tireless struggle to curtail the aberrant behavior of others earned her halo, wings, and immediate assignment to the choir in the Heavenly Kingdom.

But sloth is sin, and Crumm would never be accused of letting unhallowed dogs lie. She immediately resumes her crusading ways, suggesting and requesting serious reforms in an otherwise absolute paradise.

This divine satire unfolds entirely through a series of reports, letters, internal memos, and certificates. It's clever, cutting, and cheeky. Unfortunately, it seems to be the author's only published story.

Some Day They'll Give Us Guns by Paul W. Fairman, art by Ed Emshwiller

The aliens landed and soon took over. The adult Earthlings are under strict control. It's the young—the untainted youth—who hold promise in one day meeting the standards of the conquering Septonians. So their parents are on notice, and tiptoes, to ensure they say nothing that might warp their offspring's developing minds—that's for the Septonians to do. Yet, despite their superior intellect and technology the Septonians may have underestimated Earth's youth.

Paul W. Fairman (1909–1977) wrote dozens of science fiction stories under his own name and his pseudonyms: Clee Garson, E.K. Jarvis, Ivar Jorgensen, and Robert Eggert Lee. He served as Editor on several science fiction digests, including *If* (1952), *Amazing Stories* and *Fantastic* (1956–1958), the only three issues of *Dream World* (1957), and for the single issue of *Amazing Stories Science Fiction Novel* featuring Henry Slesar's novelization of *20 Million Miles to Earth* [see *TDE14*].

Full Circle by H.B. Hickey, art by Ed Valigursky

A two-pager about robots in the year 20,362, so advanced they're self-repairing, fuel agnostic, self-adjusting, self-replicating, and function flawlessly in any climatic conditions. Once thousands of these babies have been deployed, what could possibly go wrong?

From the story's intro: "Like so many, Mr. Hickey [a pseudonym of Herbert B. Livingston (1916–2016)] turned to writing after a good many false starts in other directions. He sold haberdashery and music lessons, sewing machines and cigars, photographs and radio scripts, before he finally got around to selling editors. He now lives in California with his wife and two sons, where he turns out western-, detective-, and science-fiction with equal facility—and all excellent."

The Runaway by Louise Lee Outlaw, art by Robert Kay

May Barton's leisurely days as a happily married housewife are over by the time our story begins. Her problem—or is it her husband's—is "the strange, shadowy double that drifted from him like a ghost."

She's never broached the subject with him, but his "double" keeps coming back and it's driving her mad. She seeks counsel with a psychiatrist, followed by an eye doctor, thinking there must be something wrong with her vision. But no, that's not the problem.

In desperation, she confides in her husband, and to her relief, he actually knows exactly what she's talking about. He never realized anyone else could see the demon that haunts him.

Now that the truth is out, there is yet another sort of doctor to be consulted—a mentalist. His advice provides an answer both Bartons regret.

Louise Lee Outlaw (1919–2009) followed the footsteps of her father, newspaperman Claude Raymond Outlaw, and wrote for the Florence (S.C.) *Evening Star*, the *New York Daily News*, and became a reporter for the *Philadelphia Record*. When she married, she adopted her husband's surname (Shallit), but continued to write under her maiden name, Outlaw. Her pseudonyms include Lee Canaday and Juliet Ashby.

Outlaw's fiction was published in *Collier's, Cosmopolitan, Fantastic, Redbook, Good Housekeeping, Reader's Digest*, and *Today's Woman*. Her novels include *Dream of Passion* (Silhouette 279), *One Man Forever* (Silhouette 162), *Midnight Lover* (Silhouette 258), and *Victim of Love* (Candlelight 254).

The Opal Necklace by Kris Neville, art by Leo R. Summers

As this waking nightmare opens, an old witch rebukes her daughter's desire to spurn the bayous for a life in the city. "You can't leave it," she said. "You *can't* leave it. Its water is your blood, and its air is your lungs."

Shelia Larson has good reason to fear her mother. The old crone has prepared a potion in which to dip her daughter's string of opals. Opals, the iridescent gems that portend misfortune. With the spell cast, Shelia flees the bogs of the swamp for the lights of the city.

In time, she marries Gil and tries to forget her past, but finds the grasp of the swamp smothering her will. At a carnival, Shelia tugs her reluctant husband into the snake house. "In the center of the tent there was a shallow pit surrounded by a two-foot canvas over which spectators might peer down at the writhing reptiles."

A snake-handler stands amid the serpents with a four-foot black snake coiled around his arm. Shelia demands to see it, reaching out her hand. The pit man warns her of the danger. Gil suggests they leave, but Shelia spurns his advice and locks eyes with the pit man reaching out for the viper.

"It's your funeral," the handler says as he crosses the pit and allows the snake to slither onto her arm. She caresses its scaly hide and tickles behind its jaws. She offers the serpent to Gil, but he refuses, backing away, encouraging her to return it to the pit man. At last she does, and the tainted couple leaves the tent.

As if determined to repel her husband and ruin their marriage, Shelia's wild behavior escalates in the following days. She binges on gin and pulls a stranger she met at a bar into her bed. Then she tells Gil all about it. Declares it's his fault. She falls apart, unable to leave her past. She sobs, "When I get

include *The Unearth People* (Belmont, 1964), *The Mutants* (Belmont, 1966), Invaders On the Moon (Belmont, 1970), and *Bettyann* (Tower, 1970).

The Smile by Ray Bradbury, art by L. Sterne Stevens

It may be the year 2251. "That's what *they* say. Liars. Could be 3000 or 5000 for all we know, things were in a fearful mess there for awhile. All we got now is bits and pieces."

A quip from the spontaneous conversion exchanged between the men in line for a turn to spit on the painting about to be displayed in the town's main square. Perhaps not as fun as the last functioning automobile they destroyed awhile back, but by 2251—or whatever—you get your fun where you find it.

Is there any hope for this dystopian future? Maybe; the man behind another man in line says, "Someone'll come along some day with imagination and patch it up. Mark my words. Someone with a heart." Perhaps it will be the young man in line who mourns the loss of beauty as the painting is ripped to shreds before his eyes.

The intro suggests Ray Bradbury (1920–2012) was a figure of controversy: "he's been called everything from a 'chromium-age Thoreau' to a 'hyperbole-happy hater of humanity'. Both quotes seem more precious than pertinent—but the fact remains that almost as much has been written *about* Bradbury as by him. His work has appeared in smooth-paper magazines, in the pulps, on radio and television, as well as in numerous anthologies and pocket editions."

myself back, I'm gonna go home."

Disgusted with her, Gil packs a bag and takes their dog with him. Shelia pulls the opal necklace from her neck, breaking the string, spilling the gems into her hand. She selects the smallest one and places it on the floor, smashing it to bits with an electric iron.

Outside, Benny, their pet, jumps from Gil's arms and darts into traffic. "There was a squeal of brakes, an excited snarl, a simultaneous thump and yip, and Benny lay dead and mangled in the slush."

Before the nightmare ends, another victim will pay the price of Shelia's madness.

Kris Neville (1925–1980), who occasionally wrote as Henderson Starke, published dozens of stories in *F&SF*, *Future SF*, *Astounding*, *Amazing*, *Spaceway*, and several other SF digests. His stories were collected in *Mission: Manstop* (Leisure Books, 1971) and *The Science Fiction of Kris Neville* (Southern University Press, 1984). His novels

And Three to Get Ready . . .
by H.L. Gold, art by David Stone

Somehow it seems fitting that a story by Horace Leonard Gold (1914–1996) would appear in the debut issue of *Fan-*

The opening illustration by Leo R. Summers for "Professor Bingo's Snuff" by Raymond Chandler.

Fantasy & Science Fiction October 1953 with Raymond Chandler's "The Bronze Door." Cover by Ed Emshwiller.

tastic. Gold's own digest, *Galaxy Science Fiction*, had launched about two years earlier and was already a newsstand staple. Both magazines went on to thrive, leaders in the burgeoning science fiction market of the 1950s.

Born in Canada, but raised in America, Gold maintained dual citizenship. He sold his first story to *Astounding* (Oct. 1934), as by Clyde Crane Campbell, and went on to write over a hundred others under his own name and half a dozen pseudonyms.

This story for *Fantastic* is a playful romp about a poor wretch with the unfortunate ability to cause death to anyone whose name he speaks aloud three times. When he shows up at the psycho ward, the psychologists there aren't quite sure what to do with him. Is his deadly claim hyperbole or is there really something to it?

What If by Isaac Asimov, art by David Stone

Asimov's own digest was 25 years away at the time *Fantastic* first appeared on newsstands, but the author was already one of the top science fictioneers in the field. The story's introduction provides this succinct overview:

"While Dr. Asimov's forte is the robot's place in tomorrow's universe (Earth is pretty small potatoes in stories of the future!), he drops Metal Men this time to give

you a tender and compelling tale of a married couple who wondered 'what if' they had never met— and who found the answer to be strangely rewarding . . ."

The SF element here is a gadget that allows the viewer to watch an alternate past and present without the usual time travel or full-body immersive commitment. Nonetheless, it is equally effective.

Professor Bingo's Snuff by Raymond Chandler, art by Leo R. Summers

Raymond Chandler wrote two fantasy stories over a career that "almost single-handedly lifted detective fiction out of the post-Van Dine doldrums," per *Fantastic's* intro. His first, "The Bronze Door" (*Unknown* Nov. 1939), was reprinted by *F&SF* in Oct. 1953 (UK edition Nov. 1953). The second, "Professor Bingo's Snuff" first appeared in *Park East* June 1951, and was reprinted here about a year later.

The piece wouldn't work without the fantasy element, but much of the story

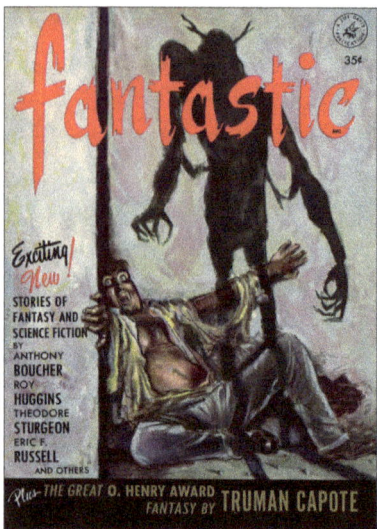 

Fantastic, Vol. 1 No. 2, Fall 1952. Cover by Leo R. Summers, back cover by George Tooker.

is crime fiction, with a somewhat softer edge than Chandler's famous hard-boiled prose.

> *"Already at ten o'clock in the morning the ice cubes in the glass, the flushed cheek, the slightly glazed eye, the silly smile, the loud laughter about nothing at all."*

And

> *"A tall, dark fellow with a sprinkle of gray in his hair. Well dressed. A bit shifty-eyed. Might be a used car salesman. Might be anything that didn't take too much work or too much honesty."*

The plot is relatively simple, with a straight through-line. It's built on the mysterious Professor Bingo—his appearance as magical as the snuff that fuels the fantasy.

At 38 pages, "Bingo's" is the issue's longest story. *Fantastic* calls it "a classic novel" on the cover. It's a terrific story and ends the title's debut issue with a satisfying, memorable flourish.

Fantastic Fillers

Most digests run short, miscellaneous content to fill out the white space at the end of stories. A few group the final bits of text on a page near the back where they share space with other story endings. The layout of *Fantastic* used this latter technique, so there isn't as much filler content as in some other digests. The minimal filler that was needed includes gag cartoons, quotes like "Science is a cemetery of dead ideas." (from Miguel de Unamuno), and humorous factoids like "The ancient Egyptians used a vertical line to represent the figure 1, a horseshoe for the future 10. . . . And 1,000,000 by a man with an astonished look on his face!"

The inside back cover was used to promote stories by Truman Capote and Roy Huggins coming in the Fall edition.

Fantastic No. 2 Fall 1952
162 pages, cover by Leo R. Summers

Angels in the Jets by Jerome Bixby, art by Paul Lundy

With "mile-high flora, hungry fauna,

TRUMAN CAPOTE

"I was born in New Orleans in 1925. Before I finally settled down to writing as a full-time profession, I did as most writers seem to—a variety of work. I wrote political speeches, danced on a river boat, painted flowers on glass, read scripts for a film company, studied fortune-telling with the celebrated Mrs. Acey Jones, worked for the New Yorker, and selected anecdotes for digest magazines."

ERIC FRANK RUSSELL

"I'm 46 look like 56—feel like 36. Educated by the late Robert Ingersoll and the late Charles Fort. They boiled away all the abstruse ignorance squirted into me by the British educational system. Dressed in khaki, I followed General Patton through Europe during the last war Chief hobby needling my agent. Major ambition: to entertain so many magazine readers so well, someone will have a momentary regret when I'm put down the hole. Minor ambition. to type with more than two fingers."

ROY HUGGINS

"I graduated from a Portland, Oregon, grammar school with the distinction of being voted 'the sloppiest kid in school.' I bummed around for a few years after finishing high school, graduated Phi Beta Kappa from UCLA, and then went into industrial engineering. I sold my first story in 1946, when I was 30, and have been going strong ever since. Right now, I'm directing a motion picture at Columbia Studios."

Contributor bios, inside front cover of *Fantastic* No. 2 Fall 1952.

a yellowish-red sky that often rained, grey rivers that wound smoothly to a tossing grey sea," the planet resembled a smaller version of Earth—at first. But upon closer inspection, this planet somewhere in Messier 13, with its perfectly breathable atmosphere, hid a secret. Captain Murchison G. Dodge of the starship Lance, named it "Deadly."

An airborne discharge from an alien fungus that once inhaled causes madness. The first to fall is Mabel Guernsey of Team 411. She trips during the third day of exploration and compromises her oxy-mask, and almost immediately succumbs to mania. She's isolated and locked in one of the ship's storage bays with a guard posted outside the door.

But Mabel is a beautiful woman, and one of the spacehands, a guy named Kraus, whom nobody liked, couldn't resist the draw of an attractive woman, now provocatively irresponsible. Of course, he only succeeds in freeing her and exposing himself and the crew to madness.

When Captain Dodge returns in a one-man crewboat, the Lance is gone. Now he's the only human standing between utter chaos and salvation.

"A native New Yorker, Jerry Bixby [1923–1998], 27 and unmarried, is a seasoned and capable magazine editor. While his fiction output is small, it sells at once and invariably gets anthologized."

Bixby also wrote as Jay B. Drexel, D.B. Lewis, Harry Neal, and Alger Rome. By the 1960s he'd seen several dozen stories published in over a dozen science fiction digests and pulps. He also wrote horror and western stories, and screenplays for films and television, including *It! the Terror from Beyond Space* (1958), and later four episodes of *Star Trek*.

His editorial roles included work on *Planet Stories*, *Galaxy*, *Thrilling Wonder Stories*, and *Startling Stories*.

I'm Looking for "Jeff" by Fritz Leiber, art by Ed Emshwiller

Why "Jeff" is in quotes on the story's splash page is a mystery. But the woman looking for him is a bit of a mystery herself. Pops, the bartender at Tomtoms describes her like this:

"Name's Bobby," he began abruptly. "Blonde. About twenty. Always orders brandies. Smooth, kid face, except for the faintest scar that goes all the way

across it. Black dress that splits down to her belly-button." Her likeness is captured beautifully by Ed Emshwiller in his illustration for the story.

Bobby is a ghost and only certain people can see her, like Pops and Martin Bellows. Martin doesn't see her right away, but he finds her after he's hit a few taverns and swallowed a few drinks.

First he finds Bobby, then he finds Jeff—and then he finds out what's what. A bittersweet ghost story with just enough tension and dread to keep things moving.

Fritz Leiber (1910–1992) was a master of short and long fiction in science fiction, fantasy, horror, sword and sorcery—often in stories that crossed multiple genres. Like this one, a supernatural crime story. He was inducted into the Science Fiction Hall of Fame in 2001 and received the World Fantasy Award for lifetime achievement in 1976.

The Sin of Hyacinth Peuch
by Eric Frank Russell, art by R.L. Summers

The story intro sums up this 19-page screwball dramedy aptly. "If you like belly-laughs based on biology, stranglings strewn with sex, tenterhooks that are titillating, then we heartily recommend this story of a French town beset by a killer from beyond the stars—a killer that seeks as victims those whose blood runs hot. Death follows death as the townspeople bar their doors; yet all the time the answer lies in the twisted mind of Hyacinth Peuch, the village idiot."

Light on character investment, Russell manages to hold reader interest through his witty prose.

"Now, the Widow Martin weighed one hundred kilos, had a black mustache and once had killed a hog with a backhand blow intended to discourage it from her

16

Ed Emshwiller's illustration for "I'm Looking for 'Jeff'" by Fritz Leiber.

vegetable patch. Germaine Jou-
bert, the village gossip, often swore
the unfortunate animal had performed three somersaults before it
closed its eyes and expired with an
expression of exactly like that of the

late Henri Martin in his last moments, a similarity that might well
be no coincidence."

Eric Frank Russell (1905–1978) was
a UK author who broke into American
pulps in the pages of *Astounding* in

Courtesy Borden Publishing Company

Illustration by Heinrich Kley from his portfolio feature.

1937. He subsequently sold dozens of stories and novels. His *Sinister Barrier* was reprinted many times, including as *Galaxy Novel* No. 1. Russell was posthumously inducted into the Science Fiction Hall of Frame in 2000.

The Star Dummy by Anthony Boucher, art by Tom Beecham

Anthony Boucher (1911–1968) was a busy man when he wrote this story for *Fantastic*. He was editor of *Fantasy & Science Fiction* and author of a review column on detective fiction for the *New York Times*.

His story concerns a ventriloquist whose unique brain waves make him receptive to an alien being who came to Earth in search of his one true love. The performer figures out how to help his other-worldly friend and pick up a nice piece of fame and fortune for himself at the same time. It's a light-hearted romp, well-told with some nice turns of phrase to add spice. For example an analyst responding to the notion of science fiction declares: "That escapist dianetics-spawning rubbish?"

Famous Fantasy Masterpieces
by Heinrich Kley (1863–1945)
A five-page portfolio of the renowned artist's pen and ink artwork, highlighting his satirical images, circa 1908.

The Sex Opposite by Theodore Sturgeon, art by David Stone
What begins as a crime story—a double murder—unfolds in a cascade of wrinkles to a newspaper reporter and a medical consultant to the police. The bodies are rushed to the consultant's lab, but there are complications unfit to report. The victims were Siamese twins. The murderers separated them during the murder.

Readers are kept in the dark when a stop at a bar at the end of a long day, transforms the narrative into a blissful asexual romance between the consultant and a remarkable beauty that seems to appear out of nowhere.

"Music came. Only some of it was from the records. He sat and listened to it all. Rudy came with a second drink before he said anything, and only then did he realize how much time had passed while he rested there, taking in her face as if it were quite a new painting by a favorite artist. She did nothing to draw his attention or to reject it. She did not stare rapturously into his eyes or avoid them. She did not ever appear to be waiting, or expecting anything of him. She was neither remote nor intimate. She was close, and it was good."

Theodore Sturgeon (1918–1985) successfully ties these seemingly dis-

Ed Emshwiller's illustration for "Beatrice" by Dean Evans..

parate strands into a satisfying whole with a few deft strokes of fantasy scientification.

Beatrice by Dean Evans,
art by Ed Emshwiller
Evans' prophesies of supermatic I.D. Boxes, desks equipped with messaging machines, and bar cabinets that play prerecorded reminders to drink in moderation, in the future of 1999,

may well have amused readers in 1952. But by 2021, they seem awfully dated, their details bogging down the friction between a wimpy, "mild as cheesefood" husband and his gorgeous wife. You guessed it, after ten years of marriage to the brilliant little twerp she's cheating on him with their apartment building's super, and when he finds out there's futuristic hell to pay.

Dean Evans was a pseudonym of George F. Kull (1911–1963) who wrote for *Amazing Stories, Galaxy,* and a few other magazines under that byline. Stories written under his given name appeared in a very similar list of pulps and digests.

Aside from the story, its narrative reveals an interesting factoid about postal delivery. "What with all this economy wave at the Post Office around the country, we were getting one delivery a day and that not before the middle of the afternoon."

From the *Universal Service and the Postal Monopoly: A Brief History,* page 18, USPS October 2008: "To save money in 1923, the number of daily residential deliveries in many cities was cut from four to three, and in 1930, from three to two. For a few months in 1934, some residential areas received only one delivery a day, and this was made permanent in 1950."

Man in the Dark by Roy Huggins, art by Gaylord Welker

Howard Browne explains: "When I started getting stories together for *Fantastic,* I called my friend Roy Huggins and asked him if he could do a detective story with fantasy elements in it. 'Sure,' he said. When the time came to turn it in, however, he told me he was too busy writing a screenplay to do the story, but I already had the cover of the magazine plated, with his name on it, so I wrote 'Man in the Dark' under the 'pseudonym' of Roy Huggins—and cashed the check myself!"

The result was a terrific detective yarn, without an element of fantasy, despite the claims of its introduction:

"*Whether or not you like Man in the Dark will depend on how you interpret the word 'fantastic.' The fact that a man's wife telephones him two hours after she is reported dead in an automobile accident is certainly fantastic enough.*"

The story's fantasy angle is supplanted with clever twists, credible characters, and solid writing. Browne's knowledge of Hollywood and production informs much of the background for "Man in the Dark."

Miriam by Truman Capote, art by David Stone

Reprinted from *Mademoiselle* June 1945, "Miriam" came to the attention of Bennett Cerf and led to a publishing contract with Random House. With an advance of $1,500, Capote moved to Monroeville, Alabama (where he was raised) and began writing *Other Voices, Other Rooms,* which he eventually completed; it was published in 1948.

The title character of "Miriam" is a pre-teenage girl who disarms her victim with manners and style beyond her years; likewise, her command of manipulation and audacity. Her stature and immaculate attire camouflage the monster within. Far more than the poor widow Mrs. Miller can contend.

Born Truman Streckfus Persons (1924–1984), the famous author of *Breakfast at Tiffany's* (1958) and *In Cold Blood* (1966), changed his name to Truman Garcia Capote after his mother's second husband, José Garcia Capote in 1932. His other short story appearance in a science fiction digest was "Master Misery" *F&SF* July 1962, a reprint from *Harper's Magazine* (Feb. 1949).

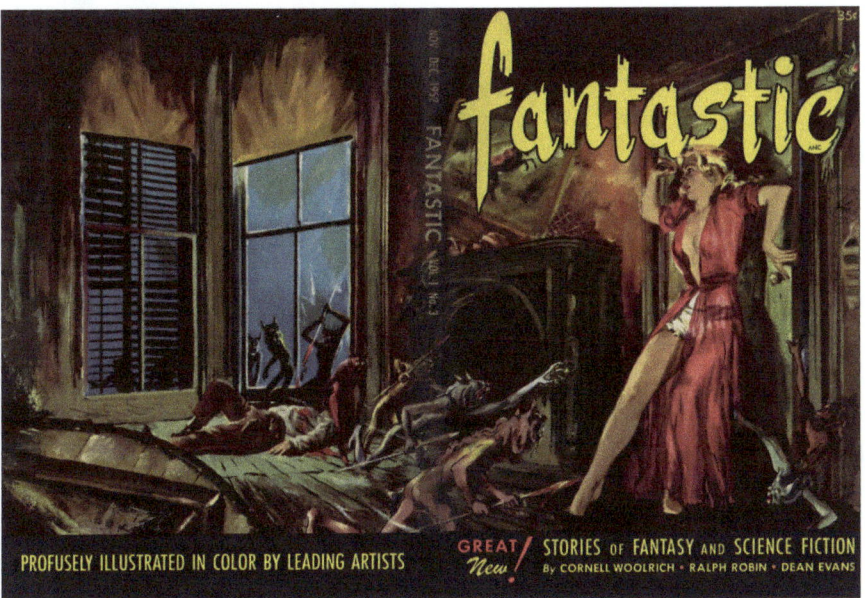

Fantastic, Vol. 1 No. 3, Nov/Dec 1952. Wraparound cover by Barye Phillips.

The Tell-Tale Heart by Edgar Allan Poe, art by Virgil Finlay

Reprinted from *The Pioneer* January 1843. This story also saw print in Robert A.W. Lowndes' *Startling Mystery Stories* No. 1; see *TDE14*, page 50.

Get Me Spillane!

In the summer of 1952, Bill Ziff called Browne into this office and asked him to get a story by Mickey Spillane for *Fantastic*. At the time, Spillane was at the hottest point in his career. [See "*Manhunt* 1953 part one" by Peter Enfantino *TDE6* pg. 90.] Browne replied, "Mr. Ziff, Spillane is a detective story writer, and he gets the kind of money that pulp magazines don't *dream* about."

But when the boss makes a suggestion, it sticks with you. So Browne called up an agent he knew and asked if he could tell him who represented Spillane. By a strange coincidence, that same agent had just recently signed him!

Brown inquired about the possibility of a fantasy story and was told "You couldn't afford it . . . However, Spillane wrote a fantasy story that's been rejected by everybody in the business."

He sent it. To quote the agent, "It's not very good." And the title gave away the plot to boot! Browne showed it to Ziff, who didn't get past page four. But Browne agreed to buy it anyway for $1,000 with the stipulation that he could make any editorial change he thought necessary.

The inside back cover announced a sensational new story by Mickey Spillane: "The Veiled Woman."

Fantastic No. 3 Nov/Dec 1952
162 pages, wraparound cover
by Barye W. Phillips

Upgraded to bi-monthly status, *Fantastic* would continue at this pace until February 1957, when it went monthly. Despite the previous hype for Mickey Spillane, his name is absent from the cover.

Ed Emshwiller's illustration for "The Veiled Woman" by Mickey Spillane..

The Veiled Woman

by Mickey Spillane, art by Ed Emshwiller

"The editors of *Fantastic* take pride in presenting the first science-fiction story by Mr. Spillane." Like last issue's "Man in the Dark," Spillane's novelette begins like a hardboiled private eye yarn, loaded with the author's trademark sex and sadism. But the big reveal near the end places it firmly, if melodramatically, in the realm of science fiction.

The story opens with a break-in. Millionaire Karl Terris is awakened by his wife. Someone is downstairs. Terris goes to investigate and shoots a burglar, attempting to crack his safe. Unfortunately, the would-be yeggman ain't alone. A beautiful woman and two armed henchmen force Terris to stand down. They're not after his money. They want "the machine." A machine capable of trapping and converting the power of cosmic radiation. But no such machine exists. Terris tries to explain, but his captor wants no part of it.

Instead, she has Terris injected with a powerful sedative and kidnaps his wife. When he's ready to give up "the machine," she'll be returned.

When Terris wakes, he begins a bruising, relentless investigation into who took his wife and where to find them. If you like Spillane's brand of crime fiction, you'll enjoy this unexpected yarn with a science fiction twist. Only it turns out, the story was written by Howard Browne.

"I threw the manuscript [Spillane's] in the waste basket," said Browne. "I went home on Friday night, and Sunday morning I came in with a 15,000-word Mickey Spillane story, 'The Veiled Woman.' I think I killed fourteen people in it."

The issue hit the stands on a Tuesday and sold 300,000 copies in three days. Then Spillane's agent called Browne at his home. Spillane was livid, threatening to raise hell in all the news services. Browne knew he had to try to defuse the situation. He called Spillane and told him who he was. He put down the phone while the famed writer ranted, "full of fascinating cuss words that I'd never heard before! It went on and on and on."

When Spillane started repeating himself, Browne picked up the phone and said, "I can understand how upset you are by all this—now let me tell you my side of the story."

Browne had bought the story in good faith, claiming he'd loved it! He was ready to print it, but happened to pick up a copy of *Life* magazine with five- or six-page spread of Spillane giving the entire story away. Browne no longer had first rights, Spillane had already told it to a national publication. In desperation, Browne wrote a new story, doing his best to match Spillane's inimitable style.

"Well, it stunk!" said Spillane. "What'd you ever write?"

When Browne replied he'd written under the name John Evans, Spillane interrupted, "You wrote the Halo books?"

Turns out Spillane had a few Halo books on his bookshelf. The rant ended, and a conversation began with two pros talking. Spillane didn't know his story would sell when he did the piece with *Life*, it'd been around for so long. He finally decided, "Let's just forget it." Lawsuit averted.

To Fit the Crime by Richard Matheson, art by David Stone

An insufferable poet with an intractable passion for words berates the family members that surround him on his deathbed. His living legacy is rewarded with a trip downstairs where he is condemned to an eternity of clichés.

Matheson's entertaining prose barely saves this one-note storyline from completely tanking. Miraculously, the story ran a second time in *Fantastic* August 1969).

Richard Matheson (1926–2013) wrote stories, novels, and scripts, perhaps most notably *I Am Legend* and *The Shrinking Man*. His screenplay for the latter was

his entrée into film, where he went on to write screenplays for *The Twilight Zone* (original series), several Roger Corman productions, and many others. He was inducted into the Science Fiction Hall of Fame in 2010.

Final Exam
by Chad Oliver, art by Bill Ashman

Symmes Chadwick Oliver (1928–1993) was born in Ohio, but spent most of his life in Texas. He studied Anthropology, earning his PhD from the University of California in Los Angeles. He did not care for the usual depiction of Native Americans in much of the media and strove to portray them accurately in his own work.

In "Final Exam," Earth has claimed the planet Mars as its own, usurping the native Martians, many of whom were fatalities of the planet-grab. The Martians are a metaphor for the American Indians and Oliver depicts a humble, gentle race that has suffered greatly under their arrogant captors' brutality.

"My anthropologist friends

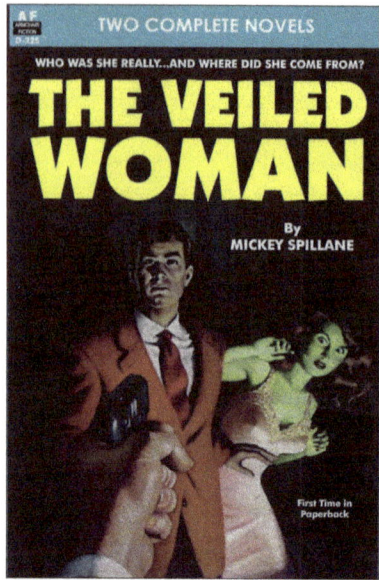 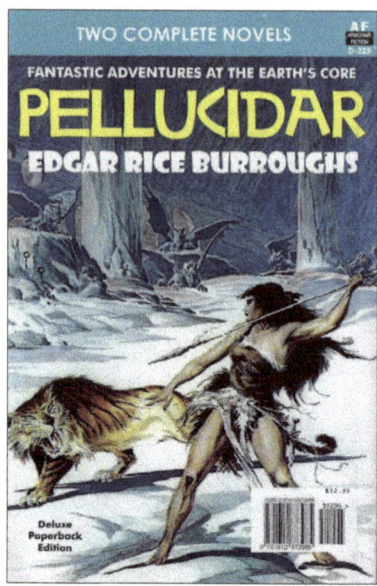

The Veiled Woman by Howard Browne writing as Mickey Spillane was reprinted along with *Pellucidar* by Edgar Rice Burroughs as an Armchair Fiction double in 2018.

tell me that such ceremonial dances always have some function in a total culture, whether or not the participants are aware of it. This was true of the old Indian dances back on Earth."

In this case, the dance is the Martians' Death Dance and the oblivious participants are the Earthlings.

Writing as Chad Oliver, he sold his first story to *Super Science Fiction* in November 1950. From there, he sold dozens of stories to *Astounding*, *F&SF*, *Satellite*, *Analog*, and several other digest and pulp magazines.

Candlesticks
by Dean Evans, art by Dave Berger

Siebert, his insufferable boss, and two others are game for eighteen holes of golf. During play, Siebert tumbles upon a groundsman known as Old Webb. The man is seldom noticed as he potters around the links, smoothing sand traps, collecting beer cans, and replacing divots. But if you take

the time to listen to Old Webb's mutterings, you might learn of his power of second sight, his ability to see the future.

Siebert listens and soon puts together a plan to bilk the boss over a series of bets along the fairways. It's a surefire setup, but is Siebert's final bet really worth the life-or-death stakes?

The intro to this story ends with a promise: "You'll get more stories by Dean Evans, if we can manage it!" Sure enough, Evans returned in the next issue with "The World Is So People," but it was his last story for *Fantastic*.

Rather than the usual large splash page illustration, Dave Berger produced five smaller illos that are sprinkled throughout the story.

The Moon of Montezuma by Cornell Woolrich, art by B. Frankenberg

This noir/horror/fantasy is chock-full of dreary imagination and creeping dread. Bill Taylor seeks his fortune in the silver mines of Mexico, leaving his pregnant wife behind in the states. She writes to him about the birth of their son, but receives no reply. In desperation, she pawns her wedding ring to buy a one-way fare to the only address Taylor left her.

When she arrives in the God-forsaken hills of her destination, the lone house she finds is empty except for an old crone and her daughter, Chata.

"Jet-black hair parted arrow-straight along the center of her head. Her skin the color of old ivory. The same glittering black eyes as the old one, but larger, younger. Even more liquid, as though they had recently been shedding tears. There was the same cruelty implicit in them too, but not yet as apparent. There was about her whole beauty, and she was beautiful, a tinge of cruelty, of barbarism."

At first, the two women are reluctant to allow their caller to enter, but when Chata's gaze finally washes over the baby, she ushers the travelers in. The stoic women claim no knowledge of Bill Taylor.

The baby is fed and laid to rest on a bed. As his mother leaves him to find her hosts, she stumbles across another room where she finds another infant, a boy, who lies motionless in death. Like her son, the boy has blond hair. It is Chata's son.

After a meal of beans and rice, Mrs. Taylor retires, exhausted from her travels. While she slumbers, Chata and her mother convene in the open-air patio within the walls of the house and begin an ancient ritual that spells devastating horror for the intruder.

A master of suspense, Woolrich drags readers into the ancient world of Aztec sacraments in pursuit of an impossible, twisted sense of order and justice. A creepy, haunting, first-rate tale of terror.

Cornell Woolrich (1903–1968)

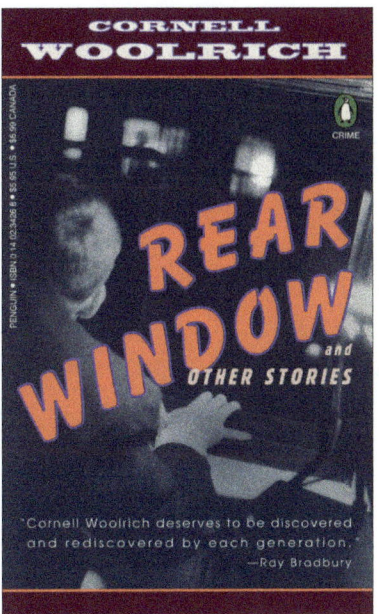

Rear Window and Other Stoires
by Cornell Woolrich Penguin Books, 1994.

wrote volumes as William Irish, George Hopley, and himself. Perhaps his most famous story, written as Irish, "It Had to Be Murder" (*Dime Detective Magazine*, February 1942) was the basis for one of Alfred Hitchcock's best films, *Rear Window*, released in 1954. The story's title was changed to "Rear Window" for the paperback anthology of the same name, published by Ballantine Books in 1984, and by Penguin Books in 1994.

The Missing Symbol by Ivar Jorgensen, art by Ed Emshwiller

What I found most interesting in this story about the first manned flight to the moon was the inner dialogue of each of its five crew members.

At first, the men heap their admiration on the engineers, scientists, and technicians who built the ship and plotted every minute detail of their mission. But then the solitude and isolation of their journey takes root. Their

Tom Beecham's illustration for "Rabbit Punch" by Ralph Robin..

commander's thoughts reflect the concerns of each crew member:

"*They know what a sheet of steel will withstand; the stress and strain on a jet tube. They know that down to a gnat's eyebrow. But what about the stress and strain on the human mind? On the man that rides the ship? Space does something to him,*

and they missed it completely."

Ivar Jorgensen was a pseudonym used by Howard Browne, Harlan Ellison, Paul W. Fairman, Randall Garrett, Tobert Silverberg, and Henry Slesar. It this case it was Fairman (1909–1977), who also served as *Fantastic*'s associate editor on this issue.

Rabbit Punch by Ralph Robin, art by Tom Beecham

This light-weight, slightly humorous fable is bolstered by a couple of terrific illustrations by Tom Beecham. The question of an end-all method of warfare—both effective and humane—is thought-worthy, but its white magic deployment is strictly played for laughs with a deadpan delivery.

A chemist and Professor of English, Ralph Robin (1914–1983) wrote about a dozen short stories for *Fantastic*, *F&SF*, *Amazing*, *Galaxy*, and *Other Worlds*. In 1976, he received the Christopher Morley Award from the Poetry Society of America. His poetry appeared in *The Saturday Review*, *The New Republic*, and *The American Scholar*.

The Celestial Omnibus
by E.M. Forster, art by L.R. Summers

Here is another story Howard Browne sourced from outside the expected stable of popular fictioneers. Edward Morgan Forster (1879–1970) was primarily a novelist. His most famous works are *A Room with a View* (1908), *Howard's End* (1910), and *A Passage to India* (1924). He was nominated for the Nobel Prize in Literature 16 times.

In this usage, "omnibus" is a horse-drawn carriage. In this case, a transport from the mortal plane to the celestial heavens. Fortunately, for the young man who takes the journey, you can make it a round trip if you're savvy enough to request a ticket home as you climb aboard. Otherwise, it's strictly one-way, as his wise old chaperone discovers.

"Omnibus" was originally published in the *Albany Review* (Jan. 1908) and the titular story in the collection *The Celestial Omnibus (and other stories)* Sidgwick & Jackson, 1911. Today, the book is available online at Project Gutenberg and in an audio download at Librivox.

The Cask of Amontillado
by Edgar Allan Poe, art by Virgil Finlay

We are never privy to the offense which Fortunato wrought upon Montresor. The latter's family shield depicts a foot crushing a serpent whose fangs are imbedded in the heel, with a Latin motto that translates to "no one attacks me with impunity."

Montresor finds Fortunato dressed as a jester at carnival and lures him to his vaults with the offer of Amontillado, a treasured Spanish sherry. His pigeon is already drunk and obediently descends deep into the dank catacombs with his host. Fortunato is tricked into entering a niche and is quickly bound in irons while Montresor seals him in with bricks and mortar.

The story was first published in *Godey's Lady's Book* Nov. 1846 and has been reprinted again and again, and adapted for stage, radio, television, film, and comic books.

The Opener of the Crypt
by John Jakes, art by David Stone

"Occasionally a story by one of the old masters so stimulates the interest and imagination of a present-day writer that it amounts to an obsession. Nothing will do but that he must carry on the plot by writing a sequel . . ."

That purported obsession extends to Jakes' first-person narrator. Drawn to the ruins of a castle in Italy, he uncov-ers the truth of the famous story that rules his subconscious. A satisfying sequel to Poe's classic.

Summary

The year 1952 saw the debut of two other digests of speculative fiction, *Space Science Fiction* and *Science Fiction Adventures*, both from publisher John Raymond. Unlike *Fantastic*, they were gone by mid-1954. Only *Fantastic* would go on to take its place among those few titles with more than a few months or years worth of issues. In 1952, it shared the newsstand with *Amazing Stories* (at the time still in its pulp format), *Analog*, *F&SF*, *Galaxy*, *If*, *Imagination*, *Other Worlds*, and the short-lived *Mysterious Traveler* magazine. *Weird Tales* was also there in pulp format as it neared the end of its long, original run.

Fantastic was indeed a fantastic fiction digest that, in its debut year, brought an eclectic mix of fantasy, science fiction, and crime stories to readers in a beautifully produced package. Browne's leadership and his roster of top-tier authors, as well as Ziff-Davis' distribution network, helped ensure its success, gaining readers in an increasingly challenging environment for publishers.

References
BlackGate.com
Galactic Central website
The Encyclopedia of Science Fiction
Incredible Ink by Howard Browne
  Dennis McMillan Publications, 1997
Sparknotes.com
University of Waterloo
Wikipedia

Special thanks to **Rick Ollerman** for his help with research for this article.

People Today
Vol. 6 No. 3 February 11, 1953
Article by Tom Brinkmann

"People are always falling desperately in love with me, or something."
–Vanessa Brown *People Today* Feb. 11, 1953 page 28 "People On the Stage"

People Today—a human interest pocket-size digest that covered crime, politics, sex, and Hollywood, the last incorporating the first three. "A Magazine About Headline People." Cover price 10¢. Dimensions: 4-1/8" x 5-7/8". Published bi-weekly by Hillman Periodicals, Inc. 353 Fifth Avenue, New York, NY.

The first issue of *People Today* was dated June 20, 1950. It continued on into the early 1960s, eventually using color covers and centerspreads. The most collectable and sought after issues are those with covers with Marilyn Monroe, Jane Mansfield and, to a lesser extent, starlets like Jeanne Carmen.

The Feb. 11, 1953 cover had Vanessa Brown as the featured "girlie" and a smaller picture of Tom Ewell, both from the first stage production of "The Seven Year Itch" by George Axelrod. It announced "One Year of Love in Hollywood see pages 16–22," and in smaller type "Vanessa Brown and Tom Ewell 'The 7 Year Itch.'"

Starting on the inside front cover was a New York crime-related piece

PEOPLE ON THE STAGE

VANESSA...

People are always falling desperately in love with me, or something." So chirps Vanessa Brown (*left*) in Broadway's sauciest hit, *The Seven Year Itch*, by George Axelrod. Sure enough, Vanessa makes a shattering impression on her neighbor, Tom Ewell (*below*) For 7 years he's been faithful to his wife. But now she's

Before summer bachelor Ewell meets neighbor Vanessa, he daydreams of her as a vamp (*l.*).

...BEAUTIFUL—AND NOT BAD

in the country. And Vanessa's here. On stage throughout the play, veteran comedian Ewell faces the philanderer's dilemma in a string of hilarious daydream scenes, mostly pessimistic Will she blackmail me? Will my wife shoot me? "In a way, I'm the straight man," Ewell told PEOPLE TODAY "The feed is as important as the comedy line, and here I get both. Vanessa is charming. She has looks and sex and talent." To critics she's "exquisite as a wild violet" and "altogether fascinating, even fresher than the average daisy," with "exactly the right air of innocent sophistication" depicted with "beautiful naturalness." Now 24, Vanessa was born in Vienna,

Real meeting brings surprises. Vanessa turns out to be a giddy teen-ager reveals she posed nude, thinks Ewell old enough to remember Sarah Bernhardt.

Author's Note: This article is basically a postscript to the "The Creature from the Black Lagoon with The Seven Year Itch" (*TDE10* June 2019). Having not been aware of this issue of *People Today*'s existence, at the time I wrote the aforementioned piece, it seems to need to be known—it is a great issue.

titled "Whistling in the Dark?" which said "As state probe of crime-ridden NY waterfront ended, the big question was: would ILA [International Longshoremen's Association] 'lifetime' boss Joe Ryan step down for hand-picked successor? The possible choice: tugboat boss Wm. Bradley."

It was the perfect lead-in for the feature on page 2, "Who Dropped the Curtain on Three-Fingered Brown?" The subject was Thomas "Three-Fingered Brown" Luchese, "top boss of the underworld," successor to Frank Costello." (The same Frank Costello that loaned the money to Gene Pope, Jr., to buy the *New York Enquirer*, which later became the *National Enquirer* in June 1957. Look for Jeanne Carmen covers and articles in 1950s issues.)

This issue's "People in the Arts" feature is "Hand of Destiny," an article about artist Mrs. Franc Root McCreary of Buffalo, New York who did pencil

Centerspread with Vanessa Brown and Tom Ewell from *People Today* February 11, 1953.

Smart, Sweet Vanessa Charms All

in Manhattan, 3½ rooms, with a fantastic view. I write and I play tennis and I swim and I dance and I sing. I'll probably be a soprano. I've had 3 short stories published. You know, trash. Now I'm working on my first play. I figure I'll be a great actress, so 20 years from now when I'm at my peak I'll write and reach another peak, and then I'll die." Meantime, there's nothing livelier than Vanessa.

Ewell daydreams of how he'll drop Vanessa ("Baby, I'm strictly a one-night guy"). Actually, she goes gladly, to look for real love.

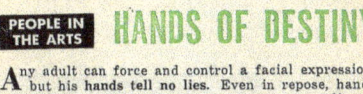

PEOPLE IN THE ARTS — HANDS OF DESTINY

Any adult can force and control a facial expression, but his **hands tell no lies**. Even in repose, hands reveal to a sensitive observer the inner personality of a man or woman. After pondering these truths a few years back, a woman portrait painter embarked on the task of creating a gallery of hands that have shaped history.

She is Mrs. Franc Root McCreery of Buffalo, N. Y., and today in her studio she has a magnificent collection of pencil sketches of the "hands of destiny" as she calls them. On the next pages a half-dozen of her sketches are shown, together with her comments on them.

DWIGHT D. EISENHOWER: the chief characteristics of Ike's hands, according to the artist, are determination, directness in thought and action, and dependability. Firmly constructed, these are the sturdy, capable hands of a man who does things rather than those of a philosopher. Strong and expressive, they show reservoirs of patience, reliability, and understanding.

JOSEF V STALIN: the most outstanding quality of this pair of hands is their inflexible heaviness, indicative of a calmly self-satisfied inner personality. Hands like these reveal the least about the hidden, inner emotions of their owner; but the artist perceives in this pair, in addition to "many inscrutable qualities," a very strong indication of the materialistic.

Artist McCreery is shown here in her Buffalo studio. She is putting the finishing touches on her conception of sculptor Rodin's famed "Hands of God." Mrs. McCreery believes that a pair of hands, by their basic structure and the use to which they are put, reveal many things about their owner: heritage and habit, appreciation and intuition, character and achievement or failure.

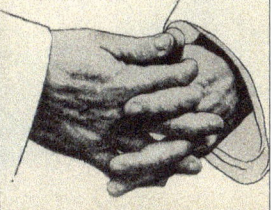

sketches of the hands of Dwight D. Eisenhower, Josef V. Stalin, Franklin D. Roosevelt, Winston Churchill, Queen Elizabeth, and Pope Paul XII. To McCreary, "Hands are an open book... Even in repose, hands reveal to a sensitive observer the inner personality of a man or woman." Each caption beside her illustrations outlined the traits she saw, in a horoscope-style profile.

The cover story on 24-year-old Vanessa Brown features prominent poses of the actress with insets of Tom Ewell hamming it up for his co-star in Broadway's "The Seven Year Itch." The lively actress says, "I write and I play tennis and I swim and I dance and I sing. I'll probably be a soprano. I've had 3 short stories published. You know, trash. Now I'm working on my first play. I figure I'll be a great actress, so 20 years from now when I'm at my peak I'll write and reach another peak, and then I'll die."

The back cover features a mustachioed and goateed Alice B. Toklas.

Readers are directed to page 34 to learn "What's Happened to..." Toklas. The half-page coverage includes her "autobiography" written by companion and collaborator Gertrude Stein, proclaims Toklas "knew every writer who was anybody, including Hemingway."

Tom Brinkmann is currently living in a family care home (you can reach him at c/o Mims Family Care Home 6337 Mims Road, Holly Springs, NC 27540), after living for a year in a subsidized-housing apartment in Raleigh, NC, and having spent that year in and out of many hospitals in Raleigh, both traditional and psychiatric. He turned 66 on June 28, 2021 and is trying to get *Pure Insanity* No. 21 (last issue) and *Squint* No. 8 and 9 (the "Isolation Madness" issues), out for public consumption. He will be interviewed by Micah Liesenfeld in an upcoming issue of the amazing mini-zine, *After That!* Special thanks to Kathleen Banks Nutter, PhD, for line editing and other assistance.

Paragon: Thoughts on William Preston's Old Man Sequence

Article by Anthony Perconti

"So to think about a Doc-like character—really, to think about any superheroic character—centered in that place, how could there not have been someone to stop it. And that's, to my mind, a question about any man-made catastrophe: What are the limits of what any of us can do?"
–William Preston

I became aware of the character, Doc Savage, through DC Comics' house ads during the late 1980s. From what I saw in those small snippets, the character didn't appeal all that much to me initially. In my youthful ignorance, I thought he was built *too* along the lines of Superman (little did I know): I was, however, an avid reader of another pulp hero, the gonzo Shadow reboot by Andy Helfer, Bill Sienkiewicz, and Kyle Baker. What made me an eventual fan of the character, what converted me, was getting a hold of Phillip Jose Farmer's "biography" of Clark Savage Jr. *Doc Savage: His Apocalyptic Life* is one of those works that intentionally blurs the line between the fictional and the real. This marvelous book examined Doc's adventures, lineage and linked it with that of several figures taken from classic literature and pulp fiction. Farmer's Wold Newton family tree (now, universe) remains an undaunted accomplishment of crossover mythography. Being a habitual comic geek, in the late 1990s, I picked up two series that featured homages to Lester Dent's Man of Bronze. Warren Ellis and John Cassaday's character Doctor Axel Brass, from their meta-fictional *Planetary* and Alan Moore and Chris Sprouse's highly charming *Tom Strong*. What Ellis and, to a greater degree, Moore did, was take the essence of this classic character, put their own unique spin on it, and made it their own.

Moore, much like Farmer before him, took the skeleton of an established hero from a previous generation, recon-

Doc Savage Vol. 1 No. 1 March 1933 pulp magazine. Cover by Walter M. Baumhofer.

Blacklight was a brain surgeon (perhaps more accurately, a vivisectionist). An individual that revoked the Hippocratic Oath and performed all manner of unethical and inhumane procedures on his fellow human beings.

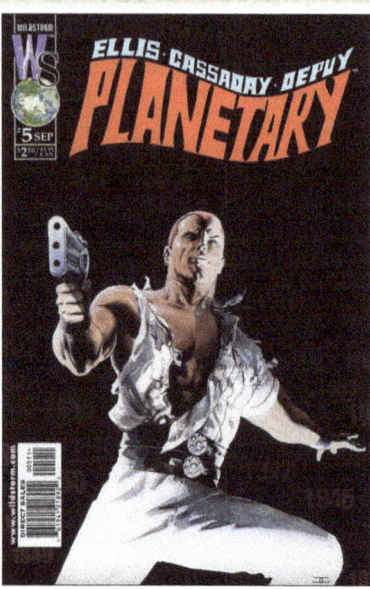

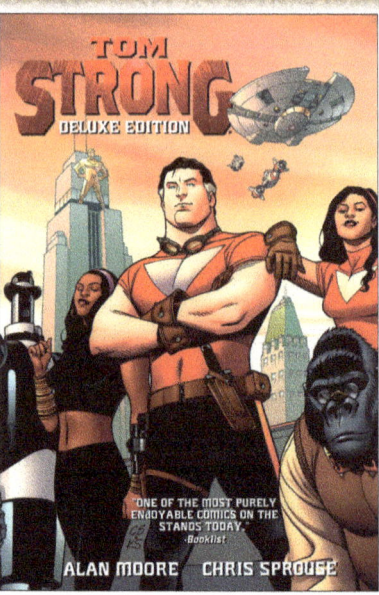

Planetary No. 5 by Warren Ellis and John Cassaday.

Tom Strong Deluxe Edition by Alan Moore and Chris Sprouse.

figured the components, while remaining true to the character's core concept and updated it for a new (and presumably, younger) audience. In addition to these aforementioned writers, William Preston has crafted his own unique homage to the bronze man of science. "I'd loved the character since my father handed me a copy of *The Czar of Fear* (absent a front cover) when I was maybe 14. I was a comic book reader, still a Batman and Superman fan at that time, but beginning the shift to Marvel comics with their deeply intertwined narratives. I say I loved Doc, but I think I loved the idea of the character more than the execution." Preston's the Old Man sequence, to date, consists of four stories that were published in *Asimov's Science Fiction* magazine from 2010 to 2014. These four tales take the concept of the genius hero into interesting new territory that certainly crosses into the realm of the literary. Preston uses the concept of the pulp hero to examine some heady themes, including (among others): the American War on Terror, the concept of free will, the nature of heroism and the moral and ethical implications of criminal rehabilitation. Preston's prose never talks down to the audience. These tales are thought provoking, yet simultaneously highly entertaining. The Old Man sequence is the thinking person's iteration of a classic pulp hero, updated for the post 9/11 world.

The four stories that comprise the current sequence are all conveyed from several viewpoint characters that have engaged with the Old Man in one form or another. Preston does not let the reader into the interior headspace of his enigmatic hero. This decision allows the audience to experience this character from the "person on the street" perspective, enhancing the sense that the Old Man is a truly extraordinary human being. "Helping Them Take the Old Man Down" takes place in the months following the destruction of the Twin Towers.

Orleans, where Randolph patiently bides his time, awaiting the call to action.

> "Violence and terror ground down ordinary people as if their lives had no purpose but to be pressed under history's terrible weight. Good people could not allow that. There at his back, past the shower wall, past the building, people acted to lift the heel of violence."

Randolph's transformation becomes apparent. Like all of those other members of the wide-ranging and diverse network, he becomes an adherent of the Old Man's philosophy and cause (The Work). Ready and waiting to do his small part in making the world a better place.

Like Alan Moore and Phillip Jose Farmer before him, William Preston has taken the framework of a previously established pulp character and made it his own. The Old Man sequence is a novel interpretation of the Doc Savage template, designed and geared towards a modern audience. Preston examines the vagaries of the human condition through the seemingly innocuous medium of pulp fiction. It is an ambitious piece of storytelling that follows in the footsteps of Michael Chabon's *Gentlemen of the Road*, with a dash of *The Amazing Adventures of Kavalier and Clay*, Tom DeHaven, *It's Superman!* and Isabel Allende's *Zorro*.

It strikes the perfect balance between highbrow and lowbrow entertainment.

Will Lanny find catharsis for his involvement in the capture of the Old Man? Will Lieutenant Randolph and the gang be able to stop the deadly machinations of the Improbable Man and save New Orleans in the nick of time? Preston (once again) states:

> "There's one more story I intend to tell. It's taken me a long time to get to it, or at least to get to a plot that I'm happy with, one

with exciting moments as well as moments of emotional and intellectual impact. Events in my own life caused me to balk at finishing the story; then events in the life of our nation gave me further pause. But I have, I think, finally figured out the story itself and the role of its protagonists. Every one of these stories has tackled a different time period with different protagonists, and this will be no exception; the Old Man (given various monikers) is the one consistent presence, and I think I have a way to tie together everything I've written about him and those who've encountered him. Readers who came to the character cold will, I hope, appreciate where I'm taking things as much as readers who always understood the character's roots as a Doc Savage homage or a superhero homage. That fifth story will be the last one."

Until that day, sir. Until that day.

NOTES

1. My sincere thanks to William Preston in going above and beyond in answering my questions about the Old Man and the four stories that make up the current sequence.

2. The Old Man stories are all readily available through Amazon. You can find them and more of William Preston's work on his Amazon page.

> **Anthony Perconti** lives and works in the hinterlands of New Jersey with his wife and kids. He enjoys well-crafted and engaging stories across a variety of genres and mediums. His articles have appeared in several online venues and he can be found on Twitter at @AnthonyPerconti.

MANHUNT
DETECTIVE STORY MONTHLY

Side Street
James T. Farrell
author of
STUDS LONIGAN

EVERY STORY NEW!

SEPTEMBER 35 CENTS

Plus —
**HAL ELLSON
RICHARD DEMING
DAVID ALEXANDER
RICHARD MARSTEN
ANDREW J. BURRIS**
— and others

A Complete Novel by **CHARLES WILLIAMS**

Manhunt Detective Story Monthly Vol. 3 No. 9 September 1955

MANHUNT
DETECTIVE STORY MONTHLY

1955 part three
Synopses by Peter Enfantino

Illustration by James Sentz for "The Big Day" by Richard Marsten.

Vol. 3 No. 9 September 1955
144 pages 35 cents

Uncle Tom by David Alexander
(5000 words) ★★ illo: Tom O'Sullivan
A tale of race relations in the deep south, narrated by an African-American boy facing integration and a cloudy future.

Cast Off by Jonathan Craig
(4000 words) ★★ illo: GHP
Steve Manning and Walt Logan investigate the bludgeoning death of an antique dealer. Was the murderer his mistress or the rival antique dealer who wanted to buy him out? The fifth episode of the Dragnet clone offers little in the way of action or plot.

The Big Day by Richard Marsten
(5500 words) ★★★★ illo: James Sentz
Three men plan the perfect bank robbery. Staking out the building for weeks, they track the employees' movements daily to the minute. It's the perfect caper. Until it isn't. As in most heist stories, "The Big Day" for Carl, Anson, and Jeremy unravels due to the tiniest unplanned incidents. As with most stories written by Evan Hunter, the minutiae is detailed (but never boring) and captivating; though no background is given for the three masterminds, all three are engaging characters.

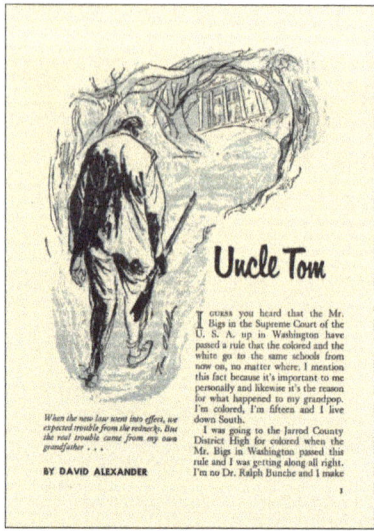

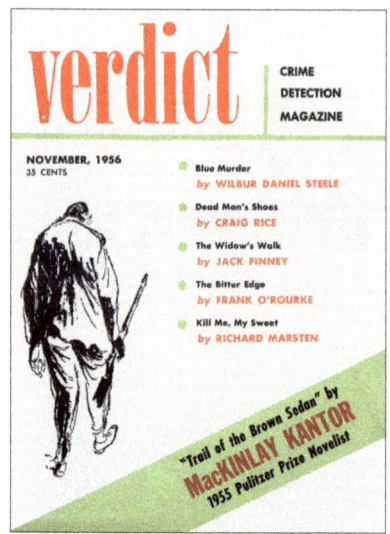

Manhunt's editors must've really liked Tom O'Sullivan's illustration for "Uncle Tom" by David Alexander, they used it again on all three covers for their second iteration of *Verdict Crime Detection Magazine*. Shown above is No. 2, November 1956.

Pickup by Hal Ellson (2000 words)
★ illo: Ray Houlihan
A rare non-JD tale by Hal Ellson about a man who becomes obsessed with a young girl who hangs out at a candy store. Though it's thankfully void of Ellson's JD-lingo, the story is, nonetheless, equally annoying due to its monotony.

Side Street by James T. Farrell (1500 words) ★★ illo: Dick Shelton
Tommy Brandon waits outside the apartment he and his girlfriend live in as, inside, she has an abortion.

The Muscle by Philip Weck (1800 words) ★½ illo: Ray Houlihan
A short-order cook eyes the three goons who have walked into his diner and ponders who in the restaurant they've come for. The answer is very predictable.

The War by Richard Deming (10,000 words) ★★★½

illo: Tom O'Sullivan
Gambling entrepreneur and playboy Clancy Ross is visited at his nightclub/casino, The Club Rotunda, by Janice Talbot, the wife of his close war buddy, Jim. Janice explains that Jim witnessed a mob murder committed by mafia big-wig Bix Lawson and was, himself, murdered in their apartment only a week before. Now the mafia has pinned Jim's murder on Janice and fronted money for her bail, with an eye on killing the girl and framing it as suicide.
Clancy Ross might be a cut-throat businessman but no one, not even the mob, messes with his best friends. After one of Lawson's bent cops threatens Clancy (and leaves the casino with a busted nose), it's all-out war that climaxes with thrown grenades and a truly surprising twist.
"The War" is our first look at the charismatic Clancy Ross, who holes up in the third-floor office of The Rotunda like a slightly darker version of Bruce Wayne, using his vast wealth and

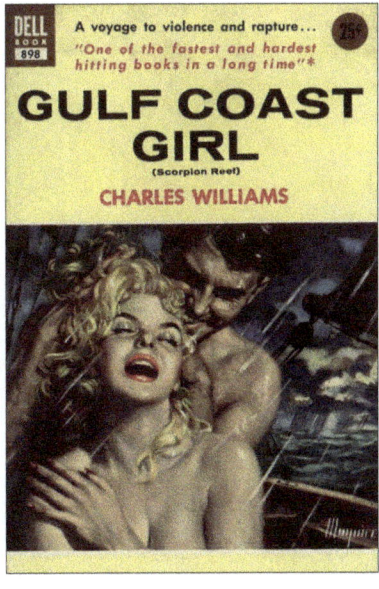

cunning to right wrongs. The most interesting aspect of Ross is that Deming avoids the usual traps of the PI story by giving Ross a different vocation (but with the hardboiled sentiment of a PI) and, as we discover in the end, a mean disposition. Ross will appear five more times in *Manhunt* and get the full-length treatment with *She'll Hate Me Tomorrow* (Monarch, 1963).

Flight to Nowhere
by Charles Williams (20,500 words)
★★★ illo: Tom O'Sullivan

A boat, the *Freya*, is found drifting in the Gulf of Mexico, unmanned. The only clue left aboard is the captain's journal. It tells the story of professional scuba diver Bill Manning and his meeting with the beautiful blonde, Shannon Macauley. The woman hires Manning to recover an antique shotgun from the bottom of the lake. When Manning finds the weapon, his suspicions are aroused when he notices that the gun has been in the water only a few

hours. Turns out the woman is looking for a diver to help her and her husband retrieve millions in diamonds from a downed plane in the Gulf of Mexico.

When a band of thugs turns up looking for the same plane and Mr. Macauley ends up a corpse, Manning starts questioning the honesty of the beautiful blonde. This leads to an exciting climax when the thugs force Manning to pilot his boat to the supposed crash site.

Though there's a solid plot in here that keeps you turning the pages, I couldn't help the feeling that this was a Reader's Digest Condensed novel. That's really not far off the mark since "Flight to Nowhere" was expanded and released in hardcover by MacMillan the same year as *Scorpion Reef*. The following year, Dell paperbacks released it with a beautiful Robert Maguire cover as *Gulf Coast Girl*. "Flight to Nowhere" seems rushed. Passages are missing, action scrimped on (though its downbeat ending retains the power of its

Manhunt Detective Story Monthly Vol. 3 No 10, October 1955.

big brother). Think of it as a warm-up to the main event, the novel *Scorpion Reef*. Much like a short feature that's sculpted into a major film.

There's still a lot of good writing here, as the memorable final passage in Manning's journal shows:

    "*...that last, haunting flash of silver, gesturing as it died. It was beckoning.*

    Toward the rapture. The rapture..."

Vol. 3 No. 10 October 1955

144 pages 35 cents

The Spoilers by Jonathan Craig
(7000 words) ★ illo: Tom O'Sullivan

Mel Traynor has his head caved in with a camera and there's no shortage of suspects. Could it be the teenage girlfriend? The jealous wife? The wife's boyfriend? Steve and Walt try to run the various suspects through the strainer (as they do in every entry of the "Police Files" series) and see what happens. Craig continues his formulaic series with wearying results. The Dragnet-style chitchat (Manning repeats his "It would be easier if I asked the questions" mantra to suspects in every PF story), the rote, mechanical writing and plot, the interchangeable cast of suspects. I'll repeat—a little characterization never hurt *any* story. After six episodes, you'd think a *Manhunt* editor would raise the issue with Craig.

Field of Honor by Robert Turner
(2000 words) ★★★ illo: Ray Houlihan

Robert Turner ventures into Evan Hunter country in this JD tale of two rival girl gangs, highlighted by a bloody showdown. The story's a good one, told at a fast pace, but a bit too preachy at times for my taste. When it comes to giving sermons, Hunter can hit the ball out of the park, Turner can't.

In Memory of Judith Courtwright
by Erskine Caldwell
(3000 words) ★★ illo: GHP

Why did 18-year-old Merle Ran-

Illustration by Tom O'Sullivan for "The Spoilers" by Jonathan Craig.

dolph kill himself with his father's shotgun and what does it have to do with school teacher Judith Courtwright? It's a slice of Southern life told in the Erskine Caldwell style but, this time, the author has nothing new to say.

I Saw Her Die by Gil Brewer
(2500 words) ★★½ illo: Ray Houlihan

Hewitt claims he saw the brutal killing of a woman in a new development

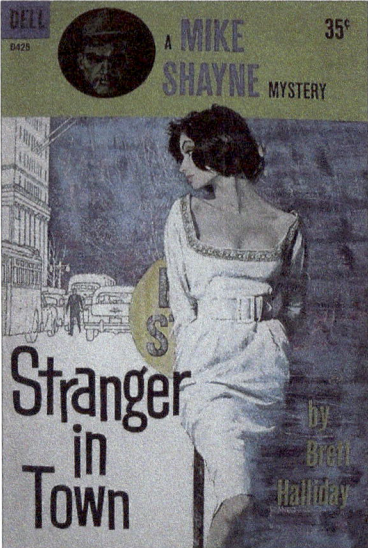

of homes, but more importantly, the killer saw him. Two detectives take him out to the site but there's no body or even a sign of violence. But Hewitt saw something.

Blonde at the Wheel by Stephen Marlowe (5500 words) ★★★

Fred wakes up in the passenger seat of a convertible driven by a beauty named Petey. How did he get there? No idea. Fred has a rare form of amnesia that strikes with no warning and can last for days. The blonde at the wheel isn't as alarming as the dried blood on his Polo. The blood, the girl explains, came from some kind of fight the night before, a tangle she has no info about other than from the limited mutterings of an amnesiac. Fred insists they turn the Buick around so that he can face the music but, after stopping at a roadside cafe and reading the headlines of the morning paper, Fred doesn't know what to do. Did he murder the wealthy Fred Pearson at the Buena Vista Motel? Is it only coincidence that this dive is where Petey has a room? And why does Petey have a man's suit in her closet?

Those questions and more will *not* be answered by Stephen Marlowe in the maddeningly ambiguous climax. Well, maddening for some, but not for this reader. Sometimes the best mystery is the one unsolved. Marlowe keeps the pace at breakneck speed, constantly teasing us with clues that might be answers but sometimes end in dead ends and crisp dialogue between the frightened Fred and the seemingly golden-hearted Petey.

Tell Them Nothing by Hal Ellson (8000 words) ★★ illo: James Sentz

The dynamic of a street gang changes when one of the JDs finds a gun. Suddenly, he's a big man on the street. The tense situations and interplay between the four youths are lost within the usual Hal Ellson staccato and silly street lingo.

The Hunter by John A. Sentry (2000 words) ★★½

A serial rapist sits in a bar sizing up his next "conquest," not realizing he's about to meet his match.

A Stranger in Town by Brett Halliday (19,000 words) ★★½ illo: Tom O'Sullivan

Just finished with a case and heading back to Miami, Michael Shayne stops in a roadside bar in Brockton for a well-deserved drink. His placidity is interrupted when a gorgeous gal stumbles into the bar and whispers "I'm sorry" to him just as three goons lay into him. Beaten unconscious, Shayne just misses becoming Brockton's latest hit-and-run with a well-placed knee. The private eye manages to escape, with one goon left behind as roadkill, but the big question is: why is Mike Shayne the target of this attack?

As Shayne digs deeper, he discovers the town has a dirty little secret, something hidden deep in the walls of the

Manhunt Detective Story Monthly Vol. 3 No 11, November 1955.

sanitarium located on the outskirts of Brockton.

Thoroughly engaging despite padding (Halliday tends to repeat himself quite a bit) and a contrived finale. "A Stranger in Town" was expanded into the novel of the same name and published by Dell in 1961.

Vol. 3 No. 11 November 1955
144 pages 35 cents

Big Frank by Bryce Walton
(4500 words) ★★ illo: Tom O'Sullivan

Big Frank Connel is a traveling salesman who has a side job when he can pull it off: strangling female hitch-hikers and burying their bodies along the

Illustration by Tom O'Sullivan for "Big Frank" by Bryce Walton.

the harbor.

A very average adventure redeemed only by an (literally) explosive finale, "Time to Kill" has the feel of a condensed novel; it's rushed and lacking in characterization. The 13th (and final) Marsten story to appear in *Manhunt*.

Fat Boy by Hal Ellson (3000 words) ★ illo: Lee

Character study of Ronald, a bullied obese boy and his day at the beach with "friends." I'm not sure what the point of this story was other than to inflict nastiness upon this mentally and physically challenged teenager. The climax, where Ronald heads to the house of one of the girls in his group, with murder on his mind, seems tacked on in order to be picked up by the editors of *Manhunt*.

Vanishing Act by W. R. Burnett (8000 words) ★½ illo: Ray Houlihan

Ex-police reporter Bob Stuart runs into taxi driver Lou Jacks, who tells the man a strange story about Dan Polling, a mob lawyer he gave a ride to recently. Something just wasn't right about the man's demeanor and it hasn't sat well with Lou. With a bit of prodding, Bob goes to the man's apartment with Lou, and the lawyer's wife answers the door. She has no idea where her husband is and this intrigues Bob enough to agree to investigate. The next morning, the police arrive and haul Bob off to the precinct. Eventually, after much interrogation, Bob learns that Lou is dead and the Pollings have disappeared.

A very long and arduous read, "Vanishing Act" is like one of those 1940s bottom-billed crime movies with smart-alecky Bob and the tough-but-fair lieutenant who doesn't actually believe for a moment that Bob is responsible for Lou's murder but puts on a charade, anyway. The climax is the obligatory expository (something about an armored truck heist years be-

roadside. But Frank gets sloppy and the latest hitcher is there for a reason.

I'll Do Anything by Charles Beaumont (3500 words) ★★ illo: Ray Houlihan

If Julio wants to join the Aces, he'll have to stick a switchblade into a man who disrespected the Aces' leader. No one in the group believes Julio has the stones to commit murder but he may just surprise them yet.

Time to Kill by Richard Marsten (10,000 words) ★★ illo: Tom O'Sullivan

Hal Thompson has had enough of the Navy and so, while on a mountain climbing excursion in a small village in Japan, the sailor deserts and takes refuge in a house owned by a kindly old man, his wife, and their attractive daughter. Thompson convinces the trio he's surveying a local volcano and manages to evade the ensuing search party. Thompson falls for the lovely young Nara, but danger rears its head when he discovers that the old man plans on blowing up the destroyer anchored in fore) and the showdown between Bob and the bad guys.

Woman Hater by Sam Merwin, Jr.
(5000 words) ★★★ illo: Lee
Captain Mike Conway is called to the Grand Plaza to hush up a killing. Seems local boy made good Lyon Wister (nee Willy Lyons) has beaten a man to death in his hotel room and that won't look good on the front page of *Variety*. Wister is the hottest star in Hollywood and so his PR man asks Mike to haul the body away and forget he ever saw it. Since it looks like the dead guy was pilfering Wister's room, Mike agrees, but something picks at his brain. When the dead man's wife turns up missing, Conway digs deep into Lyon Wister's background and discovers that delivering beatings is number one on Lyon's list of hobbies. Gripping with a great hardboiled lead character and a climax that delivers.

The Trap by Robert Turner
(1000 words) ★★ illo: James Sentz
A couple of teen hoods attempt to rob a gas station, but the manager is waiting for them.

The Man Between by Jonathan Craig
(10,000 words) ★★ illo: Tom O'Sullivan
Detective Steve Manning investigates the murder of a sporting goods store manager and discovers there's no shortage of suspects. The seventh installment in Craig's "Police Files" series, "The Man Between" is no better or worse than the previous six; the pacing and dialogue remind one of a mediocre 1950s detective TV show.

Low Tide by Cole Price
(1500 words) ★★★ illo: Ray Houlihan
Harry discovers that his business partner, Chuck, is sleeping with Harry's wife. Harry concocts a revenge plan but, too late, learns that his wife is one

Illustration by James Sentz for "The Trap" by Robert Turner.

step ahead of him. For such a short story, "Low Tide" is enthralling and ends with a nice kick in the teeth.

Vol. 3 No. 12 December 1955
128 pages 35 cents

First Offense by Evan Hunter
(5500 words) ★★★ illo: Ray Houlihan
A cocky teen faces his first police line-up and becomes less self-assured as the process unfolds. One of two 1955 *Manhunt* stories selected by David C. Cooke for *Best Detective Stories of the Year* (Dutton, 1956).

My Son and Heir by Stephen Marlowe
(4000 words) ★★★★ illo: O'Sullivan
Ex-FBI turned PI Chester Drum

Illustration by Ray Houlihan for "First Offense" by Evan Hunter.

Senator wants the PI to dispose of the body and help him save his political career. No wisecracks, no luscious dames, no happy ending; this PI story is quite unlike any other.

Stephen Marlowe's Chester Drum was a very popular character, the star of 20 novels published by Gold Medal between 1955 to 1968 (one co-written by Richard S. Prather and co-starring Shell Scott).

Custody by Richard Deming
(3000 words) ★★★ illo: Tom O'Sullivan

When the police summon Harry Maddon to the home of his ex-wife, Hazel, he fears harm may have come to his son, Tommy, at the hands of Hazel or her new husband, both violent alcoholics. His son is safe but the cops explain that Hazel has fatally shot her husband during an argument; the woman claims she doesn't remember. Harry takes Tommy home, but once he questions his son about the incident, he realizes his ex-wife may not be the shooter. Also selected by David C. Cooke for *Best Detective Stories of the Year* (Dutton, 1956).

Outside the Cages by Jack Webb
(4500 words) ★ illo: James Sentz

The cops have stashed away an animal trainer in order to keep him safe before he testifies in a big mob trial. His boss at the zoo is having a problem with his tiger at the zoo, so he appeals to the cops to let him borrow the State's witness for a little while. Meandering and silly.

The Jokers by Robert Turner
(2500 word)★★★ illo: Tom O'Sullivan

A group of college boys think it would be a whole lot of fun to play a gag on Georgie Grootch, the religious custodian at their university. Since Grootch has never "gone out" with a woman, they hire exotic dancer Lil-

is rudely awoken by Senator Ohland, mad with worry about his son Roy. Seems the young man took a girl up to the family cabin and may have hurt her. The Senator will pay Drum five hundred bucks to accompany him to the cabin. Drum agrees but, upon arriving at the cabin, discovers the situation has not been properly explained to him. Roy has strangled the girl and now the

Manhunt Detective Story Monthly Vol. 3 No 12, December 1955.

lie Lamar, the Snake Dancer, to show Grootch what he's missing. Lillie steals into Georgie's room one night while the boys listen at the adjoining wall. A woman's scream sends the group scrambling for the exit but, later, after Lillie fails to emerge, they return to the scene of their crime just in time to bump into Grootch exiting the furnace room. When pressed as to the where-abouts of the dancer, the custodian only mutters that he's sent the woman to the fiery pit she deserved. The set-up has been used before, but the grim finale makes the trip worthwhile.

The High Trap by Floyd Mahannah (8000 words) ★★★

While driving down the desolate road that leads to their ranch, Tom and

Kay Lander come across a man parked by the side of the road, across from a deserted Air Force runway. When a jumbo jet makes a surprise landing, the man forces Tom and Kay by gunpoint to the tarmac. They learn that the man is a part of a group of hoods who have hijacked the plane and its millions in diamonds. A host of passengers, including the owner of the ice, exit the plane and are ordered to start walking across the desert. Tom and Kay, however, are taken hostage and loaded onto the plane as insurance. Very soon, Tom learns the hoods are going to parachute off the plane with Tom and Kay as sacrifices. A suspenseful edge-of-your-seat adventure thriller made all the more intriguing when the thugs begin to turn on each other and Tom must devise a way for him and his wife to escape.

Kill Me Tomorrow by Fletcher Flora (11,000 words) ★★½ illo: Ric Estrada
    Peter Roche, the Senator's son,

comes home for Christmas to discover dad has married a woman half his age. A real head-turner, Etta immediately catches Peter's fancy, and the two become "really good friends" almost overnight. Etta shares Peter's disdain for the Senator but they both enjoy his money and decide that three's a crowd. Etta lets on that the Senator is in financial straits so there's only one way for Etta and Peter to cash in; the gorgeous but devious gal concocts a complicated plan wherein she fakes her own death and then "comes back from the dead" to kill the elderly Roche.

Peter murders a prostitute and runs Etta's car off a cliff with the corpse in the front seat. Etta hides away for a spell and, when they feel the time is right, the duo proceed with the finale of the plot. Things go fine until a nosy inspector figures out the con and slaps the bracelets on the murderous pair. What is essentially, one of mystery fiction's oldest plots manages to work here through snappy dialogue and effective

The Best Stories of 1955
1. Moonshine by Gil Brewer (March)
2. Memento by Erskine Caldwell (March)
3. Blood Brothers by Hal Ellson (April)
4. Solitary by Jack Ritchie (July)
5. The Big Score by Sam Merwin, Jr. (July)
6. The Big Day by Richard Marsten (September)
7. The War by Richard Deming (September)
8. Flight to Nowhere by Charles Williams (September)
9. My Son and Heir by Stephen Marlowe (December)
10. Surprise! Surprise! by David Alexander (December)

characterization. Oddly enough, the focal point of the crime, the Senator, is only discussed and never actually materializes in the action.

Surprise! Surprise!
by David Alexander (4500 words)
★★★½ illo: Ray Houlihan

All the boys down at the Eighth Precinct know that Joe Bacci's wife is stepping out on him; the worst part is that the guy-on-the-side is a detective in the same squad room. Joe just ignores the catty comments but, eventually, the lid is going to blow. It's a testament to David Alexander's writing that a story as choppy as "Surprise! Surprise!" is so effective. Alexander slows the narrative down now and then to let us know about the atrocities committed in the precinct:

A couple of lovers on West Third made a suicide pact and turned the gas on and they were lying in each other's arms deader than the mackerel in the Fulton Fish Market

when we found them. That wasn't all. They hadn't stuffed the cracks in the doors too well and the gas had seeped through to the next flat and asphyxiated a three-months-old baby that was sleeping in its crib.

Joe Bacci's adulterous wife meets with a grim fate, but these interludes are what make this story click.

Peter Enfantino is cofounder and coeditor of the *bare•*bones pop culture magazine. When not obsessing over the latest issue—or other Cimarron Street Books—he writes about various horror and war comic books on <barebonesezine.blogspot.com>, covering Warren Publishing (*Vampirella*, *Eerie*, and *Creepy*), Atlas/Marvel pre-code horror books (*Strange Tales, Stories to Hold You Spellbound, Suspense, Mystic, Uncanny Tales*, etc.), and DC's war comics (*G.I. Combat, Our Army at War, Our Fighting Forces, Star Spangled War Stories*, etc.).

Murder Mystery Monthly No. 31 June 1945

If I should Die Before I Wake by William Irish
Review by Jack Seabrook

"He [Cornell Woolrich] is quite simply the premier paranoid among crime writers. His is the realm of the impossible coincidence, precieved as a cosmic joke at the expense of man. Even if he writes of thugs and dives and dark city streets, he is miles away from any kind of naturalism; in his world there are magical corresondences between things rather than logical relations."

–Geoffrey O'Brien *Hardboiled America* Expanded Edition Da Capo Press, 1997

The cover of issue No. 31 of *Murder Mystery Monthly* notes that it is "By the Author of *Phantom Lady*," William Irish, a pseudonym for Cornell Woolrich. Reviewing this collection in the *San Francisco Chronicle*, Anthony Boucher wrote that the "cover illustration captured almost perfectly the existential terror and loneliness of the Woolrich world." The illustration depicts a man who is wearing a hat and has his collar turned up, standing with his back to the viewer, on top of a globe, looking over the edge, surrounded by dark clouds but with a halo of light surrounding his body.

The cover lacks a date, issue number, or price, though the spine features a yellow number "31" in a black circle. The back cover advertises the previous and subsequent issues in the series. On the top left of the cover is a yellow box with "Murder Mystery Monthly" in black and a picture of a skull with an incongruous mop of white hair atop its head.

The inside cover claims that "the six novelettes included in this volume are all new," a statement that is not true. Five of the stories had been published

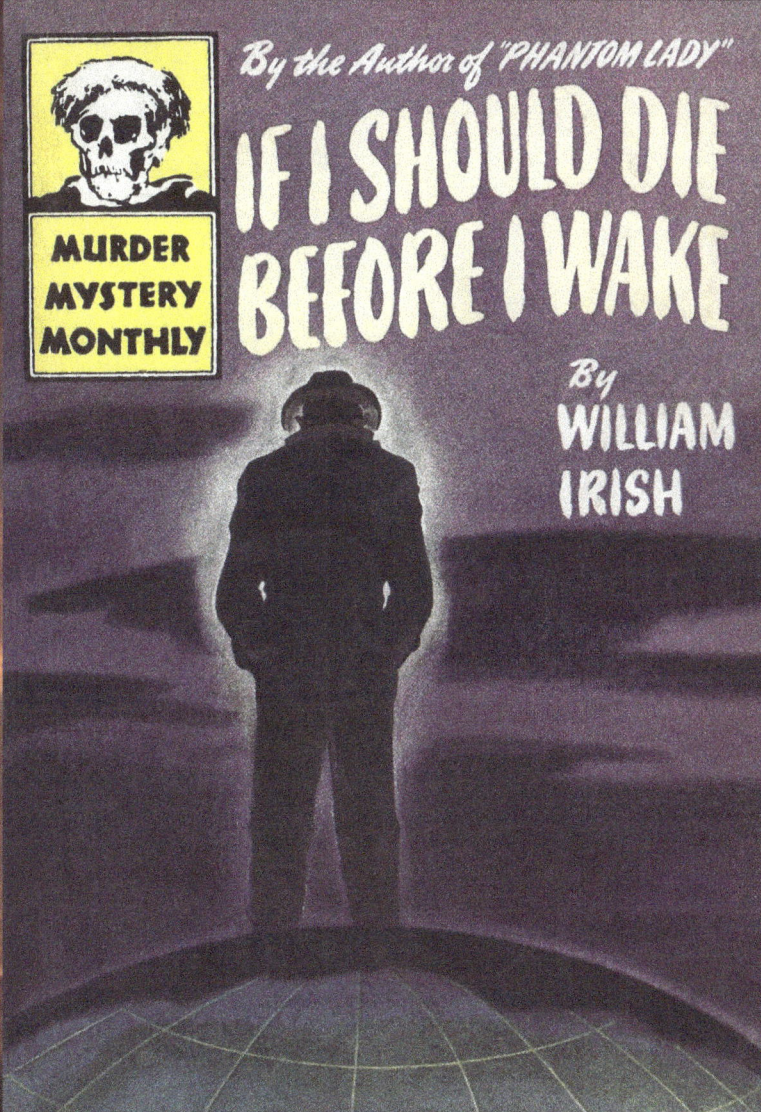

Murder Mystery Monthly No. 31 with six short stories by William Irish (Cornell Woolrich).

in pulps in the 1930s and 1940s and one was published in a different digest that was released right around the same time as this one. In his classic book about Cornell Woolrich, *First You Dream, Then You Die*, Francis M. Nevins notes that the author was known to sell old stories as if they were new to unsuspecting publishers in the 1950s, so it's possible that he took these stories and sold them to Avon, claiming they were new. It's also possible that Avon was being disingenuous.

The title page features the only date

Inside front and back covers of *Murder Mystery Monthly* No. 31.

"[Anthony] Boucher, perhaps the only critic broad-minded enough to notice softcover originals, described the 25-cent volume as 'various in quality but containing at least two of the finest Woolrich-Irish opuses—which is about as fine as terror-suspense comes currently.' (1 July 1945)
–Francis M. Nevins "Boucher on Woolrich: When Titans Touched" <mysteryfile.com>

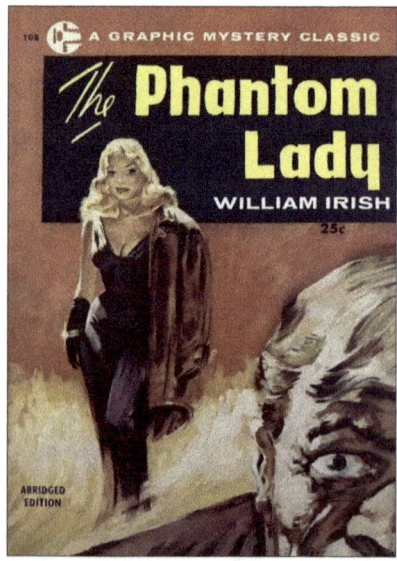

Phantom Lady by William Irish: Pocket Book 253, 1945 and Graphic Mystery Classic 108, 1955.

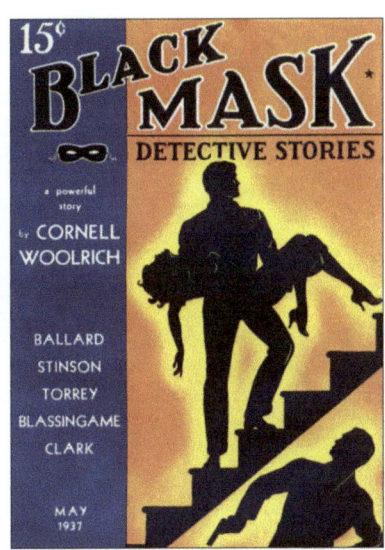

Detective Fiction Weekly July 3, 1937 with "If I Should Die Before I Wake."

Black Mask May 1937 with "I'll Never Play Detective Again."

to be found, which is a copyright date of 1945. There is also a WWII paper drive ad. The June date comes from Nevins's book and presumably can be inferred from the date of Boucher's review, which ran on July 3, 1945.

The first story starts on page 11, which is puzzling, because even if one counts the cover, inside cover, title page, and table of contents, the first story would begin on page 5. The last interior page is 128, so perhaps Avon was trying to make it look like the digest was longer than it actually was. The inside back cover lists 25 other issues of *Murder Mystery Monthly* that are available for 25 cents each; that's the only place where a price is mentioned.

Of the six stories in this issue, all but the last were originally published under the Cornell Woolrich byline, making one wonder why they are published here under the William Irish byline. Perhaps it was to cash in on the popularity of *Phantom Lady*, which had been published as by William Irish in 1942 and adapted for film in 1944, or

perhaps it was part of the attempt to pass the stories off as new. The six stories are as follows.

If I Should Die Before I Wake
★★★★

Twelve-year-old Tommy keeps his promise to classmate Millie not to tell about the man who gives her candy, even after she disappears. Two years later, the same man starts giving candy to Jeanie Myers, who also disappears. No one will listen to Tommy, so he has to find her by himself. Suspense builds to a terrifying climax in this story that is told from a child's point of view and with his voice.

Francis M. Nevins called it "one of the most chilling suspensers in the literature," and it was adapted for the radio show, *Nightmare*, on August 25, 1954, starring Peter Lorre as the killer. It was also adapted into an Argentinian film, titled *Si Muero Antes de Despertar* (1952). The story first appeared in *Detective Fiction Weekly*'s July 3, 1937 issue.

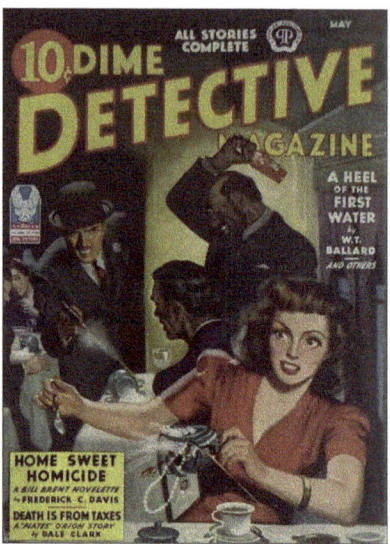

Detective Fiction Weekly Jan. 25, 1936 with "Change of Murder."

Dime Detective Magazine May 1943 with "Mind Over Murder" ("A Death is Caused").

I'll Never Play Detective Again
★★

When a seventeen year old girl dies after pricking her thumb on a thorn from a poisoned rose, Dick Walsh learns more than he wished he knew about his best friend, Tom Nye.

Nevins calls this "a very strange story" and speculates that it was written in the 1920s and revised for publication in the 1930s. It first appeared in *Black Mask*'s May 1937 issue.

Change of Murder ★★★

In Chicago, Brains Donleavy pays Fade Williams to provide him with a solid alibi for murder but things don't go as planned.

This story features entertainingly Runyonesque dialogue. Nevins comments that the ending was borrowed from Cain's *The Postman Always Rings Twice* (1934) and that it is telegraphed in advance. It was first published in *Detective Fiction Weekly*'s January 25, 1936 issue, and it was adapted twice for television, first as "Change of Murder"

on *Colgate Theater* (May 21, 1950) and second as "The Big Switch" on *Alfred Hitchcock Presents* (January 8, 1956).

A Death is Caused ★★★

An unhappily married woman plots to use her husband's pathological fear of snakes to cause his death, but things don't go quite the way she anticipated.

Woolrich's tale anticipates Roald Dahl's story, "Poison" (1950), in its use of the fear of snakes. "A Death is Caused" was first published as "Mind Over Murder" in *Dime Detective*'s May 1943 issue. It was adapted for radio as "A Death is Caused" on *Molle Mystery Theatre* (October 12, 1945).

Two Murders, One Crime ★★★

Gary Severn is misidentified as the murderer of a policeman and electrocuted. When Donny Blake later confesses to the crime, the District Attorney hushes it up in order to maintain public confidence in the police. Detective Rogers quits the force and becomes Blake's shadow, leading to an unexpect-

Black Mask July 1942 with "Three Kills for One" ("Two Murders, One Crime").

Mystery Book Magazine August 1945 with "The Man Upstairs."

ed outcome.

A long story with several twists and turns, Nevins calls "Two Murders, One Crime" a "perverse, malevolent and hopeless . . . image of life" and a "masterpiece." It was first published under the title, "Three Kills for One" in the July 1942 *Black Mask*. It was loosely adapted under the title, "Framed for Murder," for TV's *The Mask* and broadcast on February 7, 1954.

The Man Upstairs ★★★

Mrs. Collins rents a room in her home to a poor bookseller named Mr. Davis and tells no one that her stepbrother Jerry is hiding in the basement. Jerry is a murderer who escaped from prison and, when Mr. Davis disappears, Mrs. Collins has to take matters into her own hands.

Nevins writes that "The Man Upstairs" is "vividly readable and reasonably suspenseful." It was published in the August 1945 *Mystery Book Magazine* under the same title, also as a new story by William Irish; it's hard to tell

which digest came out first or whether they came out at about the same time. It was adapted for TV's *Suspense* and broadcast on April 5, 1949.

Sources

FictionMags Index
IMDb
Irish, William. If I Should Die Before I Wake. *Murder Mystery Monthly* No. 31 [June 1945].
Nevins, Francis M. *Cornell Woolrich: First You Dream, Then You Die.* NY: The Mysterious Press, 1988.
The Old Time Radio Network
Wikipedia

Jack Seabrook is the author of *Martians and Misplaced Clues* (1993), about Fredric Brown, *Images of America: Hopewell Valley* (2000) about New Jersey history, and *Stealing Through Time: On the Writings of Jack Finney* (2006). He writes about comic books and Alfred Hitchcock TV shows for the blog <barebonesez.blogspot.com>, has had numerous works published in various books, and appears on a DVD of *Invasion of the Body Snatchers* discussing Jack Finney.

11 True Crimes

Article by Richard Krauss

"It is generally recognized by now that Joseph Gollomb is the outstanding chronicler in this country of crime and its exponents."
–Henry Montor writing about Gollomb's *Crimes of the Year* in "Views and Reviews" *The Sentinel* June 26, 1931

A digest-sized paperbound book, *11 True Crimes* was the second in a short-lived series published by the Green Publishing Company of New York, copyright Horace Liveright, Inc. The cover and spine use the numeral 11, while the title page spells out: "Eleven True Crimes." Kevin Hancer's *The Paperback Price Guide* No. 2 lists nine titles for Green Publishing, numbered 6–14. *11 True Crimes* was the seventh of the series. The other eight titles are mystery novels.

Horace Brisbin Liveright (pronounced "live-right")(1884–1933) married Lucille Elsas, daughter of Herman Elsas who owned a paper compa-

ny that eventually merged into International Paper. The elder Elsas bankrolled Liveright's early career in publishing. In 1917, Liveright founded Modern Library and Boni & Liveright with a partner, Albert Boni. The former was a reprint line of European modernists, the latter a line of originals by modern American writers.

By the 1920s, an interest in theater led Liveright to begin stage productions. His initial efforts were unsuccessful, but he staged a major hit in 1927 with the first American production of *Dracula* with Bela Lugosi and Edward Van Sloan, which spawned the famous 1931 movie, sans Liveright's involvement.

Liveright's publishing success included books by T.S. Eliot, Ernest Hemingway, William Faulkner, Hart Crane, Dorothy Parker, and S.J. Perelman. Liveright wanted to publish these contemporary authors, while Boni favored sociopolitical works. The company partnership ended with a coin toss, with Liveright the winner and sole proprietor.

In 1925, Liveright sold Modern Library to Bennett Cerf for $200,000. Cerf and his partner Donald Klopfer changed the company's name to Random House two years later. In 1928,

11 TRUE CRIMES

by JOSEPH GOLLOMB

F.D.C.

THE SEAL OF A GOOD BOOK

$2.50 BOOK
for 25c

Liveright renamed Boni & Liveright, to Horace Liveright, Inc. And the name was changed yet again to simply Liveright, Inc. in 1931. *Crimes of the Year* by Joseph Gollomb was published in a 354-page hardcover edition by Horace Liveright in 1931. The 128-page digest was a reprint (with much smaller type) of the hardcover's first eleven chapters. Not included were two others: "Chicago Contributors" (Al Capone and "Bugs" Moran) and "The Mad God of Palm Island" (Robert Harry Curry). Oddly, the page headers of the digest are "Crimes of the Year" rather than "Eleven True Crimes." (Perhaps it was originally intended to be a full reprint of the hardcover, but when only the first eleven chapters would fit in the typical digest length of 128 pages, the name was changed late in its production.)

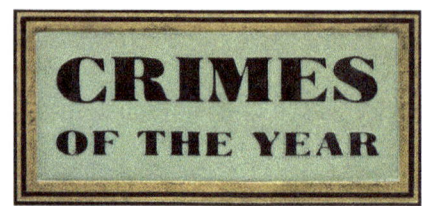

Also absent from the digest is Gollomb's short foreword:

"Every modern war forges new weapons and a new technique. Crime too is war, even when committed in time of peace; it is war against the individual as well as society. Is modern crime also creating new weapons and new technique? If so it behooves society to know it.

"In this book are the outstanding crimes committed within the year in different parts of the world. What have they to say to us?"

The specific year of *Crimes of the Year* is never firmly stated, but when dates are given, they run from 1924 to 1930.

The undated copyright notice in *11 True Crimes* is by Horace Liveright, Inc., implying it was published in 1931 when that was the company's name. However, Kenneth R. Johnson's "The Digest Index" groups the titles from Green Publishing with a few earlier digests (No. 1–5) from Larkin; Roosevelt & Larkin, Ltd.; R.W. Voigt; and The Spotlight. Johnson concludes the digests "cannot have been issued any earlier than 1943." Liveright died in 1933, but The Black and Gold Library hardcover series he began continued under the Liveright Publishing Corporation under Arthur Pell, who had partnered with Liveright in 1930. Unfortunately, the exact year of the digest's publication is unclear.

A fox head emblem appears on the digest's cover with the letters "F.D.C." printed across its face, with the first two periods doing double duty as irises for the fox's eyes. Circling its head is the proclamation "The Seal of a Good Book." It's very similar to the fox-head logo used on Fox Feature Syndicate's mid-1940s comic books like *Everybody's Comics* No. 1. (Perhaps Victor S. Fox had an interest in Green Publishing—or something else, as yet undocumented.)

The author, Joseph Gollomb (1881–1950), was born in Petrograd Russia, and immigrated with his family to New York in 1891. His father died shortly after they arrived, leaving his socialist mother to raise him in New York's Jewish tenements on the Lower East Side. His fictionalized autobiography, *Unquiet*, published by Dodd, Mead, and Co. in 1935, details his experiences there. He was a member of the Socialist Party of America and the Industrial Workers of the World. He taught English to Russian Jewish immigrants at the socialist Rand School. His niece was the actress Judy Holliday (1921–1965).

As a successful journalist, he wrote for New York's *Evening Post*, *Evening World*, the *New Yorker*, and for the foreign bureaus of the Associated and United Press. His research led to his nonfiction books *Crimes of the Year* and *Armies of Spies* (1939). He also wrote true crime articles for *Flynn's Weekly Detective Fiction*, *The Black Mask*, *Detective Story Magazine*, and others. His short stories appeared in *Argosy Allstory Weekly*. His mystery novels include *The Girl in the Fog* (1923), *The Portrait Invisible* (1927), and *The Curtain of Storm* (1932). His career also encompassed screenwriting where his credits include early shorts and the full-length films *More Deadly Than the Male* (1919) and *Murder at the Vanities* (1934).

Chapter 1: The Perfect Mystery

The tragic life of Isadore Fink began in Poland. At seven, his mother died. At ten, his father. He paid his way to whatever family was willing to board him in return for a full day's chores and taking in laundry. By the time he was grown, he'd scraped together enough for steerage to New York, where he worked sixteen-hour days on the lower east side as a laundry helper. After ten years of toil, he finally had enough to realize his dream of a laundry of his own.

It was located at 52 East 132nd Street in Harlem. A store front tenement with two rooms for living space that he rented to an older African American woman for a meager rent. Always a wary young man, he secured every point of egress: an iron bolt on the door between his shop and his renter's rooms, closely spaced bars on the shop's rear window, and the transom above the front door nailed shut all around. The front door itself had two locks upon his arrival, and he added a third.

One night in February, he left his shop to deliver a package of laundry to a customer, locking his shop securely as he left. On his return trip, he stopped at the cigar store across the street, bought some cigarettes, and chatted for a few minutes with the clerk. When he left, the clerk recalls him crossing the street, entering his shop, and pulling the shade on the door's window. His light went out at about half-past ten.

Not much later, Isadore's tenant woke to the sound of gunfire. Three shots in rapid succession from inside the shop, followed by what must have been the sound of a body falling to the floor. She threw on her wrapper and

ran out into the tenement's hall, yelling "Police!"

Fortunately, a cop on his beat heard her cries and came running. Once he understood the trouble, he tried the front door to Isadore's shop, but it was locked tight. He then tried the adjoining door in the tenant's rooms, but it too, was bolted shut on the shop side.

By now, a small crowd had formed outside the shop. The policeman enlisted the aid of a young man, lifting him up to the transom. It too was immovable, so the cop handed his club to the youngster to break the glass. The boy was able to squirm inside, slide down, and unlock the front door.

The policeman rushed inside, flipped on the light switch, and found the body of Isadore Fink, blood still oozing from two bullet wounds in his head and one in his hand.

The crowd was asked to phone the local precinct while the patrolman assessed the situation. At first, it seemed a suicide, but after a thorough search, no gun was found. When a sergeant and two detectives arrived, they too were baffled. They searched the shop from top to bottom and found no weapon. The Isadore Fink murder was never solved. A true life locked room mystery with no motive, no evidence, and no apparent means of escape for the gunman.

The case has been documented many times over the years. One theory is that Isadore himself locked the door moments after the gunman fled, then staggered back into the shop and collapsed. Maybe—but we'll never know for sure.

Chapter 2: Scotland Yard's Latest

Vivian Messiter's life was longer and happier than Isadore Fink's. Messiter was born and raised in England, but moved to American when he reached adulthood, seeking to optimize his employment opportunities there. He did indeed find work, but moved from state to state, seeking to improve his lot. He also found a wife, but his marriage ended in divorce. When World War I began, he served in the Canadian infantry, until he was wounded. He was discharged and required the aid of a cane to walk for the rest of his life.

At the age of 57, he returned to England and was hired as an agent for the Wolf Head Oil Company in Southampton. He lived alone in a boarding house and kept to himself. He was a man of routine, so when his landlord discovered he had not slept in his bed the previous night, she began to worry.

She wanted to alert the police, but her husband dissuaded her, fearing their tenant would not appreciate the intrusion of the authorities when he surely would return. However, in the succeeding days, when his employer did not hear from him after repeated telegrams and letters, the Oil Company assumed he'd left, and sent a replacement to their garage in Southhampton.

When the new man unlocked the doors, he found the body of Messiter lying beside a delivery truck, his head battered in from blows on the back of his head and forehead, presumably from the hammer found behind an oil drum.

The Southampton police did a thorough investigation, but coming up empty, contacted Scotland Yard to take over the case.

"*The fiction version of what has made Scotland Yard celebrated would indicate that it pos-*

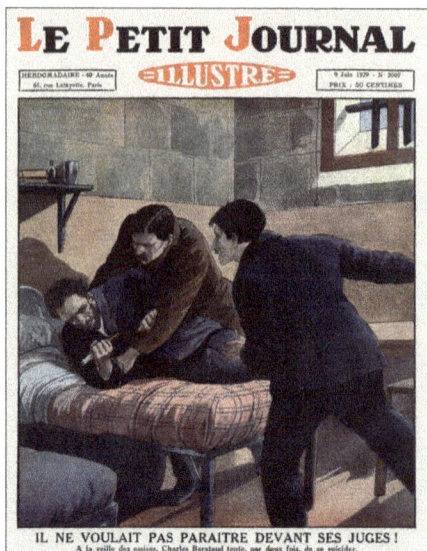

IL NE VOULAIT PAS PARAITRE DEVANT SES JUGES !
A la veille des assises, Charles Barataud tente, par deux fois, de se suicider.

sesses some diabolical cleverness in dealing with criminals and their works; a more true conception would ascribe much of the success of Scotland Yard to an infinite capacity for taking pains."

After a remarkably meticulous investigation following a series of slim, potential leads, the assigned squad at last uncovered a promising suspect: one William Henry Podmore, a three-time loser. He was arrested and charged with murder, but escaped conviction. However, he was sent to prison to serve out his term on a prior robbery conviction.

In prison, he bragged about the Messiter murder to fellow inmates and their subsequent testimony, combined with the previous circumstantial evidence, was enough for a conviction in Podmore's second trial. He was sentenced to death by hanging.

Chapter 3: The Loving Son

The insurance business is all about premium payments. But while the cash flowing in is always accepted, the cash flowing out may be excepted.

When Sydney Harry Fox's mother died of suffocation and shock, it was found an accidental death. However, when a clerk reviewed her life insurance policy it was discovered young Fox had renewed it mere hours before it was to expire. This triggered an investigation, and the company's agent soon learned Fox's path was lined with lies, scams, and fraud. They handed over their findings to Scotland Yard, who launched a massive investigation.

The evidence they found was extreme. Fox was a swindler who'd served multiple terms in prison. When his mother's body was exhumed it was found she died from strangulation, suffered bruises to her larynx, and there were no traces of soot in her lungs from the fire in her room—meaning she died before the fire began.

Fox was arrested and tried for murder. The jury found him guilty, and he was hanged at Maidstone Jail on April 8, 1930. Fox's case has been dramatized on radio and television, most recently on the BBC series *Murder, Mystery and My Family* (season 5, episode 6, July 5, 2021) that concluded his mother died of heart failure and the fire was indeed accidental.

Chapter 4:
The Youth with Smiling Eyes

Joseph Gollomb knew how to repurpose his work. He sold this chapter to the *Syracuse Herald*'s magazine section for their March 8, 1931 edition with the headline: French Mother's Love Saves Son From Guillotine But His Bragging Brings Justice and He Pays Penalty.

It's the sordid story of Roger Voron, an unabashed layabout whose own mother kicked him out of her poor house at the age of 24, when he refused to earn his keep by any measure whatsoever. He first turned to his grandmother for shelter, but the older woman knew him too well and ordered him away.

The powerfully built lad made his way to Paris, where he lived on the streets until he met a poor old woman. She told him her raggy clothes and hovel were choices she made in her appreciation for the value of money. She was actually better off than most. She was taken in by Voron's sad story and offered him her home until he was able to find work. In return, he strangled her and sought to find her fortune. Either she'd hidden it too well or had lied, for he fled with only a small coin.

He returned to his mother's home in Loire, pleading for a second chance. The secret murder had changed him. He secured a job and worked hard to earn his keep—at first. But too soon, his languid habits returned. He threw in with another scheming lout named Hermette and together they plotted the murder and robbery of Voron's grandmother. This time the buffoons were caught red-handed thanks to the old woman's dog.

At the trial, Roger's mother revealed he was a bastard. His victim was, in fact, not his grandmother by blood, so his crime had not been matricide. Her plea swayed the jury, saving him from the guillotine. Instead, he and his accomplice each received a 14-year sentence.

In prison, Roger met an older inmate named Bebert and ingratiated himself with the man, bragging about his murders. He gave Bebert so much detail about the murder in Paris that Bebert attempted to use his knowledge as a negotiating wedge with the warden. The effort failed, but the facts soon pointed to Roger, who was tried and convicted for the

crime. And this time, the guillotine showed him no mercy.

Chapter 5:
A Grim Tale of Vienna Woods

Rushing toward their station to avoid an impending downpour, three police officers were jarred by the report of a weapon that came from inside the Lainzer Tiergarten. It was followed by what appeared to be a small fire amid the trees. As the officers ran to investigate, the downpour drenched the area, extinguishing the blaze. Within smoldering embers was a body. A woman shot in the head, her body badly burned. The heavy rains had washed the crime scene of all footprints.

The remaining evidence showed her killer had emptied a bottle of benzine over her body and set pieces of solid alcohol (calcium acetate) on her chest to incite the blaze.

According to Gollomb, the Vienna police were renown for their intelligence and tenacity. Unable to identify the badly burned victim, they enlisted the aid of a sculptor, a dermatologist, a dentist, a hairdresser, and other experts to recreate an accurate wax likeness of the victim built upon her bone structure.

"Photographs (of her likeness) and descriptions of the dead woman's teeth were printed in the technical dental journals and the cooperation of the profession was asked." But without result. So they embarked on personal visits to every dentist in Vienna. An officer sat with each practitioner as they went over their files to find a match for the victim's dental work. When a good match was finally found, the dentist was shown the likeness and identified the woman as Elsa Fellner. She was a dancer who had married a Romanian, but divorced him. She was enjoying her unattached freedom, but she feared her husband even after the divorce. He was a jealous man and had once threatened to kill her. Thus, Andreas Fellner was the investigators' first suspect.

However, once arrested, he proved a poor one. He confirmed the likeness was indeed accurate and identified a bracelet from her remains. But his alibi on the date of the murder (July 17, 1928), was airtight. He had been traveling when his car broke down and had been helped by two Italian police officers who had documented the event in their reports. Fellner was cleared and released. He advised the police that Elsa enjoyed the company of several men and one of them might have felt jealous about the others. The police had determined Elsa had left Trieste a few days before her murder, so they launched a review of all the telegrams sent between the Trieste and Vienna in that time frame on the theory that she had arranged to meet someone there.

At last, they found a telegram from "Elsa Donau" to Gustave Bauer that fit the theory. "Donau" was not "Fellner" but they proceeded with the only lead they had. When Bauer was approached, he was aloof and uncooperative. Nevertheless, police searched his effects and found he kept journals about his romantic relationships, one volume for each of his lovers. Unfortunately, none mentioned Elsa Fellner or any other Elsa. When Bauer's former valet was found and questioned, he recognized the likeness as a woman Bauer had told him to meet at the train station from Trieste. They soon found other witnesses who could attest that Bauer did indeed know Fellner, despite his earlier denial.

Since their brief affair, Bauer had moved on and was engaged to be married. When Fellner told him she was coming to see him, he feared she would upset his betrothed. Thus, he arranged

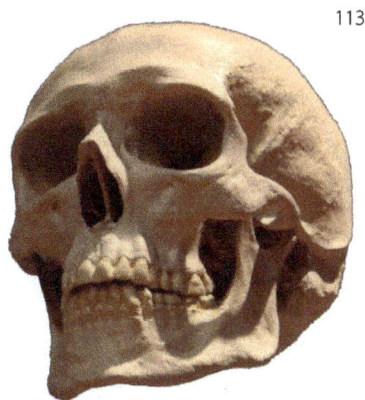

a rendezvous in Lainzer Tiergarten. He was arrested in Berlin and wrote two letters which he gave to a fellow prisoner to post upon the man's eminent release. They never reached their destinations—a friend and a former mistress. Instead, the police read his desperate pleas for an alibi for the date of the murder. At the time of Gollomb's report, Bauer's trial was set for the fall.

Chapter 6:
The Killer Who Laughed Last

Limoges, located in southwest-central France, is known for its fine, decorated porcelain. Charles Barataud, son of a wealthy porcelain manufacturer, was arrested for the murder of a taxi driver, Etienne Faure. The crime began as a plot to rob a wealthy lumber merchant out of 600,000 francs, by tempting him with the bargain sale of a plot of timber land. But first, Barataud needed to steal a car. He chose Faure's taxi and lured the man to a remote woods on the pretense of a stalled car. As Faure peered under the hood to inspect the engine, Barataud struck the back of his head with a hatchet.

Barataud loaded Faure's pockets with stones and hurled his body into a nearby river. Later that night, his plot to murder the lumber merchant and his associate, and steal the 600,000 francs was foiled by the criminal's ineptitude. Barataud's hatchet was no match for the merchant's pistol. Barataud dismissed the entire affair as a joke and drove the taxi back to the site of the murder, rolling it into the same river in which he had dumped the body.

An investigation began as soon as Etienne Faure and his taxi were reported missing. The details of how the French Police traced the murder to Barataud were not revealed, but when they brought him to the Commissariat of Police, he readily confessed, trading his signed confession for a last chance to say goodbye to his father.

He was taken home and allowed to return to his room for a change of clothes. Unbeknown to the authorities, in his room, his closest confederate, Bertrand Peynet was waiting. Barataud called a lawyer, and pretending to be Peynet, explained that his friend Barataud had been arrested, but was innocent. He knew this only too well. And rather than see his friend tried, the two had decided to die together.

Barataud snatched one of his hunting rifles from a rack and aimed it at the stunned Peynet. Meanwhile, the lawyer called the Barataud home and told the police that the two men intended on

committing suicide at that very moment! The police heard a shot as they rushed toward the room. Too late, Peynet was dead. Barataud claimed his friend had shot himself and he was about to take his own life, but the rifle misfired. And then he calmly rescinded his earlier confession, insinuating that Peynet had been the killer.

It took sixteen months for the trial to begin. The jury found Barataud guilty of the murder of the taxi driver and the death of his friend—but with extenuating circumstances. The jury foreman yielded his position to a small-town notary who botched the delivery of the verdict and saved Barataud from the guillotine. The murderer received a life sentence instead.

The New York Times reported violent rioting erupted in Limoges at the erroneous verdict. Twenty-five people were injured, with several probably fatally. The military was called in to quell the uproar. On May 4, 1961, *Le Populaire* reported Barataud's death from tuberculosis while still in prison. The case inspired the book: *Charles Barataud, criminel ou martyr?* by Annie Brousseau (Lucien Souny, 1995).

Chapter 7: Nemesis in Texas

The amateur is as common in detective fiction as the professional, but in true crime investigation not so much.

However, in the case of the murder of Exa Johnson Payne, it was due to a newspaper reporter that her killer was finally brought to justice.

On the fateful day, Arthur D. Payne walked to his office with his daughter, Bobbie Jean, in tow. Within the hour, he received an urgent call from the police, his wife had been killed in an explosion while driving. His son was in critical condition and rushed to a hospital. The police determined a high explosive had been placed in the car and ignited by a time-fuse. They pledged to work overtime to find the culprit responsible. But as the days and weeks passed, they found no likely suspect or motive for the crime.

However, Gene Howe the crusading editor of the Amarillo *Globe-News* was so moved by the murder he took it upon himself to offer a five hundred dollar reward to spur the hunt, and pledged to have himself deputized to see what he could do with the case. His editorial struck a nerve immediately with Payne, who added five thousand dollars to the pot. This prompted Howe to contact A.B. Macdonald, a reporter with the *Kansas City Star*, a well-known crime reporter with a reputation for solving crimes that baffled the police.

As soon as Macdonald arrived in Amarillo, he went to work. His first interview was with Arthur Payne, who offered full cooperation providing the names of all the secretaries he'd employed over the past two years. He also learned Exa and Arthur each had $10,000 life insurance policies for each other, and the insurance company had held payment pending their own investigation into the murder.

Howe was not convinced Macdonald had found a motive. "I've studied the man and whatever else you may make me believe you couldn't convince me that Payne killed his wife for her insurance," he asserted. So Macdon-

ald pursued another angle—that of another woman. Howe balked at this, too. Amarillo was a small town and Payne was too well known to carry on with someone else without gossip. But Macdonald wasn't convinced. He began to interview Payne's past secretaries. When he got to Verona Thompson, something clicked. Payne had described her as rather commonplace, but when Macdonald met her, she was more attractive than he was led to believe. He soon discovered she'd lunched and traveled with Payne on several occasions—always for business.

Following a hunch, he pressed her. "I know, for instance, that you've been seeing Payne since you quit working for him; that you've been off on trips with him that have nothing to do with business; and I know other things." He told her Payne had been arrested for the murder of his wife, and if she knew what was good for her, she'd better start cooperating. He was bluffing, but his claims clearly unsettled her. He pushed harder, and she broke down completely, revealing a clandestine affair with Payne and their plan to marry after he'd divorced his wife. Although he said nothing about the murder, he told her, "Our lives, yours and mine, depend on your silence."

Macdonald met with Howe and the mayor, Ernest O. Thompson, and they decided to arrest Payne for murder. He was taken at his home and caught a glimpse of Verona Thompson in the district attorney's office as he was processed. A search of Payne's offices revealed two identical letters written by a man who described himself as a burglar. They detailed a flimsy story about dynamite placed in the wrong car and how the murder was just a terrible accident. His conscience had prompted his anonymous confession.

Mayor Thompson didn't fall for the phony letters and ordered Payne put in solitary confinement in "the cooler," an isolated cell in the basement. The sobering burden of detention and solitude took their toll. Payne called for the Mayor and agreed to confess. He wrote nearly 60,000 words detailing his love for Verona, and several previous attempts to kill Exa with poison, an automobile accident, a shotgun, and finally explosives.

News of his sensational confession appeared in newspapers around the world. As the case came to trial, he assaulted a guard and was again locked in solitary, where he committed suicide rather than face the electric chair. Gollomb's report clearly identifies the murderer as Arthur D. Payne, but at FindAGrave.com, he is listed as Alfred Day Payne, Sr., author of a 20,000-word confession.

Chapter 8:
The Mystery of Chung Yi Maio

Organized crime and corruption are the underlying tentacles that grasped the lives of Chung Yi Maio and his wife Wai Shung Siu. Maio was the son of a wealthy Peking (Beijing) merchant. His father fell victim to the chaos and civil war that racked China in the early twentieth century, losing his wife and most of his kin in its wake. He converted all his assets to cash, willing his bankroll to his son, and then committed suicide.

Determined to break with the past, Maio left China for America to study law at the University of Chicago. In the spring of 1928, he visited some friends in New York, where he met Wai Shang Siu. She, too, came to America with a sizable inheritance. To two fell in love and Maio began his law practice in New York serving Chinese merchants.

As time went on, his career grew more and more enmeshed with his clients. He kept the details of his activities secret from Wai Shung as he grew more dour.

When it came time to wed, he explained, "We will marry and go away—at once! But I am in a difficult position; I am running away from some of my—business responsibilities. You will indulge me then if I keep our traveling plans secret—not only from my business associates but also from our friends."

Publicly, they made one set of travel plans, but secretly they followed another. Nonetheless, when they arrived in Glasgow on a steamer, Maio turned pale when he noticed two Chinamen on the dock who seemed to be scrutinizing the newlyweds.

The couple honeymooned at the Borrowdale Gates Hotel outside the town of Keswick, England. On the afternoon of June 18, the couple left the hotel for a walk. Three hours later, Maio returned alone. When a clerk asked about his wife, Maio replied she had gone on to shop in Keswick, since he was feeling ill and needed rest. When Wai Shung had not returned by eight o'clock, the clerk visited the couple's room and asked if he should send a car for her. Maio declined, saying his wife could take care of herself.

Meanwhile, a farmer working near the shores of Lake Derwentwater had noticed a large umbrella on the beach. He observed what he thought to be a pair of woman's feet visible at the edge of the canopy—feet that hadn't moved in hours. Upon closer investigation, he discovered the body of Wai Shung, a necklace of plaited string and picture wire encircling her bruised neck.

The police zeroed in on Maio immediately, and he was arrested that night. At trial, his lawyer argued he had no motive for the murder. Wai Shung's fortune had been willed to her family in China, not her husband, and he knew it. Nevertheless, he was convicted and was hanged at the Strangeways Jail in Manchester in the fall of 1928.

The epilogue to this tragedy is only rumor, but one theory has it Maio had joined a tong in New York. Wai Shung's father had made powerful enemies in the Kwangtung Province in China before his death by natural causes. Wai Shung was his favorite daughter and the benefactor of his plundering. She had been marked for execution by the tong for retribution. Maio was compelled to carry out the inevitable murder or face certain death himself.

Chapter 9:
The Drudge Who Turned Bandit

Gollomb uses just about every form of the word "drudge" to describe Irene Shrader and her life—from wretched childhood to desperate adult. If Irene rated a ten in drudgery, the love of her life, Glenn Dague, came in at eight or nine.

They met when he sideswiped her with his car. She was on foot. It wasn't at all serious, but their meeting ignited a flame. "The two strangers looked at each other—and in each other two commonplace human beings discovered a miracle." They became lovers. "He left his family, his job, respectability, everything to join Irene." He worked his tail off to support her and her toddler, Donnie, fathered by her ex-husband, another drudge two couldn't earn enough to support himself, let alone a wife and baby.

Dague worked every job he could manage. "One day, while working for a tree 'doctor,' he fell from a forty-foot ladder, was laid up for weeks and thereby lost his job." Irene did her best to care for him, but the day came when there was nothing left. She knew her only recourse was to sell herself. When the realization hit Dague, he cried, "This is the end! God's curse is on us! He will not help me get bread for you and the boy honestly. Very well, I'll go out and take it by force!"

Irene accepted this axiom and went with him. They purchased two decrepit pistols from a pawnbroker and began a crime spree that would drive them to headline infamy and a cross-country flight from Wheeling, West Virgina, all the way to Arizona. Their three-week crime wave fueled dozens of robberies, gunfights, murder, and a massive manhunt involving law enforcement and bounty hunters across the country.

Gollomb records their flight in riveting detail, at times using Irene's own words, transcribed from her diaries written in prison while awaiting her execution. This exceptional chapter is worth the price of the book all by itself.

Chapter 10: A County of Crime

Williamson County, in southern Illinois, was a case study in the perversion of justice during most of the 1920s. Its citizens were "a lean, hard, narrow-minded, intense race who held life cheap and who could nurse a dispute over a mongrel hound or a personal slight till it grew into a blood-feud for generations." Armed with pistols, rifles, machine guns, a self-righteous sense of entitlement and a blind allegiance to one's beliefs, the county was known as "Bloody Williamson" for over three-quarters of a century.

The first conflict Gollomb details was between union coal miners and a strip miner excavating a large vein at ground-level with steam shovels. William J. Jester, who owned the non-union operation, was prepared for conflict. He hired a small army of out-of-town muscle to protect his mine. Three union men were shot and killed when they tried to breach his encampment.

Outrage at the shootings spread and men were gathered from all around Williamson and its neighboring counties. "It was estimated that as many as five thousand armed men . . . gathered on those hill tops during the night." The battle began in the early hours. Although the hired guns were well armed, it wasn't more than a few hours before they were overwhelmed by the sheer number of their opponents.

After surrender, the Lester miners were marched into the woods. "When the orgy was over, twenty-two mutilated bodies were taken to undertakers . . . and the hospitals . . . were filled with more than sixty wounded men."

Wholesale arrests of union miners were made—seventy-six were charged with riot, intent to murder, and murder. As the cases were prepared for trial, no witnesses came forward. Seventy-six indictments dwindled to five. At the trial of one of the accused, Clem

Clarke, the jury read their statement, "We find the deaths of the decedents were due to acts direct and indirect of the officials of the Southern Illinois Coal Company and to gunshot wounds at the hands of persons unknown." The verdict shocked the country, but not Williamson County.

The next conflict was over Prohibition, with each side roughly equal. The wet side united the miners and the towns. The dry side had farmers, churches, the county districts, and the rise of the Ku Klux Klan. "Williamson County became as fertile ground for its recruiting agents as any other backward section of the country."

The Williamson movement found its leader in S. Glenn Young, a veteran of law enforcement in the Blue Ridge Mountains, who survived multiple gunfights there. "Every man I ever killed was in self-dense," he asserted.

"Over the county they scattered, revolvers strapped to their hips, rifles in their hands. The doors of a hundred speakeasies were smashed in, their owners were dragged out half dressed and with them several hundred employees and their families were hustled off in cars to the jail in the Klan town of Benton."

The reaction to the assault was the formation of a group who called themselves Knights of the Flaming Circle. The sheriff of Williamson County, George Galligan, was a supporter, but not their leader. The man who assumed that position was Ora Thomas, a bootlegger from Chicago, who had just finished a term in prison. Galligan made him his deputy sheriff.

But the dry factions were relentless. Young attempted a coup and notified the citizens of Herrin they were under marshal law and that he was now chief in Herrin's city hall. Sheriff Galligan, who had escaped during the night, appealed to the governor for troops to restore the rule of law.

The Klan caught up with Galligan in Carbondale and arrested him for the murder of Cæsar Cagle, a constable and Klansman, who had been assassinated the night of February 8, 1924 in Herrin. Galligan was hauled in to Herrin, where Young locked him up. However, soon after truckloads of state troopers arrived, Galligan was freed, and order was restored. It wasn't the first time it took intervention from the state to set things right.

The conflicts and clashes between Young's Klansmen and Thomas' Circle weighed heavily on the country. Its reputation as "Bloody Williamson" spread, depressing its businesses and outlook. The business community pressured both sides to end their crusades. Young was forced out and Thomas would soon be dismissed.

As Young left Williamson for Chicago, animosity followed. He was ambushed on the road and left wounded in the leg, his wife blinded. He recognized his attackers as Carl and Earl Shelton. He managed to drive to a doctor and alerted his Klan friends what had transpired. The Shelton brothers were arrested within the hour near Herrin.

On August 30, 1924, Sheriff Galigan and his men arrived at the garage where Young's car had been impounded. It was evidence needed in the Shelton's trial. The Klansmen at the garage disagreed, and another gunfight erupted, leaving four Klansmen and three anti-Klan dead.

"The Shelton brothers were brought to trial; just as previously, among other defendants, they had been brought to trial for the murder of Cæsar Cagle. And as before, they were acquitted."

The business community kept the tensions in Herrin tamped down but not resolved. In January 1925, Glenn Young returned to open a restaurant. His Klan cronies made it their headquarters.

When Ora Thomas got news of Young's return, he took it as a sign for him to relocate too. It wasn't long before the hatred the two rivals felt boiled over. When Young led two Klansmen into the cigar store of the European Hotel, he came looking for trouble, and he found it. The only survivor was

Lige Green, an unarmed anti-Klansman. Young and Thomas had finally killed themselves and the two Klansmen with Young were also dead.

State troops declared martial law again at the request of Galligan and A.M. Walker, Chief of Police in Herrin. The troops stayed to keep order at the funerals for both of Williamson's infamous rivals. The rest of 1925 passed with relative quiet.

The final conflict in the county erupted from the ranks of racketeers. A transplant from New York, by way of Chicago, named Charlie Birger, arrived in Williamson in 1922, just prior to the Lester mine massacre. He built his business bootlegging, and his business was booming. He specialized in booze and gambling only, and wanted no part in extortion, prostitution, or drugs. Unfortunately, the Shelton brothers, whom he hired early on, wanted their cut of any illicit trade they could exploit.

When Birger discovered the bothers had strayed far from his orders, the kindling for a war between gangsters ignited. Both sides suffered casualties. Several elected officials affiliated with one side or the other were assassinated.

The first relief came in the form of United States deputy marshals. The Shelton brothers robbed a U.S. Post Office messenger of $25,000 at Collinsville, Illinois in 1924. It took two years for the government to track them to Williamson country, where they were arrested.

At their trial, Charlie Birger was a key witness. He testified the brothers had planned the post office robbery, and he had tried to dissuade them. They were found guilty and sentenced to 25 years in Leavenworth.

Birger's triumph was short-lived. He was arrested at his home for the murder of Mayor Adams of West City, an execution he'd ordered that was carried out by his henchmen.

The new county sheriff, Oren Coleman, had only one allegiance: to uphold the law. Coleman was methodical and his campaign to uproot corruption in the county made relatively swift progress. Klan leader Arlie O. Boswell got two years for conspiring to traffic liquor. The mayor of Herrin, Marshall McCormick, and the city's chief of police, John Stamm, received similar sentences on similar charges.

Bootlegger Charlie Birger was convicted of first degree murder and sentenced to hang. He died on April 19, 1928, at the age of 47.

Chapter 11: *The Women of Nagyrev and Tiszakurt*

The reported facts of a community's wholesale murder spree requires the suspension of disbelief. The factors paving its way combine into a trifecta:

1) Isolated communities (Nagyrev and Tiszakurt, Hungary) of the early twentieth century with little access to telephone or telegraph. The nearest railroad line 25 miles away. Primitive roads prone to flooding and winters that leave the two villages snowbound for months at a time.

2) Uneducated rural citizens. (Gollomb suggests they were simpletons.) The men, fueled with inferior wine, abuse the women. The women suffer in relatively silent, but simmering anger.

3) Upon his demise, the modest plots of land a farmer owns must be divided among his heirs, leading progressively to smaller and smaller parcels. The more children, the poorer their prospects, so more children become a liability rather than an asset.

These factors created demand for the illegal practice of abortion. Most midwives of Nagyrev and Tiszakurt were reticent to offer abortions, but one was not—Susi Olah, who soon rose to popularity and influence among the women of the isolated area.

"There were no doctors in the region and midwives were the only 'medical' help available, even in illness that had nothing to do with pregnancy. When Susi's ministrations turned out fatally for the patient there was only the 'halotkem' to diagnose Susi's mistakes."

In Susi's case, the "halotkem" was her son-in-law. He simply verified a death and issued a death certificate. The number of deceased patients eventually caused some reaction and Susi found herself arrested and tried nine times—but always acquitted for lack of evidence.

Susi's track record even gave her pause. One day, when she noticed how quickly flies expired after being caught on flypaper, she discovered it was treated with arsenic. A "tea" made from several strips of flypaper could be an effective treatment for unwanted pregnancies. Susi would deliver the child and instruct the mother to dose her infant with the fatal liquid.

Susi's popularity soared. So much so, the area's other four midwives became irrate. Susi gathered them together and proposed dividing the region into sections, thus ending any competition between them. To celebrate their new found cooperation, Susi served tea and

soon became the only midwife standing. The "halotkem" ascribed natural causes to the midwives' deaths.

Fortified with her success and tired of her sickly husband, she soon found herself a widow. Her son accused her of murder, and days later, the young man was seized with violent stomach cramps after eating. By this time, Susi was no longer at home. Her son grabbed a revolver and went on the hunt. He found her in front of an inn. He pointed the weapon at her, fired, and collapsed to the ground. Susi remained standing—unhurt. Her son survived the poison, but fled the district in fear of his life.

Susi's "tea" continued to gain popularity and was now used on both unwanted infants and husbands. She was the catalyst for murder, but not the murderer. "For a score of years men all over Nagyrev and Tiszakurt died with a suddeness inexplicable to the other men." The doom spread to ailing seniors, sickly children, and the handicapped.

The beginning of the end came in 1924, when Mrs. Ladislas Szabo was charged with killing her father and his brother. She claimed innocence at first, but soon broke down and began naming others in hopes of deflecting guilt. Among them was Susi Olah.

Susi and scores of prisoners were taken to Szolnok for questioning. She proved a wary suspect and the district-attorney reluctantly released her. On her return to Nagyrev, she immediately set out on a tour to visit her customers, warning them to keep their mouths shut. When she returned home, she heard a commotion outside. The police were arresting the women she'd visited along her street, and they had her home surrounded.

But they did not advance, apparently thinking they would wait for her to lead them to yet more of her customers. They were disappointed, for she never left her house again. She had hanged herself inside a clothes closet.

Back in Szolnok, 31 women and three male accomplices were tried for murder by poisoning. Five of the women awaiting trial followed Susi Olah's example and took their own lives. Those convicted were given sentences that ranged from life to five years of imprisonment.

Summary

In the opening paragraph to Chapter 13 of *Crimes of the Year*, Gollomb writes: "Among the crimes I have recounted in this series there are murder mysteries of New York, machine-gun massacres in the underworld of Chicago and other reverberations of the steely clash that assails our senses and often our very bodies in this western civilization of ours."

Gollomb selected sensational crimes to report, but his narratives are not sensationalized. His stories are dramatized with dialogue and intimacies to increase their appeal, but they are largely accurate accounts. Details of some of these cases can be corroborated with sources online. As Henry Montor wrote in 1931, Gollomb was an outstanding crime reporter. *11 True Crimes* remains a useful resource on fascinating crimes and a history lesson on corruption, protection, and influence peddling.

References

CanalBlog.com
CoolCatDaddy.com
Encyclopedia.com
FindAGrave.com
IMDb.com
MyComicShop.com
NYTimes.com
sites.owu.edu
Wikipedia

The Digest Enthusiast No. 15 is dedicated to the memory of

Vincent Paul Nowell, Sr.

April 20, 1938–October 22, 2021

Vince began contributing to these pages in 2018 and never missed an issue. He'd begun an article shortly before he passed peacefully at his home in Simi Valley. Vince is survived by his wife of 31 years, Carole Nowell.

Vince was a true fiction enthusiast and loved to write about the history of science fiction magazines, peppered with his wry sense of humor. His pseudonyms included Ward Smith. Thanks for being part of this adventure, pal. You and your work are missed. Vince's obituary can be found on the Reardon Simi Valley Funeral Home website.

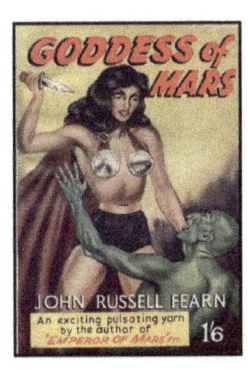

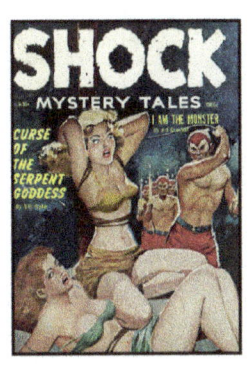

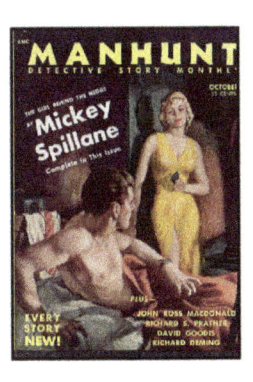

Crime On My Hands
as by Carl G. Hoges,
Phantom Book No. 506
1952. Cover by
George Gross.

Carl G. Hodges:
Crime On My Hands

Overview/Synopsis by Richard Krauss

At 21, Carl Garrett Hodges (1902–1964) began his career as a writer when his story, "The Quarrel" appeared in *Mystery Magazine* (June 15, 1923). Born in Quincy, Illinois, where he attended school, he sold five additional stories to *Mystery Magazine* through January 1925. The gap between his next published yarn, "Haymaker Shuffle" in *Fifteen Western Tales* Oct. 1942, may be explained by his work in public relations for the Illinois Department of Public Welfare; his stints as executive-secretary for the National Association of Petroleum Retailers and superintendent of the Illinois Information Service; and as a columnist for the *Peoria Star*.

In the latter half of the 1940s he created the husband and wife team of Dwight and Gail Berke, whose adventures debuted in "Sixteen Pounds of Murder" in *Thrilling Detective* (October 1946). Dwight was sports editor at *The Journal* and dug up scoops on crooked horseracing or other unsportsmanlike crime. Gail was *The Journal*'s photographer. She recorded evidence and was helpful in solving the couple's cases. The Berkes starred in five novelettes and one short story for *Thrilling*.

By the early 1950s, Hodges turned his attention to mystery novels. He served as vice-president of the Mystery Writers of America, Midwest Chapter. He included a meeting of the organization and several of its members in his novel, *Naked Villainy*, published as the final of three *Suspense Novels* in 1951

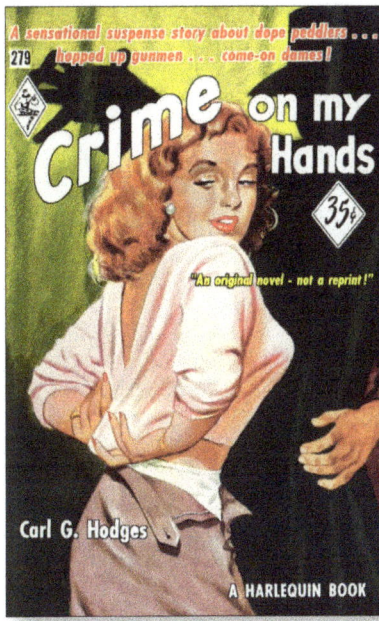

Crime On My Hands as by Carl G. Hoges, Harlequin No. 279. Cover after the Phantom Books edition by George Gross.

(see *The Digest Enthusiast* No. 4 pages 44–48). *Naked Villainy* also saw print in the UK's Phantom Classics series, as No. 581.

Crime on My Hands was his second mystery novel, published in 1952*. It appeared as a digest-sized paperback from Phantom Books, as No. 506, with a cover by George Gross. Harlequin published another edition (Harlequin No. 279), likely a follow-on as the cover is obviously a redo of the Gross original. Finally a third edition, published in the UK by Alexander Moring LTD, featuring new artwork. All editions were written as by Carl G. Hoges, without the "d."

What follows is a chapter-by-chapter synopsis of the novel. Intended primarily to entertain, but can also serve instructional for any writer looking for a detailed synopsis of how to craft a mystery. Its complex plot and numerous—and often interconnected—characters were typical of a mystery novel from this era.

*Copyright Hanro Corp. 1951

Chapter 1

At the morgue, homicide Lieutenant Ben Franklin summons private eye Jeff Hardy to verify the identity of Chicago's latest casualty.

"*Hal Benton's body was not a pretty sight. The 'cooler room' of the morgue was air-conditioned, but the stink of the formaldehyde and disinfectant and the sight of Benton's body gave me a queasy feeling.*"

Tortured and shot four times, Benton's ankles were adorned with concrete blocks to keep his body submerged in the river. Three days of saturation have distorted and bloated his features beyond recognition. Hardy can't swear it's Benton or anybody else, but Franklin is certain. The clothes and the contents of the pockets are Benton's. His secretary described the dental work Benton had done a week earlier

Crime On My Hands as by Carl G. Hoges, Alexander Moring Ltd. 1952.

in New York. Everything checks out. Franklin is certain it's Hal Benton's dead body.

The time of death aligns closely with the time of a party on the cabin cruiser Osiris, owned by Jerome Warsaw—and Jeff Hardy was at that party, as a guest of Hal Benton. Hardy explains he and Benton had been marines together in WWII. Years later, they reconnected by chance at Wrigley Field at a ballgame. Benton a changed man—from loner to glad-hander. After the war, Benton started writing scripts for comic books and eventually started publishing his own line. Warsaw was his printer. Both men were getting rich from their partnership.

Benton was the life of the party, surrounded by the type of people drawn to success. While aboard the Osiris, Hardy met a woman named Ella Granger, a stenographer for the Peerless Awning Company, and a good-looker who had caught Benton's eye.

Lieutenant Franklin admits his lack of murder suspects. Benton's relatives, if he had any, remain unknown. Hardy tells the Lieutenant he can't think of anyone who would have wanted Benton dead.

With that, Jeff Hardy returns to his office at Macaulay and Hardy, Investigations. His partner, Bill 'Mac' Macaulay had once been a detective on the Racket Squad, railroaded off the force when "*ward heelers* [operatives of a political boss] *framed a Civil Service hearing on him.*" Macaulay is almost certain crime boss Clem Dorish, who runs The Outfit, was behind his dismissal, and he'll never forget it.

At the office, Macaulay leads Hardy to his private office and introduces him to Miss Betty Conroy. Hardy is immediately shaken by the young woman's poise and beauty, but before he can quip a flirty remark, his attention is grabbed a second time by *The Tribune* laying on Macaulay's desk. Its headline: "*Macaulay and Brennan to testify before the crime committee tomorrow.*" Mel Brennan is well-known to Hardy. He's a former mouth-piece for The Outfit.

Hardy stares, dumbfounded at Macaulay—his mentor is either fearless or foolhardy.

Chapter 2

Betty Conroy excuses herself and before Hardy can question Macaulay about her, the senior partner explains he too is leaving. He needs to pick up a bowling bag at the 'Bowl' down the street. Hardy retires to his office and writes a report on the skip trace job he'd completed in Columbus, just prior to his meeting with Lieutenant Franklin at the morgue.

Report written, Hardy heads out of the building hoping to catch his partner in the Bowl's cocktail lounge. But once out on the street, he sees Macaulay is already heading back, a bowling bag swinging at his side.

Suddenly, Macaulay seems to stumble. The report of gunshots ring out, and Macaulay clutches his stomach, dropping the bag on the sidewalk beside him. Two men run toward him, guns drawn. Hardy whips out his own gat and begins shooting at them. Surprised by the unexpected challenge, the thugs duck between two parked cars as Hardy's fire shatters a window, sending shards of glass over the gunsels. One of them utters a mumbling, stuttering curse.

A little farther down the street, the engine of a double-parked sedan roars to life, pausing just long enough for the hoods to dive into the back before it speeds past Hardy and the scene of the crime. Reeling from the sudden chaos, Hardy neglects to note the car's license plate and the thugs escape while he rushes to the side of his downed partner. Macaulay's last words are "*mainline speedball*," a reference to heroin.

Before long, Lieutenant Franklin arrives to take charge of the murder scene. Hardy is convinced it was a hit job ordered by the Outfit. Both he and Franklin wonder if the murder of Benton and Mac are connected, but at the moment there's no evidence to link them.

Chapter 3

By the time Jeff Hardy finishes up with Franklin and heads home to his apartment, the last thing he expects is a visitor. Yet, there he is, a bronze-skinned muscle man with a large head and feet so small his blue suede shoes are barely visible under the cuffs of his slacks. "*The only thing missing in his get-up was a 'stick' of marijuana that had put that glitter in his eyes.*"

The unexpected visitor's manner is arrogant. He pushes past Hardy as the PI opens his door and demands to use the phone. Before Hardy can react, his unwelcome guest has already connected to his party and tells whoever it is that he's been delayed.

The thug turns to Hardy and declares he's got a message from the "*big man.*" Hardy immediately thinks of The Outfit and tries to verify the message is from Clem Dorish. But the stranger is evasive. "*I come to tell you the big man wants 'eet' back. Quick.*"

Hardy draws a blank and says as much, then tells the punk to leave. The thug smiles, reveals he knows Hardy was Macaulay's partner—a man who talked too much—and if Hardy doesn't hand 'eet' over, he'll die too.

Hardy is distracted as the thug's left hand emerges from his pocket, and doesn't see the punk's right quick enough to evade it. His fist explodes against Hardy's chin. The PI goes down, and he goes out.

When conciousness returns, Hardy's eyes slowly focus on a cylindrical object on the floor. It's a roll of nickels. The thug had wrapped his hand around it to increase the force of his punch. When Hardy went down, the punk must've left it. As the PI gathers his wits, he realizes his apartment has been searched. Then the phone rings. It's Ella Granger, the woman Benton was sweet on, the one Hardy met at the party on the Osiris. She invites him over. He agrees because he'd like to ask her some questions.

On his way over, he stops at his office. Its been ransacked. Somebody looking for "it" he surmises. The only place left intact is the "secret" compartment under the icebox, where Macaulay normally kept his bowling ball, and where Hardy had stowed it after he'd retrieved it from the crime scene. Hardy searches the bag and examines the ball, but finds nothing unusual or helpful.

Hardy calls Lieutenant Franklin to report the break-ins and search of his apartment and office. "*If what they wanted was here* [in the office], *they got* it." Franklin has a hunch the punk at Hardy's apartment is a guy named Elio. He fit Hardy's description, and he's one of the Outfit's boys. Hardy tells him about Granger's invitation and that he's leaving to meet with her. Franklin says, "*Let me know how it turns out.*"

Chapter 4

After meeting Ella Granger on a swanky yacht like the Osiris, her skeevy neighborhood comes as a surprise to Hardy. However, the inside of her apartment recalibrates his impression yet again. She greets him in a skimpy robe and pours him a drink. She's already half in the tank herself and has no intention of letting him drink alone. Initially, he's distracted by her obvious charms, but Hardy swallows some rye courage and gets down to business. He questions her about the stuttering thug who murdered Macaulay.

She reacts to the question as if it were an insult. Then she dims the lights, licks her lips and smiles at Hardy. "*Do we have to talk shop?*" she purrs. A moment later her arms encircle Hardy's neck and she presses her lips against his. Distracted by her embrace, Hardy feels something hard and round pressed into the middle of his back. He hears just enough to realize the ambush comes with a stutter. Then he's struck on the back of the head and rolls off the davenport onto the broadloom carpet, greeted by blackness.

Chapter 5

Hardy wakes with a sore noggin, naked as a jaybird. He assumes his clothes were removed, to be searched top to bottom. As if "it" could be sewn into the lining of his pants. He calls headquarters and reports the fiasco to Franklin, who can hardly control his laughter. The Lieutenant sends over a plainclothesman who finds Hardy's clothing and wallet in the hall outside

the apartment—with the lining cut wide open.

The next day, Hardy visits Central Station hoping to reach Bob Murtaugh, a Narcotics investigator. A young woman there—"*about twenty-two, ordinary brown hair, ordinary clothes*"—was chatting with the grey-haired Irishman at the desk as Hardy walks in.

The Irishman informs Hardy regretfully that Murtaugh is out, whereabouts unknown, but perhaps he can help. He introduces himself as Lt. Haley. The woman stares at Hardy "*like I had just swallowed a goldfish.*" The look on her face doesn't escape Haley's notice, and he rolls his eyes to the side, signaling her to leave; which she does.

After Hardy explains his investigation, Lt. Haley delivers a short treatise on the current state of the dope peddling business in Chi-town—with heroin at the top of the illicit heap. The junkies and pushers are easy to nab, but nothing sticks to the big shots that run things. Clem Dorish and The Outfit are key targets, but so far the Narcotics Bureau's efforts to gather evidence has stalled.

Haley tells Hardy about the woman who left when he arrived. Her name is Rosie O'Grady, a dope peddler and cigarette girl working the De Luxe Cocktail Lounge on West Madison. "*We're letting her get by because she's close to Elio. Maybe by watching her we can finally land Elio.*"

Lt. Haley's parting comment on Murtaugh: "*He was getting close to pay dirt on The Outfit. I'm afraid he's dead.*"

Hardy returns to his office and a jangling phone. It's Betty Conrad. Hardy agrees to meet her at her apartment. It's hot, so he turns on the fan in the office. The breeze flips the pages of the calendar on the wall, so Hardy re-secures the paper clip on the bottom of the folio to prevent its pages from flapping.

When Hardy arrives at Miss Conrad's, she dressed in a silk robe, her eyes red from crying. She'd seen the morning paper. She reveals her real name is Bertha Macaulay. Bill Macaulay was her father!

Chapter 6

Using the stage name Betty Conroy, Bertha Macaulay had worked as a singer at the De Luxe Cocktail Lounge, doubling as a spy for her father. She'd learned the names of the city and state officials in Clem Dorish's pocket. And she shared Dorish's unlisted number with Narcotic's man Bob Murtaugh, enabling him to secure phone taps to gather evidence.

She hadn't seen Murtaugh in a week. Her pop had told Murtaugh he had all the evidence "*in a safe place where it would be easily found if anything happened to them.*" Bertha had a copy of it as well—six sheets of paper. But, last night while she was working at the club, her copy was stolen.

Hardy leaves Bertha at her apartment and heads for his office. He calls Franklin and brings him up to date. They're both concerned for Bob Murtaugh's safety. Franklin has learned the identity of the thugs that shot Macaulay: Dale "baby bandit" Mester and a stuttering goon name of Lou Bergen. The police force is on the lookout for both.

Hardy hangs up and notes the mugginess of the office. He flips on the oscillating fan in the reception room. The rush of hot air riffles the pages of the pin-up calendar on the wall. The paper clip holding the pages together has slipped off again. As he re-secures it, the phone rings.

It's the printer, Jerry Warsaw. He's scared. He'd just received a phone call. Somebody wants to sell him the identity of Bill Macaulay's killers. Besides Hal Benton's comic book line, Warsaw also prints the *Madison Booster*,

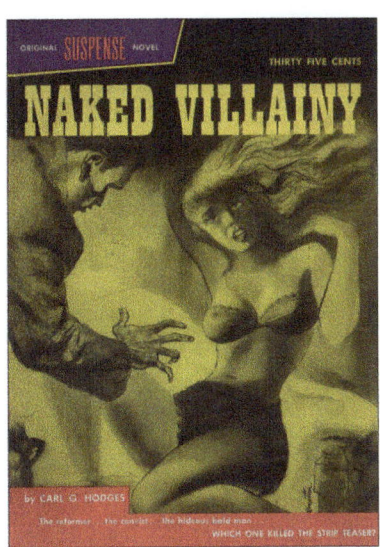

Suspense Novel No. 3 *Naked Villainy* by Carl G. Hodges, Farrell Publishing 1951.

the newsweekly for the West Madison neighborhood. The caller claimed to have the evidence Macaulay planned to present to the Crime Committee. Warsaw explained he only prints the paper; he doesn't edit it. He suggested the caller talk to the police, or perhaps Macaulay's partner, Jeff Hardy. The caller told Warsaw to call Hardy to '... *see if you were interested.*"

"*You did right,*" said Hardy. "*If he can give me proof who killed Mac, he can have every dime I've got.*"

Warsaw is nervous. He'd prefer to let the cops handle things, but Hardy wants to get his hands on the killers before the cops do. Reluctantly, Warsaw agrees to relay Hardy's willingness to pay the bounty, when the man calls back.

Chapter 7

The De Luxe Cocktail Lounge is next door to the Warsaw Printing Company in Skid Row. As Hardy walks down the street toward Warsaw's he spots an old informant he's relied on in the past,

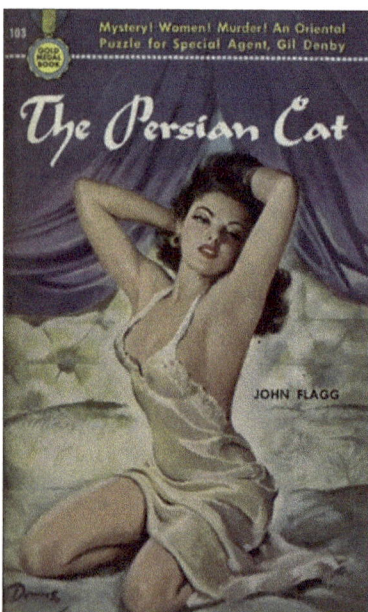

huddled in a darkened doorway. Blind Joe is a con man who sees better than he lets on. Joe verifies the name of the stuttering thug Hardy's looking for is Lou Bergen, one of Clem Dorish's boys. What's more, the dish Bergen's playing around with is Ella Granger.

Jerry Warsaw's office is up on the second floor, above the printing plant. Behind the office are his living quarters, so the man is nearly always on the premises. By the time Hardy arrives, Warsaw's mysterious caller has phoned a second time. Warsaw is to be picked up at one of a half-dozen places he's been given. Only the caller knows which one. "*At nine-thirty he'll bring me to meet you* [Hardy] *at Union Station ramp. Then I'm to take you to him.*"

It sounds screwy, but Hardy agrees to meet Warsaw at 9:30 that night. Then Hardy returns to his office. He calls Bertha and arranges to meet her at Barney's, the diner next to his office.

Bertha is already seated by the time Hardy walks in. A slender man is hassling her. The guy claims the Big Boy wants a word, and she's coming along with him. Hardy doesn't waste time asking questions, he joins right in with his fists. After Hardy decks the man, a cop rushes in and creates an unfortunate diversion by colliding with a chair and sprawling on the floor. The slender man jumps up and dashes out the back door. Who was he? Bertha knows him from working at the Lounge, it's Dale Mester, the 'baby bandit' who works for Dorish. Hardy tells the cop to call Franklin. "*Tell him Dale Mester's on the loose. He's wanted for the murder of Bill Macaulay.*"

Chapter 8

When the dust settles at Barney's, and the couple finishes a quick bite to eat, Hardy takes Bertha to the morgue where he's arranged a farewell viewing of the young woman's father. After an emotional farewell, she waits in the car while Hardy keeps his rendezvous with Jerry Warsaw at the Union Street ramp.

Warsaw is late. He's carrying a faded copy of the *Madison Booster* under his arm. Hardy glances at it and asks why the printing is so light. Warsaw tells him, "*That's the first run on tomorrow's issue. They always come off the press like that. The first hundred or so till we get a good ink distribution.*"

Warsaw also comments on his wariness about the man they're to meet. He leads Hardy back the way he came, dropping the newsweekly in an ash can as they pass by it. They also pass by Hardy's car. Bertha looks frightened, as if she wants Hardy to stop. He gives her a reassuring glance and continues on with Warsaw. The two men turn onto another street. Half a dozen parked cars line the curb. A black Chevvy among them, with its motor running.

When Warsaw reaches the coupé,

he opens the door and screams. The driver is dead from gunshot. Hardy takes over, searching the body and the car, being careful not to alter the crime scene. He finds no trace of Macaulay's evidence. Whoever shot the man must have taken it. He sends Warsaw for the cops—Lieutenant Franklin, if available.

When Franklin arrives, he identifies the victim as Mel Brennan, the man who was to testify before the Crime Committee, alongside Bill Macaulay. Now, both murdered. Franklin orders Hardy and Warsaw to come down to the station to make their statements. The two men walk over to Hardy's car. Once they're inside, Bertha tells Hardy she saw Dale Mester run past while she waited.

Chapter 9

Hardy and Warsaw give their statements to Lieutenant Franklin at HQ. Hardy adds Bertha's sighting of Dale Mester moments before they discovered Mel Brennan's body, making the thug suspect number one. Franklin believes Brennan stole the copy of Macaulay's evidence from Bertha's apartment and tried to turn it into some quick cash. Now Mester has it.

Hardy and Bertha drop off Warsaw at his plant, on their way to the De Luxe. Again, Bertha cools her heels in Hardy's sedan, while the PI ventures into the club. A poster of lounge singer Betty Conroy (Bertha Macaulay) hung in the entrance's recess.

Inside, a nearly naked cigarette girl stops Hardy. She calls out his name loud enough to catch the attention of the broad-shouldered, pug-nosed man seated at the bar. The man gets up and pushes through the door that leads to Clem Dorish's office.

It takes Hardy a minute, but then he recognizes the frail, it's Rosie O'Grady, the woman he'd seen at the Narcotics Bureau. He reaches for a pack of ciga-

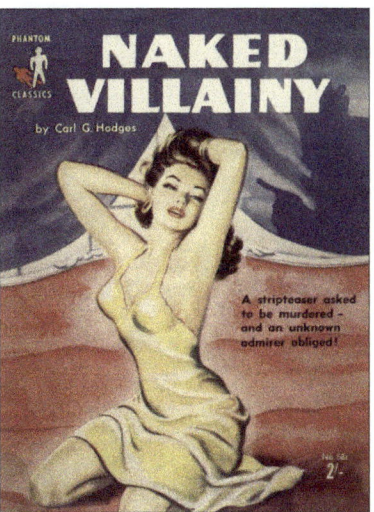

Naked Villainy by Carl G. Hodges, Phantom Books No. 581. Cover after *The Persian Cat* painting by Willard Downes. [Note: This cover was in bad shape and heavily retouched. The shadow on the curtain may not be a100% accurate recreation.]

rettes, but she covers his hand, and is told, "*Not that one.*" It's loaded with a "*cap of heroin.*" Then, she hands him an untampered pack.

Hardy gives her a look and follows the route of the pug-nosed man. Once through the door, he spots the pug-nose doing hall duty at the base of a flight of stairs. Hardy brushes past unmolested and climbs the stairs. Up top, there's only one door, so it must be Dorish's office. Inside are a man, a woman, and a dog.

The man is Elio, the woman, Ella Granger. Hardy asks for Clem Dorish and is told he's not in.

"*I can see that,*" says Hardy. "*If he were he'd get awfully mad at his honey pie being pawed by one of his hired hands.*"

Elio circles the large walnut desk. A black Doberman is chained to it. Hardy grins. He knows now it was Elio driving the getaway car for Mester and Ber-

Thrilling Detective April 1947 with Hodges' "Murder Breeds Murder" the second Dwight and Gail Berke adventure.

gen when they shot Bill Macaulay. Elio, eyes glittering, starts the fracas with a poorly timed kick. Hardy side-steps and grabs Elio's leg. The leg twists, Elio squeals, but squirms free. The thug returns to the fray and is rewarded with Hardy's fist crashing into his chin. Blood squirts from his mouth. His eyes glaze, yet he rushes forward again.

Hardy rams his knee into his assailant's groin. The thug squeals and drops his hand, trying to hold in the pain. Hardy digs into his pocket and wraps his fingers around the roll of nickels.

The Doberman is raising hell, but there's nothing it can do while chained, except bark and foam at the mouth.

Hardy nails Elio with his nickel-hardened fist, with every one of his one-hundred-and-ninety pounds behind it. Granger stoops to untie the dog's chain, but Hardy slaps her so hard she plops down on the floor, whimpering.

Suddenly, Rosie, the cigarette girl, bursts into the room to fawn over the downed and out Elio. Hardy takes his leave unmolested. As he passes the pug-nose on his way out, he asks about the dog. It's kept at a kennel in Oak Park, and brought over to the De Luxe every night at 9:00 pm.

Hardy returns to his car and takes Bertha back to his place—her place is too dangerous now. She's staying with him whether or not she likes it. "*She didn't say anything. But she was thinking plenty.*"

Chapter 10

Hardy and Bertha carry on a flirtation throughout the novel. They continue the pattern upon rising from bed (Bertha) and sofa (Hardy), interrupted yet again by circumstance. This time it's a phone call from Franklin to review the case—mostly for the benefit of readers—since the Lieutenant's only news is he's sending Macaulay's possessions over to the former investigator's office.

Hardy goes there to meet the officer/currier. The delivery is meant for Bertha, but Franklin couldn't locate her and knew Hardy could. Hardy takes Macaulay's keys to the bowling alley and checks out his locker there. Unfortunately, he finds no evidence, only a bowling ball and a pair of bowling shoes.

That evening, Hardy and Bertha monitor the De Luxe from Hardy's parked car. When the Doberman arrives at 9:00 pm, they follow the deliveryman back to the kennel. When they arrive, they sneak up on the place and peek in a window. Unfortunately, they are discovered, and taken at gunpoint inside where they meet the Big Boy, Clem Dorish.

Chapter 11

Hardy confronts Dorish, demanding the crime boss turn over Mester and Bergen for the murder of Bill Macaulay. Dorish remains calm, claiming innocence. "*If I were you I'd curb my* curiosity," he says. "*I would surmise it would be much healthier. You might suffer if you persist.*"

Hardy tries to provoke Dorish, reminding him Ella Granger is in bed with Bergen, and apparently with Elio as well. But to Hardy's surprise, the crime boss doesn't seem to care. This makes the PI wonder who's footing the bill for Granger's swanky apartment.

After an exchange of barbs and threats, Dorish allows Hardy and Bertha to leave in peace. They hoof it back to Hardy's car. Only she'll be driving back alone. Hardy slips out to sneak a ride with Dorish's flunky, hoping he'll be taken directly to Mester and Bergen's hideout. In the meantime, Bertha will call Franklin with the license plate of the thug's car, a lead the police will track down in a heartbeat. [Really?]

While the flunky's still inside with Dorish, Hardy slips into the back seat of the delivery car and hides under a conveniently placed tarp. In a few minutes, they're underway. Hardy attempts to track their route as best he can while remaining hidden. Once they park, Hardy creeps out and follows the driver into a dilapidated brownstone where he discovers the body of Dale Mester. The driver must've seen it too, as he beats it down the fire escape, only to be picked up by the cops, who've miraculously located the car from Bertha's tipoff.

Hardy searches the room before the cops join him and discovers the ashes from five or six sheets of paper, burned in a waste can. He's certain it's the copy of Macaulay's evidence stolen from Bertha.

Chapter 12

Franklin joins Hardy, and they review the crime scene. The Lieutenant thinks Mester killed himself. Hardy believes he was murdered. Mester must've stolen the evidence from Mel Brennan, after killing him. Then he tried to ex-

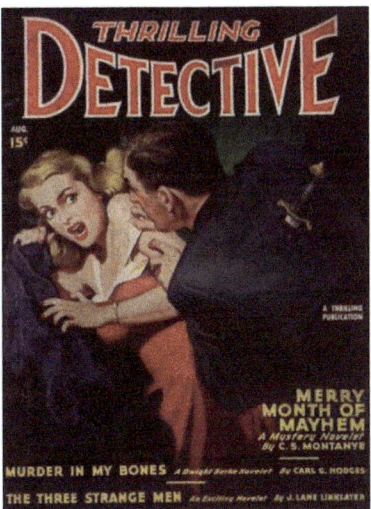

Thrilling Detective August 1947 with Hodges' "Murder in My Bones" the third Dwight and Gail Berke adventure. Cover by Rudolph Belarski.

tort someone, and that someone had him shot, and burnt the evidence. The scene yields two guns. Hardy bets ballistics will prove one killed Bill Macaulay, the other, Mel Brennan. Sure enough, hours later at headquarters, his supposition is confirmed.

Before Hardy leaves the station for the night, he calls his own apartment to check on Bertha. When she doesn't answer, he rushes home to find she's gone. He fears someone has kidnapped her. Before he figures his next move, the phone rings. It's Jerry Warsaw, the printer. Miss Macaulay is with him—and she's hurt.

Hardy takes a cab over to Warsaw's print shop and rushes inside. Lou Bergen is waiting for him. Bergen relieves Hardy of his firearm and ushers him upstairs.

Chapter 13

Inside Warsaw's office, Clem Dorish sits behind the massive desk, surrounded by Jerry Warsaw, Elio, Rosie

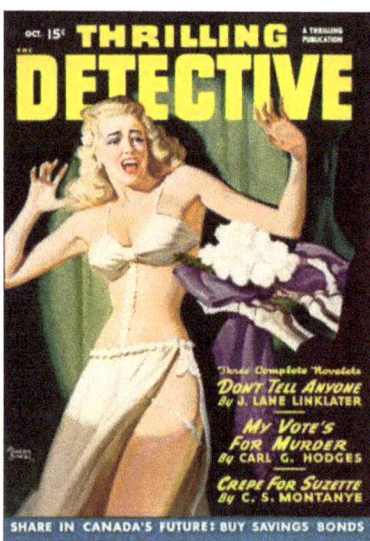

Thrilling Detective December 1948 with Hodges' "My Vote's for Murder" the sixth Dwight and Gail Berke adventure. Cover by Rudolph Belarski.

O'Grady, the broad-shouldered man from the De Luxe who told Hardy about the kennel, and Ella Granger. Lou Bergen joins the party. After a bit of posturing and gnashing of teeth from the congregation, Dorish proposes a trade: Miss Macaulay for the original copy of the evidence Hardy's partner gathered.

Unfortunately, Hardy admits he doesn't have it—and he's looked everywhere, including Macaulay's bowling locker. At that, Dorish offers to trade Bertha for the bowling ball—the one Macaulay was carrying when he met with his unfortunate accident.

Hardy agrees, but wants proof Miss Macaulay is unharmed. Dorish orders Bergen to fetch the girl. She's been held in Warsaw's living quarters behind the office. Bergen brings her out. She rushes over to Hardy, a combination of love and relief in her eyes.

Dorish clarifies the deal he's offering, "*Both of you will be held for—say, one*

week—in protective custody. Then you will be released."

Hardy agrees—he's in no position to bargain. Dorish has Bergen take Bertha back to Warsaw's quarters. When the thug returns, Hardy is to lead him and Elio to the bowling ball, so off they go.

At Hardy's office, the PI ponders various ploys for a chance to escape, but no dice. He sees Elio eyeballing the calendar girl and quips, "*Go ahead and paw her awhile. Make like it's Ella Granger.*"

Elio can barely restrain himself after Hardy's insulting remark, but Bergen intervenes. Hardy takes the momentary diversion to stick his finger in the rotary dial of the telephone, twisting the "O" all the way home and shoves the whole shebang off the top of the desk.

The noise recaptures the thugs' attention on Hardy. Bergen motions with his gun, "*The bowling ball, Bub.*" Hardy opens the drain board under the icebox and hands over the bowling bag from beside the drip pan. "*Well, I'll be damned!*" says Bergen. "*The boys went over this place and never looked in the most obvious spot.*"

At the word "obvious" something clicks with Hardy. Suddenly he's figured out the secret of the bowling ball and the location of Macaulay's evidence. On the way out, Hardy flips the switch on the oscillating fan.

Chapter 14

Returning to Warsaw's office. Bergen hands the bowling ball to Dorish, who tries to work its mechanism by pressing down on the two finger holes. Nothing happens, so Hardy suggests, "*Why don't you let Warsaw try it? He knows more about hiding heroin in trick bowling balls than anybody else.*

"*You've had everybody in Chicago thinking you were a self-made man,*" he continues. "*Printing comic books by the millions. It was only a front. Your real job is running The Outfit. Dorish is nothing but a jerk who fronted for you while you pulled the strings. You're the master mind! You're the one responsible for Macaulay's murder. You killed Mel Brennan. You killed Dale Mester!*

"*A half million dollars worth of heroin—retail value—was brought into Chicago. Concealed in a trick bowling ball. Brought in by an international smuggler. To turn over to you. For maybe a hundred grand in cash. You didn't have a hundred grand in cash so he had to stash it someplace until you racked up that much cash. He picked a bowling locker at the 'Bowl' as the best place to cache the stuff. Thursday you let him know you had the money raised. So he turned over to you the key to the 'Bowl' and got the bowling bag full of heroin. But, in the meantime, Bill Macaulay had tumbled to the scheme and he went to the 'Bowl' and got the stuff. You had sent Dale Mester and Lou Bergen with the key. They found the stuff gone—and they also saw Bill Macaulay walking out of the joint with a bowling bag. They followed him up the street and killed him. They didn't get the bowling bag because my gun and I happened to show up and they came back to you empty-handed. The international smuggler had your hundred grand so you cooped him up until such a time that you got the heroin or you'd take your money back.*"

Mel Brennan found the carbon copy of the evidence Macaulay gave to Bertha. Brennan was stupid enough to try to sell it to Warsaw. Warsaw and Brennan drove to Union Station in Brennan's coupe. Parked on Adams Street. Warsaw shot Brennan, grabbed the carbon copy, and met Hardy around the corner on Canal Street. Inside the rolled-up copy of the *Madison Booster* print proof was the evidence and the gun. They were dropped in the trash, where Mester picked them up.

Bertha had seen Mester from Hardy's car. She assumed he killed Brennan, but he was only there to pick up the items from the trash.

Once he saw the evidence, Dale Mester decided he'd work a shakedown on Warsaw, but it didn't work. Warsaw shot him too and burned the carbon copy in the wastecan in Mester's hideout. After Dorish detained Hardy at the kennel, the same punk that led him to the kennel, led him to the body.

It's all supposition, so Warsaw isn't worried. There's nothing to say that Macaulay's evidence points to him—only Dorish. Warsaw tries to work the bowling ball, but he can't do it either. They accuse Hardy of pulling a switch, but Bergen denies it. He'd grabbed the ball as soon as Hardy uncovered it. There was no way the PI could've pulled a switch.

Hardy challenges Warsaw to bring out the international smuggler, the guy hiding out in Warsaw's quarters. Why not make him deliver the dope? Why not bring out the dead man—Hal Benton.

Chapter 15

Benton is Warsaw's biggest customer and Hardy's old friend from the war—obviously not the dead man discovered in the river, back in the opening chapter of this yarn. When he appears, he acknowledges his regret that things have come to this. He liked Hardy, but they're clearly now on opposite sides of the law. He explains the mechanism of the trick bowling ball, and then fails to trigger it. [Wrong ball fellas.]

Bertha slips into the office and stands behind Hardy as he declairs he's figured out that Benton was financing Ella Granger's apartment and bills. But the news for Benton is that while he's been in hiding, she's been fooling around with both Bergen and Elio.

"*The reaction was more than I hoped*

for," Hardy explains to readers. *"The metamorphosis of Benton from man to monster took place before I could finish my words."*

Benton slaps Granger across the face and strips her dress from her body, leaving her to cover herself with her hands. Then he orders Bergen to toss her out on the street like a prostitute. Bergen refuses and reaches for his gun. Hardy advises him to wait, the cops will take care of Benton soon.

Hardy figures the bloated corpse pulled from the river is Bob Murtaugh, the missing Narcotics Bureau investigator. Apparently, Murtaugh had caught Benton red-handed with the heroin and the trick bowling ball. Benton killed him and made the body appear to be Benton himself. His secretary had helped corroborate the dental work to confirm his identity.

Suddenly, Rosie O'Grady flashes a .22 caliber automatic and fires. Benton is hit in the shoulder. While attention is riveted on O'Grady, Hardy grabs the heavy metal fountain pen base from the desk and slams it down on Bergen's skull. Dorish reaches for a gun behind the desk, but before he can bring it out, Bertha beans him with a metal ashtray.

Despite his shoulder wound, Benton swings his gun toward Hardy. Hardy slams into Berger sending the hoodlum forward to catch Benton's bullet in the gut. Hardy holds the thug upright as Benton's slugs pepper his body, shielding Hardy. When he lets the body drop, Benton levels the gun at Hardy.

Suddenly, the broad-shouldered man catapults across the room and tackles Benton. The gun falls. Warsaw dives for it, but his wrist is ground into the floor by Hardy's heel. Warsaw squeals in pain while Hardy recovers the weapon. At last the crooks have lost the upper hand. Elio drops the knife he was holding in surrender.

The broad-shouldered man intro-duces himself as Shelby, Federal Narcotics. He'd been working to get inside the gang, but made little progress until Hardy showed up. What about Rosie? She was Bob Murtaugh's fiancé. They were to be married on Labor Day.

The distraction of the discussion gives Warsaw an opening. He hurls a chair at Hardy, forcing the gun from his hand. Warsaw attacks and puts Hardy on the floor. But the PI wants revenge for Mac, and after a terrific fight, he triumphs.

As the battle ends, Franklin and the cops arrive, bolting up the stairs to take over. They'd found the long sought evidence written on the back of the calendar pages in Hardy's office. The fan he'd let run splayed the pages open and put the evidence in plain sight. It's enough to take down The Outfit, a State representative, and a couple of police officials with safe deposit bundles too large for their salaries.

The crooks are corralled, and the good guys head to the "Bowl" where Hardy is pretty sure Mac stashed the trick bowling ball in his locker.

Chapter 16

The "Bowl" isn't open, so Hardy, the cops, and the Feds wait for the owner to show up and let them in. Once inside, Hardy locates Macaulay's locker, retrieves the fateful ball and works its mechanism. Sure enough, hidden inside the ball is the missing heroin. Lieutenant Haley from the Federal Bureau of Narcotics collects the evidence.

Bertha and Hardy head for the station, and Hardy makes his statement. That night of the party on the Osiris, Benton and Warsaw made a deal on the heroin, but Warsaw didn't have the money yet, so Benton loaded it in the trick bowling ball intent on stashing it in a locker at the "Bowl." But Bob Murtaugh trailed him and caught him red-handed. Then Benton killed Murtaugh, switching clothes and belongings to Murtaugh's body, and dumped his corpse in the river.

When Warsaw paid Benton, Benton simply gave him the key to the locker at the bowl. Warsaw sent Mester and Bergen to pick it up, with Elio driving the car. Somehow Bill Macaulay tumbled to their secret and used the house key to put the bowling ball in his own locker before the crooks arrived.

When the crooks found an empty locker and subsequently saw Macaulay walking back to his office with a bowling bag, they assumed it was Warsaw's and bumped him off. But before they could grab the bag, Hardy showed up and chased them off.

Warsaw held Benton at his apartment until he got his hands on the dope. When the newspaper reported that Macaulay would testify before the crime committee, Warsaw knew he now needed the dope and Macaulay's evidence.

When Mel Brennan entered the scene, he figured Macaulay had given the evidence to his daughter, having seen through her act as Betty Conroy at the De Luxe. He found the duplicate in her apartment and tried to sell it to Warsaw. But Warsaw killed Brennan and dumped the duplicate in the trash, which was later picked up by Mester. Mester got the same idea and then the same treatment that Brennan got. Only this time Warsaw burned the duplicate in Mester's wastecan.

The case wraps with a romantic future ahead for Jeff Hardy and Bertha Macaulay.

Summary

Crime On My Hands is a solid mystery novel. Despite its flaws and somewhat over-complicated plot, it captures its era and its early 1950s Chicago setting beautifully. Hodges' final mystery novel was *Murder By the Pack*, pub-

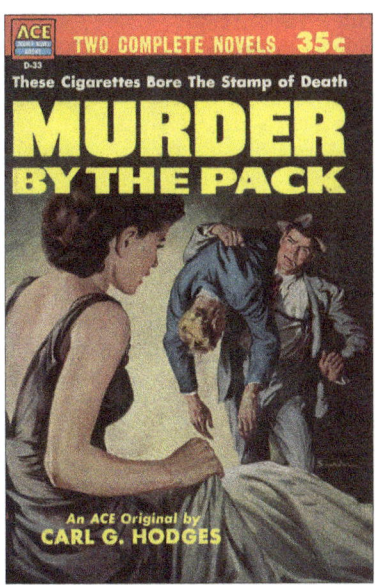

Murder By the Pack by Carl G. Hodges, Ace Double D-33. Cover by Norman Saunders.

lished as half of an Ace Double (D-33) along with *About Face* by Frank Kane in 1954.

It's unclear why Hodges drifted away from crime fiction. He served as president of the Springfield Civil War Round Table, a group he helped organize. By the 1960s he'd turned his attention to a younger audience and wrote seven historical novels as well as novelettes for Hearst Features, and articles for home and travel journals. Carl Garrett Hodges passed away on November 1964 at the age of 62 in Illinois. He was survived by his wife Ruth Matilda Hodges (nee Zuckschwert) (1907–1999).

References

AbeBooks.com
Galactic Central website
The Paperback Price Guide No. 2
   by Kevin Hancer Harmony Books, 1982
MyHeritage.com
The Thrilling Detective website

Carl G. Hodges Bibliography
"The Quarrel" *Mystery Magazine* June 15, 1923
"The Square Deceivers" *Mystery Magazine* Sep. 1, 1923
"Wang Foo's Right Eye" *Mystery Magazine* May 1, 1924
"The Last Trick" *Mystery Magazine* Oct. 1, 1924
"The Clue in the Watch" *Mystery Magazine* Nov. 15, 1924
"The Phoney Sawbucks" *Mystery Magazine* Jan. 15, 1925
"Haymaker Shuffle" *Fifteen Western Tales* Oct. 1942
"Dynamite with Cleats" *Football Action* No. 1 Fall 1944
"K Is for Killer" *G-Men Detective* Jan. 1947
"Homecoming" *Thrilling Detective* Oct. 1947
"Homicide's Their Headache" *Thrilling Detective* August 1948 (PI Bill Starch)
"The Man with Four Hands" *The Evening Citizen* May 14, 1949 (as by Carl G. Rodgers)
"Case of the Substitute Victim" aka "Substitute Victim" *The Evening Citizen* Aug. 27, 1949
The Case of a Handful of Murder" aka "Handful of Murder" *The Evening Citizen* Aug. 26, 1950
"Dead Man's Proof" *F.P. Detective Stories* Jan. 1951
"Come to Me, Killer" *Famous Detective Stories* May 1951
"The Corpse in the Santa Claus Suit" *Crime Story Magazine* Nov. 1952
"Terror in the Night" *Manhunt* Jul. 1956

Dwight and Gail Berke series
"Sixteen Pounds of Murder" *Thrilling Detective* Oct. 1946
"Murder Breeds Murder" *Thrilling Detective* April 1947
"Murder in My Bones" *Thrilling Detective* Aug. 1947
"Murder Throws a Ringer" *Thrilling Detective* Dec. 1947
"Highway Homicide" *Thrilling Detective* April 1948
"My Vote's for Murder" *Thrilling Detective* Oct. 1948

Novels
Naked Villainy *Suspense Novel* No. 3 1951
Crime On My Hands Phantom Books No. 506 1952 (as by Carl G. Hoges)
Murder By the Pack Ace D-33 1954
Baxie Randall and the Blue Raiders Bobbs, 1962
Dobie Sturgis and the Dog Soldiers Bobbs, 1963
Benjie Ream Bobbs, 1964
Land Rush Duell, 1965

Several of Hodges' short stories are reprinted in collections available on <amazon.com>.

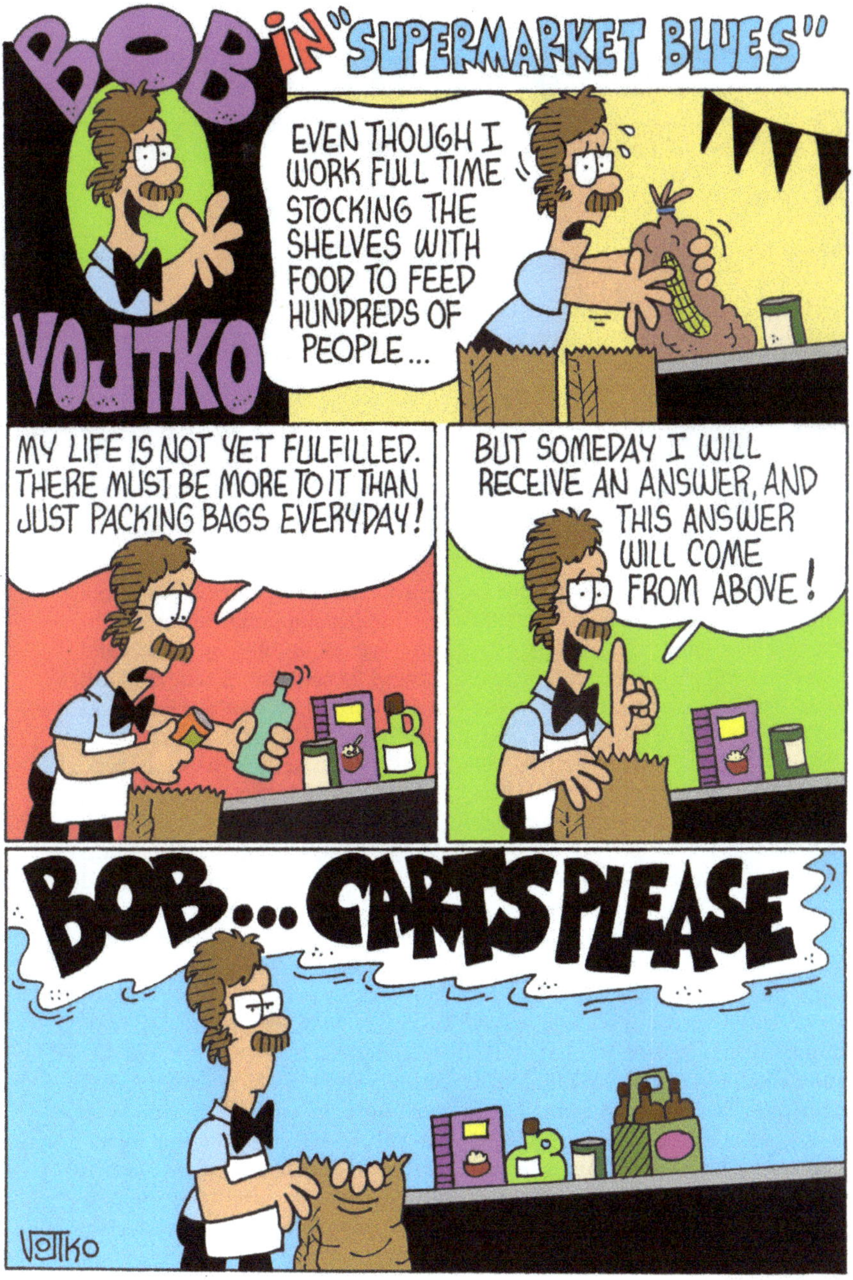

The Strange, Short Life of the Boys' and Girls' Fiction Series

Article by Steve Carper

"He [Russell Thorndike] was an actor who gained fame by writing the Dr. Syn series of adventures, described as a Batman of the 1700s, a parish priest who dressed in a scarecrow costume to pursue evildoers."

Flip through any of the numerous paperback price guides and you'll stumble over an anomaly. One and only one digest children's book line is mentioned: Comet Books, from 1948. Yet that very same year a series of digest-sized children's books, Boys' and Girls' Fiction, appeared from the Samuel Lowe Co., out of tiny Kenosha, WI.

Chicago got all the attention, but locals knew it was only the centerpiece in a 150-mile long metroplex that stretched from Gary, IN, in the south to Milwaukee, WI, then the 13th largest city in the U.S., in the north, all hugging the western shore of Lake Michigan. A series of small but bustling prosperous cities filled in the gaps. Going north, one could travel through Evanston and Waukegan, IL, and Kenosha and Racine, WI. Railroad lines connected the downtowns of all the cities like a string of pearls. In 1940, near the height of American manufacturing, tens of thousands of companies, large and small, took advantage of the area's resources and its position midway across the country, giving it the best distribution and a pool of millions of skilled and educated workers. Printer's Row in Chicago contained

such giants as R. R. Donnelley, W. F. Hall, and Rand McNally, but rising prices started pushing the trade out to the suburbs. An early example, Western Printing and Lithographing Company, started in 1907 in Racine and changed its name to the modern form in 1910. It too became a giant, printing all the Dell paperbacks and comic books (including the Disney comics, the best-selling in the world), playing cards, jigsaw puzzles, and children's stuff in various forms though its own Whitman Publishing, which produced older children's books, toys, games, and other ephemera, including the massively popular Big Little Books.

Samuel E. Lowe was born on February 12, 1884, in Posen, Germany. He emigrated to New York and became involved in what was then called boys' work, in associations similar to the YMCA. He started in one in Racine in 1915, but got hired by Western Printing the next year. Over the next twenty years he rose to the presidency of Whitman and made a reputation as one of the grand old men of the children's book business. In 1937, he married Edith Kovar, eleven years his junior, but already a well-known chil-

dren's book writer and editor under the name of Mary Windsor. They would have five boys themselves.

Maybe his new family made him look to the future, or maybe he had a quarrel with the Western executives. All he ever said publicly was that he had ideas that Western wasn't interested in, so he quit them in 1940 and started the Samuel Lowe Company in one rented room of an old hosiery mill in nearby Kenosha. Success was immediate and the firm grew to occupy three stories. A mere four years after its founding, Lowe acquired his own building spanning the length of a block and sited next to the railroad tracks that bordered downtown Kenosha, obviating the need for a separate warehouse. That the United States could support luxuries like children's and paper doll books while undergoing rationing of goods—including paper—for total war makes an implicit statement about America's wealth and isolation from the battlefronts.

Postwar prosperity worked to inflate the business even farther. By 1947 Lowe employed more than 200 workers, 70% of them women, at the plant, with plans to hire more. (A 2008 local history piece said that in 1946, Lowe had 300

workers, put out more than 200 titles, and printed 50,000,000 books. I believe these numbers are greatly inflated and that the contemporary 1947 newspaper article is a better source.) That same year he merged several local businesses into Lowe Inc., comprised of Lowe Inc., Samuel Lowe Company, John Martin's House Inc., Angelus Publishing Co., and Abbott Publishing Company. All the companies did similar children's books (Edith would have books published by several) and had been incorporated separately by Lowe in 1944. The James & Jonathan Company of Kenosha seems to have printed them all, and is confusingly sometimes listed as the publisher, even in top sources like WorldCat. At some point Lowe set up a subsidiary in Toronto, the Samuel Lowe Company of Canada, Ltd., whose books were copyrighted by none other than by James & Jonathan. I can't find any other information about James & Jonathan and the books supposedly published by them that I've checked are actually by one of Lowe's companies.

Lowe tried putting out everything and anything that could be sold to parents of very young children. According to a seller asking $500 for the lot, catalogues from his companies list

"painting and coloring books, games, toy books, general books, toy books and games, fall and Christmas books, Bonnie books, Sturdi-Bilt books, Doll books, Linen-Like books, Lolly Pop Easter stories, doll books, wheel toy books and more." A 1962 catalogue is "a folio with product linen sheets including such items as sticker fun pack, clean slates, animated cartoon profiles, cloth books, paper doll books and much more."

Lowe kept finding himself in battle with the majors, usually because they beat him to market with hot sellers. The 1942 launch of Little Golden Books from a partnership of Simon & Schuster and Western Printing was an instant smash. The first set of titles sold out all 1,500,000 copies in five months. Lowe had only released a few collections of nursery rhymes by then, so he had to broaden into a wider array of titles and accessories.

He apparently had done so by 1948, but was outshadowed when another giant, Pocket Books, pulled off a coup of its own, with the Comet Books line. Why it's the only children's digest and almost the only children's paperback series of any kind listed is odd. Hav-

ing none at all included would be more understandable; despite the obvious overlaps, children's and adult publishing have been treated as separate fields since their beginnings. (The *New York Times* didn't start a Children's Best Seller list until July 2000 and only did so because they were embarrassed that Harry Potter had the top fiction spot locked down.) My guess is that the digest-sized Comet Books gets included because it was a division of Pocket Books and eventually morphed into the mass-market-sized Pocket Books Jr. line. Other similar children's lines are still omitted, nevertheless.

Paperback histories equally slight children's lines. Only one of the half dozen or so I own bothers to reference them in its index: Kenneth C. Davis' mammoth *Two-Bit Culture*. And all he says is that there was little interest in cheap paperback children's books because inexpensive hardback reprinters had the field sewn up, presumably because hardbacks stood up to the abuse children wielded on their toys better than paperbacks, which fell apart even in the hands of adults.

Pocket Books had already seen a path around the dilemma, that of

marketing paperbacks to teenagers. It partnered with Scholastic, whose history dates back to a magazine for high schoolers started in 1920. Together they launched the Teen Age Book Club, known as TAB Books, offering generations of teens the opportunity of buying books in class and getting one free for frequent purchases. They too were an immediate success, announced in newspapers all over the country in September 1946 and signing up 50,000 teens in the first 30 days. Pocket Books at first had a strange idea of the teenage market, considering that the first five books included *Shakespeare's Tragedies*. More sensibly, Pocket tested the waters for the Comet series by releasing three titles in 1947, all mass-market-sized like the other Club selections, but with Comet Books insignia and numbered 4, 9, and 10 as they would be later on. All systems pointed to go. In 1948, the first of 34 digest-sized Comet titles were released in huge editions of 150,000. (Weirdly, Scholastic's histories insist that the Club was also started in 1948, which contradicts hard evidence from newspaper reports. I can not explain this.) Overall the Comet titles were aimed at a younger, 10–16, crowd

than TAB's core market. They sold in stores for the standard 25¢.

Surely the plans for Comet were known to industry insiders. That's why I assume Lowe made his first foray into what are now called chapter books aimed at older readers and released eight volumes in the Boys' and Girls' Fiction (BGF) series, copyright 1948 by the James & Jonathan Company of Kenosha. None are numbered and no hint as to order of publication is available. Alphabetically by title they are:

Captain Kidd's Gold
    illustrated by Jack Crowe
The Cordova Treasure
    illustrated by J. Voelz
The Flag of Distress
    illustrated by Jack Crowe
The Mysterious Trunks
    illustrated by Jack Crowe
Stories from Dickens
    retold by Russell Thorndike
Stories from Scott
    retold by Russell Thorndike
Tracked Through the Wilds
    illustrated by N. Pollard
The Vanishing Redhead
    illustrated by Jack Crowe

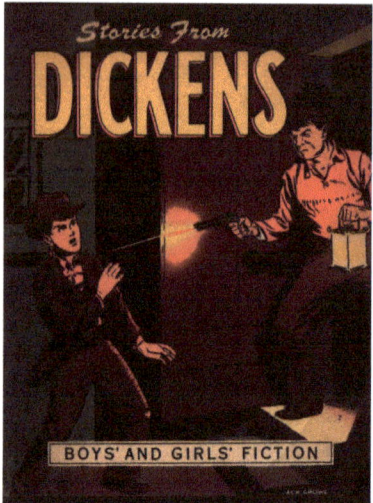

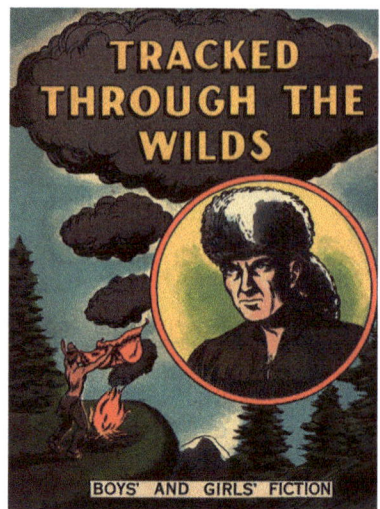

Four of the covers are signed by Crowe (*Dickens, Redhead, Kidd,* and *Trunks*). *Scott* is signed with an N. P. I see nothing resembling a signature on *Cordova, Flag* and *Tracked*. One of the many oddities about the series is that no author is given except for the rewriter of the two books by famous writers and those two books are the only ones not to credit an illustrator, although they have interior b&w illustrations just like the others. (If *Scott's* cover is by Pollard, then presumably the interiors are as well, though that's conjecture.)

All of them are just a hair smaller than standard digest size, but slightly bigger than Comet Books, at 5¼ x 7⅛", with the standard digest length of 128 pages. (Comet Books ran up to 274 text pages.) They have full-color covers with lamination and up to a dozen scattered full-page b&w illustrations inside. The back covers are bright blue except for a head shot in a circle. I'm guessing they were aimed at the 8–12 age group, with the Dickens and Scott stories more for middle schoolers (they have smaller type, less leading, and about twice as many words). The prevailing wisdom of the day was that girls

would read books written for boys, but not vice versa. Women were pictured on the covers of *Redhead* and *Cordova* but they both have boys as protagonists and rear head shots of males, and the other tales about pirates and the frontier were clearly boys' fiction in the 1940s.

Another clue that the BGF series was aimed at boys is given by the illustrators, all young local artists from an area rich in the field. Publishers of boys' fiction in those days were terrified that their product might seem to be contaminated by girl cooties. A name beginning with an initial almost always hid a woman, and J. Voelz and N. Pollard both did so.

J. Voelz drew piles of art for other Lowe Inc. companies as Jeanne Voelz. Born Mary Jeanne Nolan in 1921, and always known in private as Mary, she moved to Kenosha from nearby Waukegan when very young. Wanting to be a dress designer, she attended the New York School of Fine and Applied Art (now known as the Parsons School of Design), hated sewing, switched to illustration, and then returned home for a life as a commercial artist. She wed Vernon Voelz, a sculptor, in 1942

and they had three daughters. Her hundreds of works included coloring books, play and activity books, story books—"a lot of Santa Clauses," and scads of paper doll books, from Shirley Temple to Tricia Nixon to Diahann Carroll, so many that she is known as a giant in the field. She left Lowe in 1952 for Saalfield, a power in paper dolls. Mary died in 2009.

Nancy E. "Nan" Diestelhorst was born in 1925 and studied at the Layton School of Art in Milwaukee. She received her first children's books commissions while still in college. In 1947 she married artist George Pollard and took a staff job at Samuel Lowe. For Lowe she, like Voelz, dabbled in all the company's manifold children's ephemera. She later gained far more fame inside the field as a ghost artist for seemingly every famous character, including Donald Duck, Curious George, and the Berenstain Bears, her art appearing in about 2000 books. Husband George had the more public reputation as a portrait painter of the stars. Harry S. Truman and Muhammad Ali sat for him. Little wonder that their four children all became artists or art teachers. George and Nan did work together on some Lowe projects, including the *Janet Leigh Doll Portfolio*, a paper doll book for which Nan did the dresses and George the portrait of Leigh on the cover. That art was later displayed at the Lakeside Players Pollard Gallery in downtown Kenosha. The Wisconsin Historical Society honored the Pollards on May 23, 2006 when they were awarded the Georgia O'Keefe Award for Distinction in the Visual Arts as part of the Society's new History Makers program. Nan died in Kenosha in 2012.

The fully-named male, Jack F. Crowe, born in 1920, was a lifelong resident of Racine, WI. The many businesses in the Chicago/Milwaukee corridor required a multitude of service businesses to fill every need and Crowe worked with dozens of them as a commercial artist and advertising executive, becoming Kenosha's Ad Man of the Year in 1966. He first garnered attention when he was a 20-year-old elevator boy at the Hotel Racine, when his crayon drawings of celebrities staying at the hotel made the *Racine Journal Times*. After he joined the Army in January 1941, thinking it would be a one-year obligation, he spent the next four years in the South Pacific. Not that Crowe saw much action. A racy cartoon star-

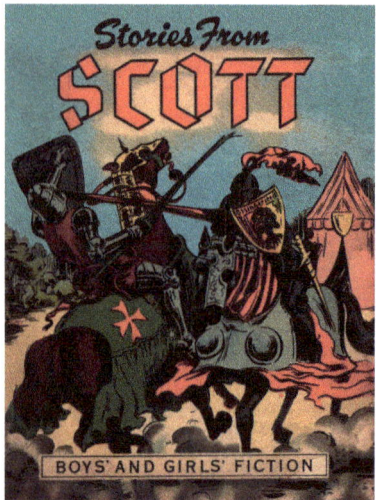

Front and back covers of the Samuel Lowe's *Stories from Scott* digest paperbacks.

ring "Windy City Kitty" became a fa-vorite in the *Yank Down Under* Army magazine in Australia and he spent the war on staff. The strip later had a short-lived incarnation as a toned-down syn-dicated strip.

He moved back to Racine, where he quickly married his girlfriend, and took a job for Western Printing before moving over to Lowe Inc. Racine and Kenosha are only ten miles apart and even Samuel Lowe himself lived there. Crowe specialized in cowboys and pi-rates and all things manly, apparently a family tradition. His father, Thomas Crowe, would become the sheriff of Racine Country and his son Christo-pher wrote the movie adaptation of *The Last of the Mohegans*. Crowe also had a daughter, Debra. Jack died in 1996.

As you might infer from the above, the BGF series was an anomaly at Lowe. I can't find any other books they did for that age group. So why did Lowe embark on such a weird outlier of a project? Probably because they were very, very cheap to do. They were re-printed to almost the last jot and tittle from the Boys' and Girls' Fiction series

published by the huge British publisher Raphael Tuck & Sons. All Lowe had to do was to remove the Tuck insignia from the back cover and change the publisher from the sonorous "Raphael Tuck & Sons Ltd./Fine Art Publishers to Their Majesties the King and Queen and Her Majesty Queen Mary/Lon-don • New York • Toronto" to "Samuel Lowe Company/Kenosha, Wisconsin," alter the copyright from 1946 to 1948, and replace the printing location of Canada with Kenosha. To the casual eye the text and illustrations and cov-ers are otherwise identical, although a close side-by-side examination reveals that the Tuck covers are slightly bright-er, either because of the quality of the ink or because the paper held up better.

One major difference is immedi-ately evident when you touch them: the Tuck BGF series appeared in hard cov-ers, normal for 1946. According to the <tuckdbephemera.org> website, The Tuck "books come in two sizes, smaller ones do not have the black bands on top and bottom of covers, no num-bers." (The dangling modifier seems to imply that the larger releases had

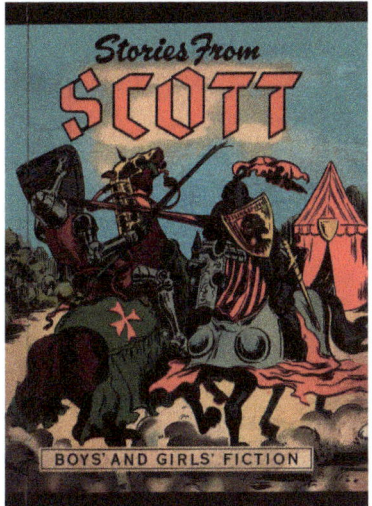

Front and back covers of the Tuck & Sons' *Stories from Scott* hardcovers.

numbers, but that's not true of my set or any images I found online.) Smaller books measure 7 x 5" with the larger ones with bands at 7½ x 5½". The Lowe reprints are sized in-between, though the black bands, clearly trimmed, range from medium large to non-existent.

The Tuck company, now defunct, had been founded in 1866 to sell pictures and greeting cards and then became the largest publisher of postcards in the world, profiting from a picture postcard boom in the early 20th century. It eventually branched into children's books, paper dolls, pop-up books, stickers, and the other children's ephemera that Lowe did on a smaller scale. The company's headquarters and its contents were completely destroyed during WWII, but they managed to keep going, shifting printing to their subsidiary in Toronto.

That seems to answer one the series' many baffling questions. Why in the world would a British company like Tuck use a bunch of just-starting-out Wisconsin illustrators for their books? The only reasonable solution is that the Samuel Lowe Company of Canada sub-

contracted the series for Tuck and put it out on the Canadian market as a test. They couldn't have been overly successful. Most of the Tuck titles are near impossible to find today, and those listed are overwhelmingly from Canada and the United Kingdom. It's also not clear whether the books were released only in Canada, or also in the UK. A New Zealand dealer also offers one.

While on the subject of mysteries, someone needs to explain why this particular set of random, old fashioned, and boy-oriented titles were created as a BGF series in the first place. It's true that evergreen classics like Scott and Dickens would probably appeal to British Empire youth, particularly if they were simplified for younger audiences. Russell Thorndike, the reteller of record, is probably the same Russell Thorndike who was a hugely popular British author between the wars. He was an actor who gained fame by writing the Dr. Syn series of adventures, described as a Batman of the 1700s, a parish priest who dressed in a scarecrow costume to pursue evildoers. That name is also on a number of children's

Front and back covers of the Tuck & Sons' *The Vanishing Redhead* hardcovers.

versions of classics for Tuck and the dating gives no reason that one person couldn't have done both, although no direct evidence links them (or distinguishes them, for that matter).

Good pirate's tales were still in vogue in that era and that probably explains two more. *Captain Kidd's Gold: The True Story Of An Adventurous Sailor Boy* dates back to 1888, when New York publisher A. L. Burt put out James Franklin Fitts's novel. Fitts (1839–1890) was an Upstate New York lawyer who served in the Civil War, went into politics, and wrote almost a dozen novels from boy's adventure to mysteries to romances. Even older was *The Flag of Distress: A Story of the South Sea* by "Captain" Thomas Mayne Reid. Reid was also American, and fought in the Mexican War. He followed that by writing nearly 100 adventure novels, set all over the world. *Flag* was published first in short form in *Chamber's Journal*, August 7, 1875, and in book form in eight volumes the next year in London, then repeatedly reprinted in the 19th century. The Lowe edition is so heavily abridged and rewritten as to be almost

unrecognizable: for one thing the original has 79 chapters and this version 18; for another the book is rewritten into the first person point of view of young Ned from the first page, although he doesn't show up until Chapter 9 of the original, and then as a minor character.

Another prolific American author of boy's adventure novels, Edward Sylvester Ellis, was responsible for *Tracked Through the Wilds: or, with Rifle and Knapsack*, a 1906 Street and Smith paperback about early American frontier life. Ellis (1840–1916), now forgotten, was a major name—or names, he wrote under an unknown multitude of pseudonyms—in the 19th century, the author of hundreds of dime novels. To me, he is most famous for *The Steam Man of the Prairies*, my choice for the first robot novel. Why none of them are listed as authors is unfathomable.

So we have two British classics and three American novels probably also in the public domain. That leaves three novels. *Cordova*, *Redhead*, and *Trunks* are almost phantoms. They appear nowhere in any records except in the Tuck/Lowe series. They aren't old, public-domain titles, nor have they ever been reprinted. No author is listed inside the books and none have been later credited. Who wrote them, when, and why remains unanswered. The books read as if they were written by different hands and they are set in different times, all in America, *Cordova* in 1867, *Trunks* in the late 19th century, and *Redhead* in the contemporary world. *Cordova* and *Redhead* have teen-age boys as protagonists, but *Trunks* features a slightly older boy who has a job as a baggage assistant for a railroad, hence the express train on the cover. Nothing seems to link them to each other or the rest of the series. Possibly they were added because a series of eight seemed more impressive than one of five, or that eight titles filled a plate better for simultaneous printing.

With six of the titles set in the United States, it's odd that Tuck would put BGF before a British/Canadian audience. The plan from the beginning might have been that Lowe would reissue them in the States but the two-year wait makes that unlikely. One possible answer is that Lowe waited to see how well the series sold, backed off at first, and then rushed to emulate the immediate success of Comet Books. Again, the lack of evidence conspires against an answer. For one thing, it's unknown when in 1948 Lowe released his series. The only clue I have is that three of my copies were signed by young Elender Lee Robertson, with one dated May 7, 1949. Elender lived in Arlington, VA, so we can presume that the series had national distribution. Whether the books were first released then or merely stayed on the shelves on some store for several months isn't clear. The "copyright 1948" printed under the table of contents itself is misleading; none of the titles are in the Catalogue of Copyright Entries for any year. Lowe, who would certainly constantly monitor

the competition, must have seen the growing teen-age market form right after the war. Waiting until 1948 implies that he finally released the books just to get some revenue back from a failed experiment. His having put them out in the cheaper wrappers reinforces that theory.

Not that BGF hurt the company. Samuel Lowe even survived Samuel Lowe, who died in 1952 at the age of 68. Edith, who had become a homemaker and full-time mother of her five boys, took over the business. She kept it going until 1980, when it quietly folded. For the next thirty years, the Kenosha newspapers regularly ran obituaries of people who had worked there, often for decades. Every single one I saw were of women, a reminder that the working woman was not a recent invention but a long-time necessity in millions of families. Edith also returned to writing children's books, several illustrated by Nan Pollard. She died in 2000, almost a half century after her husband. Today even the Lowe building is gone, razed in 1987. But it leaves a legacy of more than 1,000 books, and memories of the time when the Midwest was the industrial heartland.

New articles by **Steve Carper** appear regularly on his website <Flying CarsandFoodPills.com>. Recent article include "Food Pills in Comic Strips," "Space Age Beauty Queens," and "Pulp Robot Covers 1920s–1930s." Steve's latest book *Robots In American Popular Culture* (McFarland & Company, 2019) and companion website of the same name are essential reading for fans of science fiction and pop culture. His digest novel collection has passed 1300, not even including *Boys' and Girls' Fiction digests.*

Startling Mystery Stories No. 2 Fall 1966. Cover by Carl Kidwell.

Reader Preference Ballot: "Please rate the stories in the order of your perference, as many as possible. Ties are always acceptable. If you thought a story was bad (rather than just last place), put an 'X' beside it. If you thought a story was truly outstanding, above just first place, mark an 'O' beside it. (Then the next-best would be '1'.)"

Startling Mystery Stories No. 2
Review by Richard Krauss

"The magazine looks fine—a wanderer out of time, mysteriously produced in 1937 with a 1966 copyright date. That name! That logo! That yellow-and-black-and-red cover!"
–Excerpt from Robert Silverberg's letter about *SMS* No. 1

The Fall 1966 edition of *Startling Mystery Stories* delivers an excellent mix of reprints carefully culled by editor Robert A.W. Lowndes, along with three new stories with a more contemporary (circa 1966) feel. The reprints were decades old even in 1966, and those from *Weird Tales* are approaching 100 today—all still highly readable if you can forgive their dated cultural norms and conventions.

Introduction by Robert A.W. Lowndes

In his foreword of teasers for the stories to come, Lowndes thanks readers for their initial impressions and their warm reception of the first issue.

The House of Horror
by Seabury Quinn
"We have arranged with Seabury Quinn to present more of the adventures of Drs. Jules de Grandin and Samuel Trowbridge to you," Lowndes writes in his introduction. "Ten of the tales appear in a new hard-cover collection (see Books in this issue) and are off-limits to us; but we have free range among the other 80-odd. These stories nearly all take place in the 20's and 30's and we have made no effort to update them—only to indicate the decade."

Our story begins with de Grandin and Trowbridge lost in the countryside on an unfamiliar road. It was the proverbial dark and stormy night, and our heroes decide to seek shelter when they chance upon a large, square house of red brick, rather than fight the horrendous weather. A cliched setup even for readers in 1966, but perhaps more original when the story first appeared in *Weird Tales* July 1926. Further, there are two separate events that conve-

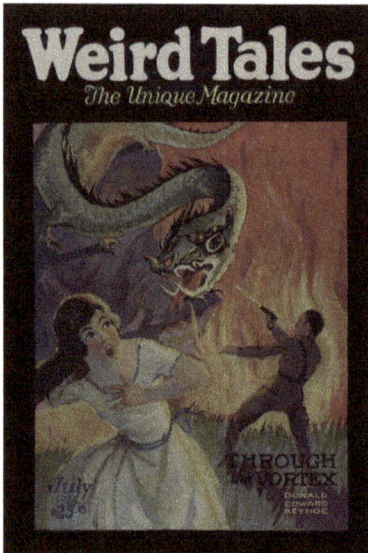

Weird Tales July 1926. Cover by E.M. Stevenson.

Grandin is sure Marston is out of ear-shot, he confides to Trowbridge that the patient exhibited no signs of illness, except the odor of chloral hydrate, and concludes she has been drugged.

A quick examination of their room reveals they are locked in and the window's latticelike frames are not wood, but "stoutly welded and bolted metal." To all intents, they are prisoners. Their thoughts on this realization is inter-rupted: "Above the hissing sound of the rain against the windows and the howl of the sea-wind about the gables, there suddenly rose a scream, wire-edged with inarticulate terror, freighted with utter, transcendental anguish of body and soul."

Unable to leave their room to inves-tigate, the pair eventually retire to their beds, the house settling into a peaceful silence. In the morning, de Grandin looks out the window and spots Mar-ston leaving the house. De Grandin picks the lock and the good doctors rush to their patient's bedside. Trow-bridge checks her pulse. It is weak, her temperature low. He checks her eyes and is shocked to find them walleyed. He determines she is the victim of some horrid surgeon.

De Grandin wakes her with an in-jection of strychnin[e]. She asks for a mirror, but is put off while de Gran-din interviews her. She is not Marston's daughter, as he claims. She was driving, when suddenly her tires were punc-tured by glass strewn across the road. She saw the light in Marston's house and went to the door to ask for help. Marston was just sitting down to din-ner and asked her to join him. That was the last thing she remembered.

She asks again for a mirror. De Grandin puts her off, and she soon suc-cumbs to the effect of the chloral again, fading back to sleep.

De Grandin returns to the entry and finds the secret controls for the front

niently occur to resolve an immediate threat and a horrid dilemma. Unfortu-nate, yet the strength of Quinn's prose overcomes these plot point imperfec-tions.

In answer to their knock, the house's door opens wide to reveal an empty entry hall. Once de Grandin and Trow-bridge are across the threshold, the door swings shut, locking itself in the process. After a moment of alarm, a voice calls out from the stairs, welcom-ing them to Marston Hall. Their host is delighted to learn his visitors are doc-tors as his daughter has taken ill with a mysterious malady. She has what Mar-ston believes to be sleeping sickness, as he can not seem to rouse her.

De Grandin examines the sleeping patient, a girl of perhaps fifteen years of age. He mixes four teaspoonfuls of a sham medication that he pours down her throat. He declares she will sleep peacefully now and he will decide upon further treatment in the morning.

Their host leads his guests to their room to retire for the night. Once de door. He and Trowbridge rush outside, wedging the door ajar with a wad of paper. In a moment they locate Marston, just in time to observe him jumping from Trowbridge's car as it edges over a steep embankment and plunges into a lake of slimy swamp-mud below.

As our heroes call out threats, Marston looks back toward the house, chuckling over his handiwork. A heavy gust of wind shakes the surrounding trees, tearing loose a tremendous branch that lands atop Marston, pinning him to the ground. De Grandin and Trowbridge rush forward to hear his dying words.

"I—I meant to kill you, for you might have hit upon my secret. As it is, you may publish it to the world, that all may know what it meant of offend a Marston. In my room you will find the documents. My—my pets—are—in—the—cellar. She—was—to—have—been—one—of—them."

By any definition, this story falls squarely into the realm of shudder pulps. The victims' torture is truly horrific. When readers' ballots for issue two were counted, "The House of Horror" was the favorite.

Two book reviews by Lowndes follow the story. The first is the collection of de Grandin stories mentioned earlier: *The Phantom Fighter* by Seabury Quinn. Lowndes concludes: "You can't go wrong with this collection." The second review is for *Strange Signposts* edited by Roger Elwood and Sam Moskowitz. "If I hadn't received a free review copy, this book is one I'd take the trouble to buy."

The Men in Black by John Brunner

A stalker is someone who watches and follows someone else out of obsession or derangement. In the case of forty-year-old muscleman/pretty

The Phantom Fighter by Seabury Quinn. Cover by Frank Utpatel.

boy Royston, the motive is money. He stalks one good-looking woman after another to enjoy her body and her bank roll.

You might imagine what would happen if some geniune Men in Black started stalking the stalker, but Brunner has done it for us in this light-hearted story of comeuppance.

This story originally appeared in *Science Fantasy* No. 17 in 1956 as "The Biggest Game" written under the pseudonym Keith Woodcott. John Killian Houston Brunner (1934–1995) was a British author of science fiction novels and short stories. His 1968 novel, *Stand on Zanzibar*, about overpopulation, won the Hugo Award in 1969 for Best SF Novel.

The Reckoning

Thanks to *SMS*'s quarterly schedule, Lowndes actually had time to count the ballots from readers on issue one and present the results here. [See Peter Enfantino's *SMS* article in *TDE10* pages 46–61 for a full accounting.]

Science Fantasy Vol. 6 No. 17 February 1956. Cover by Gerard Quinn.

Weird Tales June 1926. Cover by E.M. Stevenson.

The Strange Case of Pascal
by Roger Eugene Ulmer

This story's main event is David Pascal's nightmare. The terrible dream unfurls in increasingly unsettling waves that account for half of the story's six pages. A night terror so vivid Pascal can't help but wonder—was it real or imagined?

"Pascal" was reprinted from *Weird Tales* (June 1926). It credits "Robert" rather than "Roger." The only other story by Ulmer uncovered in my search was "The Headless Horror" from an earlier *Weird Tales* (April 1925).

The Witch is Dead by Edward D. Hoch

In Simon Ark's third adventure, the occult detective tackles the curse of Mother Fortune that is apparently killing all the students in the Hudsonville woman's college. His unnamed narrator/companion, the reporter he met in his first story, "Village of the Dead," is now married and employed by the Neptune Book company. Their reconnection in Westchester County seems a

coincidence, but despite Ark's talent for uncovering logical solutions to what appears supernatural, his inexplicable knowledge of events and phenomena gives one pause to accept the meeting as mere serendipity.

Mother Fortune was once a student of Hudsonville, expelled two weeks prior to graduation for smoking. "You must realize that at the time such a thing was unknown among young girls, and at a school like Hudsonville it would have been a most serious offense."

Fortune's threatening notes confirm her motivation: "Your cruel act of fifty years ago is at last avenged. I have cursed your school and every student in it. Before another moon has come your school will be a campus of the dead."

Ark and his companion visit Mother Fortune in her trailer. Once she realizes their visit in on behalf of Hudsonville, she sends them packing. By the next morning, she is dead; her body burned nearly beyond recognition.

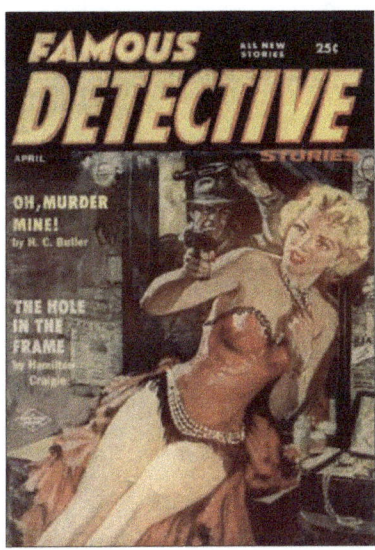

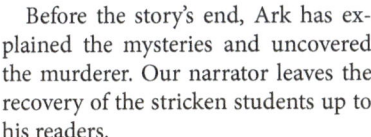

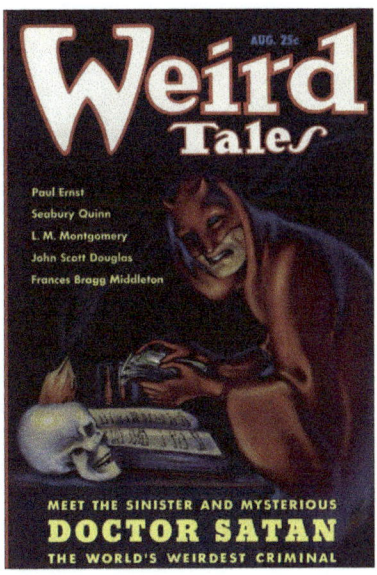

Famous Detective Stories April 1956. Cover by Norman Saunders.

Weird Tales August 1935. Cover by Margaret Brundage.

Before the story's end, Ark has explained the mysteries and uncovered the murderer. Our narrator leaves the recovery of the stricken students up to his readers.

Edward D(entinger) Hoch's (1930–2008) Simon Ark stories have been collected in three anthologies: *The Judges of Hades* (1971), *City of Brass* (1972), and *The Quests of Simon Ark* (1984). This story first appeared in *Famous Detective Stories* in April 1956.

Doctor Satan by Paul Ernst

Ascott Keane, a brilliant, independently wealthy crime-fighter, battles the weird occult mastermind, Doctor Satan, in this first of eight adventures that originally appeared in *Weird Tales* in August 1935 as the cover story. The adventure exudes pulpy excesses with shrubs exploding out of skulls and death by incineration via Satan's voodoo flame. Since this was the start of a series, it comes as no surprise the battle royal ends in stalemate, with Doc Satan escaping to fight another day.

Ernst's writing helps buoy his off-the-charts menaces, but it surprised me to find *SMS*'s reader preference poll rated this the second best story in the issue. Readers must've liked it, four more stories from the series were included in subsequent issues of *SMS*. And for those who can't get enough, the entire run of eight is reprinted in a recent volume, *The Complete Tales of Dr. Satan* (Altus Press, 2013).

The Secret of the City
by Terry Carr & Ted White

A short, straight-ahead original that could be branded fantasy, science fiction, or even horror. Losing his job after eight years jolts Arthur Wainwright III into a new perspective. Finding himself on the streets of New York City during what was once his normal working hours, he notices a ribbon of bronze embedded in the streets and sidewalks. Fascination turns obsessive as 'ol Wainwright follows the bronze strip until he pries its ghastly secret wide open on the final page.

The Complete Tales of Doctor Satan Altus Press, 2013.

Weird Tales May 1929. Cover by C.C. Senf.

The Street by Robert W. Lowndes

One of a series of poems inspired by H.P. Lovecraft's *Fungi from Yuggoth*, written by *SMS*'s editor. It originally saw print in *New Annals of Arkya*, The Phantagraph Press, 1945.

The Scourge of B'Moth
by Bertram Russell

This novelette by L.H. Hardingham, writing as Bertram Russell, originally appeared in *Weird Tales* May 1929. It is the second of only two stories for Russell on record at Galactic Central. The first being, "Death Bloom" from *Murder Mysteries* April 1929.

A monstrous entity is reaching out from the depths of the oceans to usurp the minds of men in its terrifying bid to seize control of civilization. Standing in its way are only Dr. Prendergast, our narrator Dr. Randall, and Geoffrey d'Arlancourt, a student of antiquities. The yarn is full of action, chilling atmosphere, and a heinous threat readers witness firsthand as the B'Moth's

victims fall under its control.

"*A dirty, tousled figure was dashing along the street, pursued by two policemen. He was clad in the lightest of garments that looked more like underwear or sleeping-clothes than anything else. He stumbled occasionally, but some instinct seemed to enable him to keep out of the grasp of his pursuers. He was carrying something which he balanced with great dexterity. I looked closely as he approached me and saw that it was a tank filled with water, and inside the tank was a collection of lizards, water-snakes, etc. And as he approached me, eluding his pursuers by a hair, I saw that this man in pajamas was Dr. Prendergast.*"

The Cauldron (letters of comment)

It had been only three months since *SMS* issue one hit newsstands, so the bulk of letters were yet to arrive by issue two's press deadline. Lowndes fills the space with chummy chatter, author bios, and excerpts from the very first letters, likely from readers who sent their thoughts almost immediately after they bought the debut edition. Reception was positive, boding well for a digest that would still be around five years later. The final page of the issue was the Readers' Preference Coupon, the ballot encouraging readers to rate its stories.

Lowndes acknowledges the overlaps. "It is, indeed, difficult to draw the line and at times you will very likely see stories here which you think could have gone just as well, or perhaps better, in *Magazine of Horror*—and vice versa. However, we hope and expect to have a fair amount of content in each issue which indisputably belongs in *SMS*, and would not fit well in *MOH*."

Summary

The cover's banner. promising "Unusual—Eerie—Strange" fare helps differentiate *SMS* from its companion, *Magazine of Horror*. Although even

References

DarkworldsQuarterly.gwthomas.org
Galactic Central website
JessNevins.com

"When I was your age, men were walking on the moon."

1981:
Facts & Fictions.

Pulp Modern

STORIES
CULTURE
COMMENTARY

VOL. 2 NO. 8   Winter 2022

TOM'S

Brian Asman • Misha Burnett
Roy Christopher • Jeff Esterholm • Ronin Heck
Shannon Hollinger •Tia Ja'nae • Anthony Perconti
Scotch Rutherford • Robb White

Opening Lines

Selections from the digests featured in this edition.

"When the client came, Sally was scraping her scruples off the door."
"Mother Hen" by Kim Newman *Fantasy Tales* Vol. 2 No. 3 Spring 1991

"Usually, people get committed to the psycho ward by their families or courts, but this guy came alone and said he wanted to be put away because he was deadly dangerous."
"And Three to Get Ready . . ." by H.L. Gold *Fantastic* Summer 1952

"You know how college guys are, always ready for hell or a frolic."
"The Jokers" by Robert Turner *Manhunt Detective Story Monthly* Dec. 1955

"After Tillyard and Althea were injected with the drug, they were released into the labyrinth and no one heard their names again."
"The Embracing" by David J. Schow *Fantasy Tales* Vol. 11 No. 3 Autumn 1989

"It was 1925, in a teardrop of land no map remembers, a land absorbed decades ago by other countries pressing from every side. I had come for work, a young woman sent by a man I met only once to tell the story of a people whose language I couldn't speak."
"Unearthed" by William Preston *Asimov's Science Fiction* Sep. 2012

"Some people seem to attract the torments of life because they are weak, some because they are strong, and some apparently because they meet life's bullying with a puzzled patient dignity which must enrage a tyrant; at least that was how Vivian Messiter met it."
"Scotland Yard's Latest" by Joseph Gollomb *11 True Crimes* Green Publishing Co. No. 7

"The little girl that had the desk in front of mine in 5-A was named Millie Adams."
"If I Should Die Before I Wake" by William Irish *Murder Mystery Monthly* No. 31 June 1945

"True!—nervous—very, very dreadfully nervous I had been and am; but why will you say that I am mad?"
"The Tell-Tale Heart" by Edgar Allan Poe *Fantastic* Fall 1952

"I stood on the deck of a British man-of-war and stared at the ship in front of us."
The Flag of Distress by "Captain" Thomas Mayne Reid Boys' and Girls' Fiction

"Call it what you please: blind accident, predestination, luck . . . but the thousand-to-one shot meeting of Lou Jacks, taxi driver, and Bob Stuart, out-of-work police reporter, in an all-night restaurant which neither had ever visited before, defied all the laws of probability."
"Vanishing Act" by W.R. Burnett *Manhunt Detective Story Monthly* Nov. 1955

"'I love you,' said the rock."
"A Rock That Loved" by Jessica Amanda Salmonson *Fantasy Tales* Vol. 6 No. 12 Winter 1983

"The forest was wild and lonely and still."
Tracked Through the Wilds by Edward Sylvester Ellis Boys' and Girls' Fiction

"The uniformed man in the bunker gave a last stiff-armed salute—or it should have been, but most of the stiffness had disappeared now; and the uniform with its black leather crossstrap was less than crisp, indeed it was dusty with a fine layer of concrete powder, which kept drifting down from the low ceiling as the thudding concussions crept closer and closer—and put the muzzle of his pistol to his head."
"Hell is a Personal Place" by Brian Lumley *Fantasy Tales* Vol. 9 No. 17 Summer 1987

"It would be difficult to put your finger on Old Webb's nationality for he was, after all, just a small old man—with dry cracked leather for skin, and two small slits where nothing ever showed but wind-whipped tears for eyes, and a sprinkling of very fine gray silken threads where most people wear their hair."
"Candlesticks" by John Evans *Fantastic* Nov/Dec 1952

"It was a clever, workable idea that the three killers had."
"Sales Resistance" by Andrew J. Burris *Manhunt Detective Story Monthly* Oct. 1955

"Gretch stared pensively into the bubbling murk of the cauldron; thoughts, faces, and events swirling there in an ever-changing tapestry of grey mist."
"The Woodcarver's Son" by Robert A. Cook *Fantasy Tales* Vol. 4 No. 7 Spring 1981

"The first inkling that I had of the gigantic abomination that was soon to smother the world with its saprophytic obscenity in 192–, was obtained almost by accident."
"The Scourge of B'Moth" by Bertram Russell *Startling Mystery Stories* No. 2 Fall 1966

"I guess you heard that the Mr. Bigs in the Supreme Court of the U.S.A. up in Washington have passed a rule that the colored and the white go to the same schools from now on, no matter where."
"Uncle Tom" by David Alexander *Manhunt Detective Story Monthly* Sep. 1955

"As Professor Leslie Carter understood it, there were two types of zombies in the Republic of Haiti, and he didn't believe in either."
"A Place of No Return" by Hugh B. Cave *Fantasy Tales* Vol. 4 No. 8 Summer 1981

"The morgue attendant in the white uniform took hold of the handle of the long drawer with his rubber gloves and slid it open."
Crime On My Hands by Carl G. Hodges, Alexander Moring Ltd. 1952

"It was in the days following the third crusade that King Richard Coeur de Lion, having made peace with Saladin, was treacherously taken prisoner by the crafty Duke of Austria, and England, during the two years of his captivity, was ruled by his brother, Prince John."
Ivanhoe by Walter Scott (*Stories from Scott*) Boys' and Girls' Fiction

"On stealthy feet armed men padded through the shadow-drenched streets of Blessed Paltomir, ancient capital of the League of Praterxes."
"Naked as a Sword" by Kenneth Bulmer *Fantasy Tales* Vol. 1 No. 1 Summer 1977

www.ingramcontent.com/pod-product-compliance
Lightning Source LLC
Chambersburg PA
CBHW041747010726
47507CB00008B/319